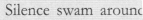

us to eye level with one a

your performance lacked

Silence swam arounc

her reply. Of which she gave none, her chin jutting out in a stubborn line that intrigued my instincts. It seemed the queen wanted to play. Good.

Her husband raised his fist as if to correct the behavior himself, but I held up a hand. "Allow me, My Lord." I had a show to put on, one I hoped would gain me his favor and allow me some much- needed alone time with his wife. "It's rude to ignore a direct question, Valora."

Gorgeous light blue eyes met my own, her pupils flaring the tiniest bit to display her irritation. Mmm, she didn't like this at all. Not that I blamed her. What would it take to prompt her rebellion? To provoke her enough to kill her own husband?

"Get it over with," she demanded. "Fuck me, if that's your choice. Use me. Do whatever it is you please, *My Prince*."

Such fire and hatred. All for someone she hardly knew. I couldn't help my resulting smile. "Enthusiasm," I informed her softly, tilting my head to the side. "That's the answer, sweetheart."

Her lips flattened. "This game bores me."

I chuckled, adoring this feisty side of her. "Does it? Shall we make it more interesting?" I slid my hand into my pocket, palming the blade I'd just used to take out half a dozen immortal men—*for her*. "Kneel."

The king wanted a demonstration, so I would provide one unlike any he could have anticipated.

Underworld Royals Series

Happily Ever Crowned

Happily Ever Bitten

Happily Ever Guarded

Happily Ever Underworld

LEXI C. FOSS
ANNA EDWARDS

This is a work of fiction. Names, characters, places, and incidents are either the product of the author's imagination or are used fictitiously, and any resemblance to actual persons, living or dead, business establishments, events, or locales is entirely coincidental.

Happily Ever Crowned

Editing by: Outthink Editing, LLC

Proofreading by: Jean Chiasson Bachen

Cover Design: Sanja Balan of Sanja's Covers

Published by: Ninja Newt Publishing, LLC

Print Edition
ISBN: 978-1-950694-20-4

"Out of suffering have emerged the strongest souls; the most massive characters are seared with scars."

– Khalil Gibran

Dear Reader,

Thank you for embarking on this dark fairy tale journey with us. We hope you enjoy Adrik and Valora.

Just a few words of warning before you begin: There are several violent undertones in this story. While Prince Adrik might be a fantasy come to life, the things Valora's husband, King Necros, does are quite literally born of Hell.

Fortunately, Valora is a fighter.

There will be death.

A lot of it.

And some very sexy scenes between Valora and her prince.

Enjoy!

-Lexi & Anna

"I DO."

Two words that signed over my soul to a monster, all to save a kingdom I knew little about. This isn't a fairy tale. No knights in shining armor, only kings fighting for power. And my heart is the key.

A GAME DESIGNED TO SHATTER EVEN THE HARSHEST OF RESOLVES.

My husband wants to debase me. To break me. To destroy my spirit. To possess every inch of my soul through acts so heinous I can hardly breathe. And he's using six men to do it. Including *him*. Adrik, Prince of Noxia.

DESIRE.

Such a wicked twist of fate. Happily-ever-after may not exist here, but amorous energy rises after a night of unbridled passion. A night I should hate, but don't. A night I long to repeat.

"I LOVE YOU."

A statement I will never say. Not even to him—my dark prince who plays in the shadows, engaging me in a forbidden dance of hope and adoration. He promises me a new crown, in exchange for my heart.

VENGEANCE.

I will not be owned.
I will rise above them all.And the only crown I will wear is the one drenched in their blood.

HAPPILY EVER CROWNED

Once upon a time in the Kingdom of Graystall, a baby cooed in delight as flames danced over her fingertips. Little did she realize that a darkness loomed, ready to steal her light. All innocence and life, a true vivacious force among the realms.

But the shadows fell, taking with them the galaxy's brightest star, leaving a salvation behind to lie in wait.

Twenty-one years later, that shadow is finally ready to rise. And with him, his destined queen.

This is the beginning of the end. A tale forged in blood and fire. The story of how Adrik met his sweet star, his Valora.

Chapter One

Valora

THIS WASN'T HOW I IMAGINED my wedding day—with darkness swirling around my long, flowing pink dress, shadowing me in the realms of the Underworld.

But I didn't live in a fairy tale. I resided in a reality underlined in duty and honor, where I accepted my fate for the greater good.

Zaya, my lady's maid, pinned a final clip into my brown hair and stepped back. "You're beautiful, Valora."

I met her pale gaze in the mirror. "Thank you." My poor attempt at a responding smile didn't go unnoticed.

She laid a delicate hand on my exposed shoulder, giving it a squeeze. "It'll be okay. It's not like you don't know him." Zaya tried to reassure me, but I couldn't discern whether knowing my soon-to-be husband's character in advance was a good thing or not.

Oh, I admired him, even respected him. But desired him, no. Yet, tonight I would give myself to him. Allow his hands to roam my body, to search and explore my skin in a manner no other ever had.

"She'll be fine," my mother—if I could even call her that—interjected and stood. She motioned for me to follow suit, her expression and manner lacking any semblance of warmth.

It didn't shock me. I hardly knew the woman, as I hadn't seen her since my third birthday—the day she and my father had sent me to live in Caluçon with my betrothed's family.

A bride in exchange for peace.

One innocent life forfeited for the lives of thousands.

To save Graystall, a kingdom I barely remembered yet cherished deep inside.

"Why you chose pink for a dress is beyond me," my mother said, her lips twisting into a grimace. "It's a ridiculous color for someone of our breeding. You should be in black. This'll bring bad luck. I'm sure of it."

"I think it's nice to have brightness now and then here," Zaya countered, but my mother shut her down with a glare so powerful it could freeze over hell.

"It's okay. I like the color. It's very me," I murmured to the girl who wasn't only my lady's maid but also my best friend and the only person I trusted in all of the Underworld.

Her halfling status often gave others the false impression that she stood beneath them, which wasn't helped by her petite frame and dull brown hair. But I saw a different side of her. A stronger side. One I adored and respected. And I considered her more like family to me than anyone else in the world.

"You can tell them I'm ready," I said softly, giving her a smile to help increase both of our confidence levels. She knew as well as I did I was nowhere near ready, but I could certainly fake it.

"Of course," she replied, taking her leave with a polite bow.

After the door closed, I frowned at my mother.

"Black may be the color to wear in Graystall, but the Caluçon Kingdom prefers color," I informed her. I bent down to take a last look in the mirror and picked up the tiara of the Royal Family of Caluçon to affix to my head. I rose taller than my mother, for in a few hours, I'd be queen of this place and her equal. "If you'll excuse me, I have to get married."

"Wait." She grabbed my hand and pulled me closer to her. "I need to know that you understand the gravity of today."

I nearly laughed. "All I've ever known is my purpose for today." *To marry Necros, King of the Dead.* There was no other recourse. I would become his indefinitely, do whatever he requested, and live and die by his rule.

She made an unpleasant noise in the back of her throat. "Valora, we're relying on you to keep our kingdom safe."

"Your kingdom," I replied flatly. "Yes, I know. But you're not the one paying the price, are you?" Most wouldn't dare speak to a queen in this manner, but I had twenty-one years of pent-up emotion over the decision my parents made on my behalf. My *mother* could afford to take a little of the emotional burden I wore for just a few seconds.

"We're counting on you to make him happy," she

gritted out through clenched teeth. "If you fail, he'll come for us."

"And wouldn't that be a shame?" I meant it to sound tongue in cheek, but deep down, I shuddered at the thought. Necros adored throwing his weight around in the Underworld and destroying other kingdoms. It would not take much for him to take down Graystall, the only realm left that valued the balance of right and wrong. A land of justice adorned in shades of black, hence my mother's distaste for my dress.

"*Valora*," she snapped, her queenly tone coming out to play. "You owe your loyalty to your people."

"Do I?" I asked, blinking my eyes innocently. I refused to let her see my weaknesses, to witness how much I truly cared deep inside. Graystall would not ever fall on my account. Of that I was certain.

"This is not—"

"You realize I've spent my entire life living here, trying to save a country I don't even know, yes?" I interjected, done with her poor attempt to command my will. "All to marry a man I don't desire," I added, leaning down to hold her icy gaze—the same startling azure color as my own. "I suggest you not talk to me about loyalties, *Mother.* Not unless you want to acknowledge your lack of loyalty to me, *your only daughter.* The sole heiress to the Graystall throne."

Not that I would be accepting my position.

My parents—the Queen and King of Graystall—had made sure of that when they promised my hand to the King of Caluçon. I often wondered if they would create a new heir in my place, but it seemed destiny had other plans for their kingdom of justice.

Her nails dug into my arm as I tried to leave. "You don't understand. There's so much you don't know. Necros can harness—"

A sharp knock preceded the door opening. I spun, ready to reprimand whoever dared disturb my quarters without sufficient approval, and fell to my knee in a deep bow. "My Lord," I breathed, shocked by the appearance of one so revered.

My mother followed suit, her voice shaking as she said, "My Lord. To what do we owe the honor?"

The dark presence lingered, saying nothing and everything all at once. My mother's flinch said he spoke into her mind, and as she left without a word, I realized he'd dismissed her.

Oh… This couldn't be good. I expected his appearance, knew he would be officiating today's ceremony, but this felt unprecedented.

"Rise, my child," Lucifer murmured, his tone oddly gentle for one so notoriously cruel.

I swallowed, righting myself on my high-heeled shoes while keeping my gaze lowered. Except his finger beneath my chin forced my gaze to meet the inky depths of his eyes. Power swirled there. Dominance. Authority. Righteous pain. Stunningly beautiful.

I shivered beneath the intensity of all those traits, my knees longing to take me to the floor again.

This being was the most revered entity in the Underworld.

And he was touching my face.

He canted his head, his long black hair falling over his broad shoulders. "You have grown into a beautiful woman, Valora," he praised. "I'm proud.

But a true queen bows for no one. Not even for me."

"I…" I didn't know what to say. *Everyone* bowed to Lucifer. He was the Supreme Being. The fallen angel who ruled us all.

His lips curled, the smile devastating. "You'll learn, my child. There's still so much that rests ahead of you. One day you'll understand my trials. One day soon." He released my face and offered me his arm. "May I escort you to the ceremony?"

As if I could tell the Devil no.

I slid my arm through his, surprised by the warmth he offered. "Thank you," I managed to say, my throat tight.

"Hmm, I'm not sure I've yet earned your gratitude," he replied, leading me down the marbled floor of the corridor. Suit-clad guards knelt at the presence of the greatest power in the Underworld, their shivers rivaling my own.

How would Necros react to seeing me on Lucifer's arm?

How would the people of Caluçon react?

"With fear," Lucifer whispered, clearly reading my thoughts. "Which is your right, my child. You'll see."

"I… I'm not sure what to say."

"No, I imagine not. Soon, my Valora. Soon." He pressed his lips to my temple as we arrived at the great hall doors, the walk somehow far faster than I ever remembered it, as if time had played tricks on my mind. And in the presence of Lucifer, that was entirely possible. "Stay strong, my sweet girl. The trials ahead, while daunting, are meant to strengthen you, not weaken you."

"I don't understand."

He smiled, saying, "I know," and escorted me through the doors into the ceremony.

My father—who should be the one to walk me down the aisle—stood off to the side with my pale-faced mother.

Everyone bowed.

Except for Necros, King of Caluçon.

He merely seemed amused as he stood waiting at the altar ahead.

"Ready?" Lucifer asked.

He didn't wait for my response. Didn't care that I screamed a resounding *No!* in my head. Just began the walk, leading me to my fate, to the powerful male waiting for my forced hand.

My future husband was over twenty years older than me, not that his features showed it. His handsome face boasted a youthful appearance, only belied by the auburn beard shrouding his square jaw. Tattoos decorated his exposed skin, granting him the symbols of authority and defining him as the King of Caluçon.

"My Lord," he greeted, nodding only slightly.

"King Necros," Lucifer replied. "Your bride is exquisite."

"I know." His forest-green eyes locked on mine. "You're stunning, Valora."

"You're looking handsome, too, My King." It wasn't a lie. In his all-black suit, he looked nice, distinguished, and full of command. But I wouldn't call him sexy. Maybe because of the age gap, or more likely a result of him raising me almost as a little sister all these years. I'd always seen him as more of a friend than a husband.

"You've taken excellent care of her," Lucifer said, releasing my arm. "I expect that to continue."

Why would he care? I wondered. This was the first time we'd even met.

"Of course, My Lord." Necros cupped my cheek, his smile fond. "And she'll take care of me."

Lucifer's responding chuckle sent a chill down my spine.

Why did I sense a double meaning in that phrase? Something important I was clearly missing?

"She certainly will," Lucifer agreed. "Let's begin."

Necros guided me to kneel with him before the room, excitement bright in his gaze. It was the kind of look most women wanted to see from their betrothed on their wedding day, but I suspected something sinister lay beneath. It had always been there between us, some hidden desire for more than just my hand in marriage.

Of course, I knew what would follow.

How he would take my body.

But I had a feeling there was just something *more.* Only, I had no idea what. Aside from being bred and brought up to serve as his wife, I offered very little. No power. No otherworldly qualities. Just a well-educated Daughter of Graystall with an affinity for justice.

The ceremony began, Lucifer's ancient words flowing around us in a series of vows and promises that tied my soul to Necros—until death do us part.

Whatever was mine, I was to share freely.

To give my husband every part of me.

To cherish him.

Adore him.

Respect and please him.

To never hurt him in any capacity.

Protect him.

And it dawned on me at some point how one-sided this deal truly was—because my husband owed me nothing in return other than protection and the throne at his side.

Our hands were bound together in a cloth of darkness forged from the crops decorating the banks of the River Styx. They had handed it down through Necros's family for generations. Special words were spoken, and before I had a chance to understand it all, I was pronounced as married.

We didn't even kiss.

Ice caressed my body, scattering goose bumps down my arms.

I knew what came next. Had dreaded it for months. But the wicked tilt of my husband's lips told me this was the part he'd been looking forward to most. For today, at least.

Consummation.

It was the only way to properly ensure the validity of our nuptials.

The merrymaking would happen later—for my husband, anyway. I'd be expected to wait for him to return to me.

Necros took my arm and led me back down the aisle. I glimpsed my mother and father sitting together but paid them little mind. I was the Queen of Caluçon now, my ties to them officially broken.

"Are you ready for me, my wife?" Necros growled into my ear. "I know I've been ready for this for several years now."

I gulped. I shouldn't show him my fear, but I couldn't help it. I was terrified.

The reason his family had raised me was to ensure my virginity on our wedding night. Necros would be the only man to touch me intimately. To fill me with his seed and ripen a child in my belly.

"I'm scared," I admitted, the words hoarse to my ears.

"As you should be." Necros laughed out loud and dragged me quickly down the corridor, away from Lucifer's oddly safe presence.

Soon, my child, his voice whispered over my mind.

I glanced back to see his serene expression, wondering if I'd truly heard him at all.

And then the hallway wall cut off my view of the ceremonial room.

A crowd followed with cheers and shouts of celebration, all of them males I recognized from society. *Necros's closest friends.*

"Fuck her good, Our King," one called, causing me to flinch.

"Show her what a queen needs to do to please her husband," another shouted, causing my cheeks to overheat.

Necros pulled me into his bedroom without preamble and pushed me flat over his bed, pressing my head and jeweled corset into the luxury mattress. Steps followed, indicating the crowd gathering in the room behind us. Tradition required everyone to witness this moment.

All one hundred plus attendees.

My new husband stood sentry at my back,

running his palm up and down my spine, waiting for all to enter.

I swallowed the bile rising in my throat and took comfort in the blankets hiding my face.

Still, I could feel the onlookers' gazes prickling my body, stroking me with an intimacy meant only for my husband. And Necros hadn't even exposed me yet…

"Mmm, my beautiful wife," he murmured, continuing to stroke me as one would an animal, not an equal. Because that was what I was to him—a new pet. A toy. One to be used and fucked and to bear heirs. Nothing more.

Murmurs of approval littered the air, urging him to get on with it.

Were my parents among them? Here to witness my shame? Perhaps they should. It was they who subjected me to this life. They might as well see my fate.

"You may proceed," a deep voice—*Lucifer*—announced.

His voice chilled me to my core. A memory slid through my thoughts, brief, a sense of déjà vu overwhelming me. *I've heard those words before…*

Impossible. We'd never even met until today.

Necros wasted no time, didn't offer me any words of encouragement, just lifted my skirts up around my waist to display my nakedness to his gaze. Lingerie hadn't been allowed. Only a dress and shoes, neither of which he bothered to remove.

"*Fuck*," he breathed. "Such a pretty pussy."

They had shaved me bare, as the ritual required, leaving my most intimate area exposed not just to my husband but also to anyone close enough to see.

I shivered, longing to disappear.

The crown in my hair jolted as I attempted to bury my head further into the bed, seeming to remind me all the more of my purpose here.

A queen meant only to serve.

The loud roar of approval told me my husband had just removed his pants.

Some part of me had hoped for some sweet words, some sort of promise that I would be okay. But it was a sad girl's dream, not my reality.

Pain unlike anything I anticipated followed, ripping me in two as Necros forced himself inside me for the first time.

I bit down on the bedspread to keep from screaming, not wanting to show any weakness in front of my kingdom. *Queens don't let anyone see them cry.*

But it hurt too badly to stop the tears from gathering in my eyes. *Just breathe*, I coached myself, flinching as he thrust in again and again. His grip on my hips tightened, forcing me to accept him and not providing me an ounce of relief.

"Damn, best pussy ever." Lust deepened his voice to a tenor I never wanted to hear again but knew would become a nightly occurrence. We were wed now, all in duty to a kingdom I knew very little about.

Why?

Why me?

Necros bucked his hips and withdrew before slamming back into me.

Tears streamed down my face, wetting the blankets beneath me, but I refused to make a sound, refused to let him see the pain no doubt etched into my features.

I wanted to hide away in my room and go back to the life I had before. One of a lonely existence dreading a future I couldn't control. Anything would be better than this torture.

A cry threatened to leave my mouth as Necros set a punishing pace with his motions.

Nothing would ever be the same again. I felt it in every punch of his hips against mine, each heavy pant rending the air, the jeers surrounding the room, and the general lechery polluting the air.

Some naïve part of me had hoped to earn respect from this union. A foolish girl's notion. A wish.

They'd never see me as a better, let alone an equal.

I was merely the king's fucktoy—a prize he'd won from the Graystall Kingdom.

"So good," he groaned, causing the crowd to roar in excitement.

He leaned forward and yanked me back by my hair, revealing my face to everyone in the room, completing my humiliation.

Lecherous gazes filled my vision. Some even appeared excited, as if the king might share. I etched each person into my memory. Memorized every smile and derogatory comment. Because one day I'd rise above this. What other choice did I have?

A dream, perhaps.

But in that moment, I considered it my life goal.

Necros shoved into me one final time and vibrated with his pleasure. Thick ropes of his hot essence coated my insides, his goal of producing an heir evident. It wasn't until his final groan—long and guttural—that he finally released my hair, allowing me to fall to the bed once more.

He withdrew sharply, eliciting a shriek of pain I couldn't swallow in time.

Chuckles followed. All underscored in evil.

I hate it here...

"My bedded wife," Necros announced. "Welcome your queen, people of Caluçon." He punctuated the words with a slap against my still-exposed ass, eliciting congratulatory cheers around the room.

I shivered from the exposure, my heart in my throat as I prayed to the deities above that this hell would soon end. Warm voices, glances that felt like strokes, and words were exchanged while I remained hidden. Until eventually the voices softened to nonexistence, leaving me.

Still, I couldn't move.

My thighs ached.

My insides screaming from the violation.

This was my duty, my purpose, but did it have to hurt so very much?

Happy fucking birthday, my conscious whispered cruelly. I supposed it was a fitting introduction to womanhood.

More tears fell, my shoulders shaking from the onslaught of varying emotions. Anger at my parents and my people. Fear of my husband and my future with him. Agony at what I'd just endured.

And an odd inkling of hope sparking from deep within, in that secret place I never told anyone else about.

I stroked the power hiding there, longing for it to

be released and not knowing how at the same time.

One day, it seemed to promise. *One day soon.*

Maybe it was just my imagination, a coping mechanism to accept such a fate.

Or perhaps it was something so much more.

I called upon that inner strength, begging it to heal my damaged heart and soul. But it remained softly whispering, cooing promises of a future I could only dream about.

Soon, My Queen. Soon.

Chapter Two

Adrik

I SIPPED THE BOURBON WITH A SIGH, relaxing into my favorite chair. "Have I told you recently how much I love you?"

Grigory snorted. "Don't tell me you're drunk already."

"Hardly." I took another calming swallow, luxuriating in the crisp flavor unavailable in the Underworld. "This is making me nostalgic." I'd spent most of last year on Earth, mostly to cultivate my more deadly talents. But I'd taken a few moments to enjoy the pleasures of life up there, including indulging in the finer bourbons of the realm.

"I thought it'd be a good farewell gift before you run off to commit suicide tomorrow," he replied, his broad face lighting up with a grin. "I wanted to bring a few humans back with me, but my mother denied the request."

"Suicide," I repeated, ignoring that last bit. Grigory enjoyed mortal company. I preferred succubi. "When I reclaim my throne, remind me not to bring you onto my council."

The big man covered his heart. "What? But I thought you loved me, Adrik?"

"Bring me more bourbon, and we'll discuss it."

"Assuming you don't die tomorrow."

I finished the contents of my drink and poured myself another. "You know, I'm starting to think you're worried about me, G."

"You're attending the infamous Caluçon Ball. Anyone with intelligence would be worried." He scratched the scruff dotting his square jaw. "Actually, no. Intelligent demons wouldn't attend in the first place."

My lips twitched. "Good thing I'm not a demon." Not in the traditional sense, anyway. I commanded the shadows of the Underworld, the pissed-off spirits in limbo. It made me a welcome entity in this realm, but not necessarily demonic.

He grunted. "Too right." He picked up his wine glass and swirled the bloody contents before downing it all in one go. Almost as if to remind me that he, too, wasn't a traditional demon. Not like Lucifer's hellhounds and minions.

I sighed, my head falling back against the padded cushion of my chair. "Necros isn't a demon, either," I pointed out, again thinking about my plan. "Just King of the Dead." And archenemy to the Shadow Kingdom he'd destroyed many years ago.

My kingdom.

I ran my hand over my face and finished my second drink, not bothering to fill it again. The last thing I needed was to be hungover tomorrow.

Caluçon would fall. I just had to play my cards right, which included indulging the king in his fucked-up games. He wanted to break his queen. Fine. I'd happily help in that endeavor. But unlike all the other contenders lined up for tomorrow night, I knew the score.

Queen Valora possessed a valuable entity inside her, one I intended to steal for myself and use to destroy the King of the Dead.

"Let me come with you," Grigory said, not for the first time. "You know I'm the better fighter between us."

I laughed. "You beat me once and that makes you my better?"

"Twice," he corrected. "And fuck yes. Now bow."

"Fuck you." The words lacked heat, as they always did. "And no, you're staying here. The last thing I need is to piss off your mother."

"Ugh, that woman is such a buzzkill." He stretched out on my couch, legs crossed at the ankles, his eyes falling closed.

"I heard that," a feminine voice said, entering without knocking.

"I know," he replied, not bothering to glance or formally acknowledge the approaching woman.

Lux, Queen of the Noxia Kingdom.

Otherwise known as Grigory's mother.

"Your Highness," I greeted, nodding in respect. Most would be on the floor, bowing. But she and I had a different sort of relationship, one that had me viewing her more in a maternal manner rather than a royal one.

She had, after all, raised me as her own.

"You boys are always causing me problems," she

said, picking up the bottle of bourbon from the table. Rather than pour herself a glass, she stole a sip from the rim and shuddered. "Rubbish."

"Liquid gold," I corrected.

She scoffed at that. "I thought I raised you better than that, Adrik." She cocked her head to the side in a chastising way while also grinning down at me. "Are you ready for tomorrow?"

"No," Grigory cut in, still not looking at his mother. They both resembled night, with their dark hair and eyes, their skin as pale as the moon. Fitting for their vampire heritage, I supposed. As I possessed similar traits, it'd be easy for Lux to adopt me into the fold. However, I never called her Mother, nor did she ever ask me to.

"You're sending my brother off to his death," Grigory added humorously.

Jackass. "Your faith in me is heartwarming," I deadpanned.

"What?" He finally cracked an eye open. "You admitted yourself that I kicked your ass recently. Doesn't leave a man all that warm and fuzzy about sending his best friend off to battle."

"You did not kick my ass."

"You bled out all over the mat," he reminded me.

"We need to work on your definition of blood, G." Except, in this case, he wasn't exactly wrong.

"They had to replace the flooring," he continued. "And you passed out."

"Because you sliced open my abdomen with a dirty blade, you prick." And it had hurt like a motherfucker. Took two days to heal, too, even with my immortality.

"You told me to give you my all."

"And you certainly did."

"And I kicked your ass," he added.

I shook my head. "After I handed you your ass the day before. And the day before that. Oh, and the day—"

"If all you two are going to do is bicker all night, I'll take my advice elsewhere," Lux murmured, her expression one of amusement, not annoyance.

"Are you going to advise him not to go to Caluçon tomorrow?" Grigory wondered aloud, knowing full well his words were useless.

"It's time, Grigory," she returned, her voice hardening just the slightest bit.

"Here we go," he replied, covering his eyes with a muscular forearm. "The prophecy says," he began in a high-pitched tone.

I chuckled. "Don't mind him. He's just trying to figure out how to survive without me."

His responding grunt neither confirmed nor denied my comment, but we both knew the truth. We'd grown up together, had learned to fight alongside each other, and had spent most of our youth causing his mother all sorts of problems. But duty always hung over our heads.

Grigory would be crowned King of Noxia in the next few years.

And me, well, I had a crown to win back from a wicked king with a deadly streak.

"You're ready," Lux informed me, her voice soft but sure. She pulled a box from some mysterious pocket in her wispy skirts and set it on the table beside my empty glass. "This is what I came to give you. It belonged to your father, and I think he'd consider you finally ready to wear it."

I sat up, intrigued. "And you've kept it this entire time?"

She lifted one delicate shoulder. "He trusted me with your life and guidance. I've raised you accordingly."

"Much to my chagrin," Grigory grumbled half-heartedly.

"Is this behavior because I wouldn't let you bring those humans down for a drink?" she asked, arching one shapely brow at her son. It didn't matter that she was half his size; lethal energy oozed from her pores, darkening her gaze to black orbs and designating her as the queen of this kingdom.

Until he ascended, she would be his better.

Even if he didn't want to admit it.

"Grigory is just upset that he has to miss out on all the fun," I told her, grinning at my oldest friend.

The big man sat up, humor lacking in his expression. "Send me with him, Mother."

"It's not your fight," she replied before I had a chance.

"The fuck it's not. His family sent him here for a reason."

"And that reason has been fulfilled. He's ready, Grigory." She stared him down, some sort of mental battle of wills happening between them.

I knew better than to interrupt one of their telepathic wars and opened the box instead.

A watch.

Of all the things for my father to leave me, this was not what I expected. I plucked it out of the box and turned it over, searching for anything unique about it.

Nothing.

Looked fresh from one of those posh stores on Earth. Even had English writing on the back denoting it was made in the United States.

How completely boring and unoriginal.

Still, it belonged to the one man I longed to know and never would, thanks to Necros's insanity.

I slid the metal over my wrist, clasping it with a silent vow of vengeance.

One I repeated every night.

Caluçon will be mine to destroy.

And when I finished with it, Necros would weep at my feet for forgiveness.

As for his pretty little wife, well, she'd cry, too. But for entirely different reasons.

If Lux had taught me anything through the years, it was that winning required sacrifice. Alas, the poor Queen of Caluçon would provide the biggest sacrifice of all.

Her heart.

"That is a symbol of fate," Lux said, gesturing at my wrist. "Your father met your mother because of it."

I arched a brow. "On Earth?"

She nodded. "You know the story about how she was sent to watch over him, but not all the details. Apparently, he sensed her following him and ducked into a store to trap her. He purchased that watch in the process before taking her to hell."

"You mean kidnapping her," I corrected, smirking.

She smiled. "It all worked out in the end, didn't it?"

I shrugged. "All I have to rely on are stories." Since they were both killed during my infancy, thanks to Necros and his father destroying the Shadow Kingdom.

"They loved each other very much," Lux assured me. "After your mother got over a few things."

Such as an angel being forced to survive in the Underworld, I thought to myself.

My father had taken my mother almost immediately, and rather than reprimand her for watching his activities on Earth, he'd stolen her. And once a heavenly being entered hell, the entity could never return.

Alas, my mother may not have *fallen* by her own choice, but her ancestors didn't care.

Which was why her side of the family hadn't bothered to help when the Shadow Kingdom was destroyed.

The dealings of the Underworld mattered little to those who didn't reside here.

"And no, Grigory," Lux continued, her sable gaze narrowing at her son. "This is not your fight."

"At least let me escort him," he argued, causing my lips to quirk upward. As if I needed anyone to *escort* me anywhere.

"You think Necros would accept that both Princes of Noxia are interested in playing with his new pet?" She tsked, shaking her head. "He'd see right through that nonsense and expect to be challenged for the throne. It'll be hard enough for Adrik to convince him on his own that he carries no political motivation, let alone for the two of you to go."

Grigory muttered to himself, shaking his head. But the giant knew his mother spoke the truth.

He finally conceded with a nod before pinning me with a glower. "You better kick his ass."

"That's the plan," I replied, relaxing into my chair while stroking the metal around my wrist. "But I need the queen first."

Lux nodded. "Her power is slowly awakening. If you can access it before Necros, he won't stand a chance."

"And since your sources spread false information on how to do that, I have the advantage." I just had to win the queen's affection. Shouldn't be too hard a task. Especially with Necros as a husband.

"You're ready," Lux said again, a smile brightening her pale features.

"I am," I agreed.

This was my destiny.

My chosen path.

My retribution.

Caluçon would burn. And my family would finally be avenged.

Chapter Three

Valora

NECROS GRUNTED AS HE THRUST into me one final time and finished. I had no pleasure from the experience, just soreness and the sticky feeling of his cum coating my insides. No doubt it would run down my thighs next. He pulled out and smacked my ass—his way of signaling that I could now lower myself to my stomach, if I wanted.

"Time to get ready, wife. Lots of important guests coming and I can't wait to show you off." He slid from the bed and pulled his pants up; he never bothered to take them off. I'd yet to see him fully naked since we married six months ago. He only wanted a quick fuck, something he required I give.

"I hope you'll be on your best behavior tonight," he continued. "Wouldn't want to have to reprimand you for showing me up."

I swallowed as I slowly sat up on the bed. The weight of his stare sent ice through my veins, the threat underlining his words palpable.

"I'll make sure I don't embarrass you," I managed to reply, my throat dry. The words sounded wrong to my ears. I wouldn't be the one doing the idiotic things. I'd be the perfect subservient wife. It was all I knew how to do—take orders and be bullied into saving the world for everyone else at my own cost.

At least I would get to meet new people tonight.

I plastered a smile on my face as my husband gathered his black leather jacket from a Queen Anne chair in my room and pulled it back around him.

"Good girl." He rewarded me with a tap to the head, similar to how one might pat a small creature. "I want you to wear color tonight. No black. Understand?"

"Yes, sir." Black would suit my mood better, but I would find something to satisfy him. Might even enjoy it.

Like a rainbow amongst the darkness, my wardrobe offered an outfit in every color, all grouped together like the meteorological phenomenon. Zaya and I had enjoyed shopping together and then sorting the clothes. It was a trip my husband had funded.

He's not all bad, I thought, chiding myself for ever thinking ill of my husband. He wasn't a bad man, really. He looked after me and gave me wonderful possessions, but sometimes monetary objects weren't everything. I wanted companionship, laughter and chatter, and maybe a little passion.

"Good. I'll be back to retrieve you shortly."

Sighing heavily, I watched Necros take his leave before standing up and wrapping myself in a gown. I could feel the evidence of yet another attempt to get me pregnant leaking from inside me. I hoped it worked this time, as the last thing I wanted to do was displease Necros. He needed this from me to secure his power.

Apart from his short visits to fuck me, I saw very little of my husband. He was busy networking with the kingdoms surrounding Caluçon.

Still, I was grateful he gave me these short moments of his life.

A tear trickled out of the corner of my eye and down my cheek.

Who the hell was I kidding? I hated it here.

My world had fallen apart since I married Necros, and I didn't know how much more I could take. I was lonely and bored and did little but read all day, every day. At least as his fiancée, I'd been busy with preparations for the future and trainings on how to be a dutiful wife. Now, it was as though my life had become little more than a vessel for my husband to stick his dick in whenever—

A quiet knock cut into my thoughts.

"Come in," I called, knowing who it would be before Zaya appeared with her head bowed. My husband never knocked.

"My Queen," she said, curtsying. She did it every time despite my telling her to stop with the formalities. Respect for authority was drilled into her by her parents. The women of her family always served the queen in some capacity, and I was grateful to have her by my side. She knew exactly what I needed to do, plus she had a wicked sense of humor that prompted much laughter together when nobody was looking.

I motioned for her to rise.

"Shall I run you a bath?"

I nodded. "Please."

She wandered off into the bathroom, and a moment later I heard the water start. I opened the closet in my room and looked at the array of dresses. My dark mood had me eyeing the black and blues of my wardrobe, but I couldn't be that woman tonight. I needed to show the might of a worthy queen. What dress to wear?

"May I suggest pink?" Zaya said from the bathroom door. "It gives you regal beauty, and I think it's your best color."

I stepped toward the fuchsia hues and flicked through the offerings. My wedding dress hung there, a luxurious ball gown I'd never wear again because of the memories associated with it. But the outfit beside it caught my eye.

Plum patterns decorated the dark pink bodice and breast cups—the form of which would emphasize my curvy figure. It all flowed into a translucent skirt that would both hide and showcase my long legs. A matching pair of gloves finished the ensemble.

Perfect.

"I'll wear this one." I showed it to Zaya, and she flashed me a playful smirk. I shook my head at her, knowing what she was thinking. "It's not like that." I didn't need to attract my husband. He came to me often enough already. But okay, maybe I wanted others to see me, too. Just to realize my potential.

Lonely indeed.

"Whatever you say, My Lady. Bath's ready."

I strode past her with my own mischievous grin and dropped my gown on the floor before climbing into the warm tub. I sank beneath the water and allowed it to wash all the evidence of my husband's lovemaking away. When I resurfaced, Zaya held out the shampoo.

“Thank you.” I took the bottle and squirted a healthy amount into my thick chestnut hair.

“It’ll be good to get out and dance a little tonight, maybe meet some new people.” Zaya fetched a strawberry-smelling conditioner while I rinsed the shampoo from my strands. Then she brushed the conditioner through the long locks.

“It will be,” I agreed. “I feel like it’s been so long since we’ve had guests. The wedding was the last time, and I didn’t enjoy that nearly as much as I’d hoped.” I flinched when Zaya found a knot in my hair and combed it with a fury. At least, I thought that was what she was doing. Unless she was showing her anger at what I’d said?

She sputtered out several words I’d not heard from her since my wedding night. It shocked me. I considered her to be mild-mannered, and she didn’t know I’d overheard her outburst that night. I’d pretended to be asleep because I hadn’t wanted to talk to anyone.

“Did you mention to the king about that idea you had?” she asked, effectively deflecting from her little tirade. “Rinse first,” she added, her ministrations with my hair done.

I ducked under the water as instructed and then stepped out of the bath. She wrapped a large, fluffy towel around me, and I dried myself while she retrieved a deodorant from a cabinet in my bathroom.

“I’ve not seen him long enough to discuss it yet,” I said, replying to her question. The truth was, I’d been reluctant to try to talk to my husband about any of the ideas I'd had to fill my time. It wasn't because I thought he'd hate them; it was just that, at the moment, he wanted me to concentrate on other duties to help him as the king—namely, the heir he desired.

"It's a superb idea," Zaya informed me. "Maybe if tonight goes well, you can try to talk to him. I know a lot of the demonic women working in the kingdom would enjoy it."

I sighed.

While traveling back from our shopping trip the other day, Zaya and I had noticed an encampment of poorer demons trying desperately to teach their children skills to better their futures. We'd stopped to chat with them and had even helped instruct some of the children.

The women were grateful and expressed a wish for someone who could train the children so they could work and help assist their husbands with bringing money into their families. I'd thought it was a right for everyone to have an education, but it seemed not.

After returning to the palace, I'd developed an idea for a program that could assist those less fortunate than myself.

Only, I hadn't spoken to my husband about it yet.

Maybe I should listen to Zaya and talk to him after the ball. Assuming everything went right tonight, of course.

I cleared my head and focused on donning the pink-and-purple dress. As with everything else in my closet, it fit perfectly.

Zaya straightened my hair before adding a curl to the ends and placed a crown on top of my head. It would be my first time wearing it to a public event, something that should have excited me but didn't due to the heaviness of the solid gold piece. I'd probably have a stiff neck tomorrow from the weight of carrying it on my head all night.

Still, there were worse things in life than being a royal.

"How do I look?" I asked.

Zaya swiped around my lips with a deep purple lipstick and stepped back to admire her handiwork.

"Stunning," she praised with a giggle. "You'll be the envy of every lady in the room and the object of attraction for all the men."

I bit my lip. "I'm not sure Necros will like that." And I didn't really want to be the center of attention, either.

"Tonight is all about him showing you off. He'll want every man in the room jealous that they can't have you, while he can."

"The prize he won in battle." I huffed and stood in front of the mirror. I did look pretty.

Yes, tonight, my husband would show me off to make everyone envious. It was why he'd suggested I wear color. It flattered me better than black. If this was his intention, then I'd make him proud, and when he was happy, I'd ask him to give me a greater role in the kingdom to help those who needed it.

"Are you ready, wife?" Necros's stern, deep tone came from behind my bedroom door.

He didn't wait for me to answer but entered as he always did and then halted on the threshold, his eyes sparkling with lust.

"Fuck me," he breathed. "I'm a lucky man."

My cheeks heated beneath the compliment, causing my eyes to drop to the ground. "Thank you."

He held out his hand for mine, yanking me to him. "Let's go before I decide to skip the entire thing and fuck you all evening instead."

"Later," I replied coyly, my insides protesting at the idea of him taking me again so soon. But I wanted him happy. Pliable. Easy to talk to. And maybe that was the only way to achieve my conversational goals.

"That's for certain." He winked at me and then, completely out of character, tenderly pressed his lips to my cheek. "You know, you're everything I wanted in a wife—beautiful, submissive, and well groomed."

He dug into his pocket and pulled out a gold bracelet studded with emeralds and rubies to match my crown.

"I know the last few months have been difficult. I'm still learning my role, but I promise it'll get better. You'll see."

He slid the bracelet onto my wrist, and I instantly felt guilty.

I'd cursed my husband more than once during our short marriage, but he was doing everything for us. For the betterment of this kingdom.

I would do better for him, too.

I went to my toes to kiss him on the lips—a kiss he didn't return. He never did.

"I'll always be what you need," I vowed.

"I know," he replied. A hint of evil lurked in his expression as his mouth curled at the sides. "And you'll prove it to me tonight. Let's go."

Necros took my hand and we left my bedroom together, the King and Queen of Caluçon ready to make their grand entrance to the assembled guests in the ballroom.

Chapter Four

Adrik

The hairs along my arms danced, warning me of the approaching royal before he stepped onto the platform above. Power oozed from his pores, shrouding the room in a cloud of energy that made it difficult to breathe.

A standard show of authority, one that called the shadows within me to the surface as if preparing for a fight. And wouldn't that be a colossal waste of training? Grigory would never let me live it down.

I lifted the blood wine to my lips and swallowed the urge to react.

Many fell to their knees beneath the onslaught of dominance, revealing those in the ballroom who posed a threat to King Necros's position. He eyed each and every one of us, his lips curling at the turnout. Hosting other royals and powerful figures in his kingdom wasn't a typical occurrence. No, we were all invited here tonight for a purpose—to help him break the beautiful woman at his side.

Innocence radiated from her as she studied the mostly male audience watching her descent. The poor little bird clearly had no idea what was waiting for her tonight, the fate she was expected to endure.

Some of the attendees were only here for the show.

Others were here to fight.

I'd come to win.

"Welcome," Necros said loudly as they reached the marble floor at the bottom of the grand staircase. He held his wife close, his muscular form highlighting her dainty appearance. How could so much power reside in such a fragile female?

One thing was for sure—when she gave me her heart, it would break her irrevocably. Likely even kill her.

The room stilled, all the focus falling on the almighty king and waiting for him to speak. Queen Valora glanced up at him with a pretty blush that crept down her neck and lower into her subtle cleavage. Definitely a gorgeous woman. Seducing her wouldn't be a hardship.

I took another sip of my wine, affecting a bored pose. Many were still on their knees, the weight of Necros's presence hanging heavy in the air. Those of us left upright were the ones he sought, the most powerful beings of the Underworld aroused by the chance to play this deadly game. The invitation for tonight had reached every kingdom, only the most daring accepting.

Or perhaps those with a death wish.

Because most would not survive the evening.

Immortality only helped us heal indefinitely, but certain weapons—like the ones used against my parents—made for a more permanent demise. I possessed two such blades, having prepared myself for the tasks ahead. Others would rely on Necros's supposed hospitality. I knew better.

"Ah, there are more of you than I anticipated." Approval deepened Necros's tone. "You can't know how much this pleases me."

Oh, I have a good idea, I thought dryly, hiding my smirk behind my glass. My opposite hand remained in the pocket of my suit pants, my thumb running over a sharp edge just in case I needed it sooner rather than later. But Necros's green gaze held only intrigue when he caught sight of me, my pale skin and drink of choice signaling my identity, not the shadows lurking deep inside.

Excellent.

"As most of you know, I was recently wed to the beauty at my side." Necros glanced down at the blushing female, his lips tilted in a sinister grin. "Valora, Queen of Caluçon. Isn't she gorgeous?" Her cheeks reddened even more as she lowered her gaze demurely. An odd reaction for someone who supposedly contained unworldly power.

What if Lux had it wrong?

The prophecy of Valora's life energy was just that—a myth. Not many knew of it. But it all stemmed from the same legend that had cost my parents their lives. Necros believed the Shadow Kingdom would overrun his kingdom of the dead, and took everyone out.

Everyone except me.

Because my mother had overheard the prophecy from the heavens, whether by fate or divine intervention, I didn't know. However, she'd used the information to hide me away in Noxia just before the attack. And part of that story foretold of a great power in Graystall, one that would rule them all.

I wondered how many others in this room knew of the tales, but most of the males were merely observing Valora with open lust, not calculation.

"Unfortunately, I have a problem," Necros continued on a dramatic sigh. "You see, while gorgeous, she's quite unskilled. Something I take full responsibility for since I kept her chaste for our wedding. But over the last six months, she's not really taken to my methods or shown any signs of improvement. So I've called you all here to help me train my wife in matters of the bedroom."

The queen's shoulders went rigid, her lips parting at the degrading speech. But her husband wasn't done.

"I mean, six months and she's still not with child. So either she's barren or something nefarious is at play. Regardless, if she can't provide me with an heir, then I'll use her for something else. Which is why I've called you all here tonight to participate in the competition at hand. There are seven nights of the week, and I only require one, which gives six of you an opportunity to claim one of her other evenings. For compensation, of course, and I will only permit the strongest among you the chance to fuck my wife."

Valora had gone white now, her body appearing even frailer among the masses. Some part of me had hoped to see a fight, or perhaps even a glimpse of her power surface, yet she remained infuriatingly subservient at the king's side, as if her stiletto-clad feet were glued to the ground.

"One more item before we begin—a consolation prize of sorts." Necros glanced over his broad shoulder toward the top of the stairs. "Maximus?"

A giant of a man appeared in a suit similar to my own, a small trembling girl at his side, with soft brown curls and round eyes filled with horror.

The queen grabbed her husband's arm, causing him to turn toward her with a warning glance. She said something too softly for me to catch, her imploring gaze making the king's mouth to flatten.

"Even now, my wife forgets her place," Necros boasted, his tone filled with disdain. "Which is why I offer her lady's maid for entertainment tonight, to those who prefer a quick fuck over the fight for a taste of royalty."

I set my glass down, the power play souring my stomach. This was all a ruse, a way to weed out the weakest among the herd before we even began. And already several were taking the bait.

Such a sad group indeed.

To think, Grigory had worried about me.

Tears blossomed in the queen's eyes, her mouth moving almost silently to plead for the female she clearly cared about above. The king ignored her, signaling for Maximus to bring the shaking girl down to his level. She appeared so young, maybe twenty at most. Her fearful gaze sought out the queen, a look of misery passing between them, much to the amusement in the room.

Jeers began, salacious commentary littering the air, leaving only a few of us silent in our preparation for the true prize.

A prize that was visibly breaking only twenty feet away.

The little bird's wings were clearly clipped before she'd ever learned to fly. She attempted to move forward, as if to shield her lady's maid, but the king held her back with a hand on her shoulder and some stern words whispered into her ear.

Whatever he said had her posture falling into perfect submission, her beautiful face angling toward the ground.

There was nothing she could do.

Nowhere to run.

And yet, a slight clench in her jaw indicated her opinion. Hmm, was that the fighter inside teasing her way to the surface? Or a way to keep herself from sobbing before the room of hungry males?

The lady's maid screamed as her clothes were ripped away, the men already on her for their bout of enjoyment.

Necros observed the debasing act with a serene gleam, revealing the king's perverse side. He enjoyed harming those beneath him, mostly as a way of remaining in power.

But what he adored more was to take out potential contenders. Hence, tonight's little game.

I slowly removed my suit jacket, folding it over a nearby chair, and began rolling the sleeves of my dress shirt while I waited. By my count, there were fifteen of us who could potentially compete. None of them posed a threat to my ability and status. But there were a few I wouldn't mind removing from the equation, mostly because I wanted the queen to remain intact and not everyone here would have her safety in mind.

Sure, the king would provide us with rules. I just doubted some of my contenders' abilities to abide by them.

Particularly, Thortus—the bulky brute with the football-shaped head. He was notorious for kidnapping humans from Earth just to rape them to death. Necros no doubt considered the asshole to be a suitable candidate for breaking his pretty little wife.

I disagreed.

Rolling my neck, I ignored the muffled cries coming from the lady's maid and focused on Necros. He held the queen's arm tightly while conversing with two of his men. Whatever he was saying had painted her skin in shades of gray.

Then he released her with a clap of his hands. "It's time."

A gladiator ring formed throughout the middle of the room, dividing those who wanted to watch from the candidates, while those seeking more sadistic entertainment played with the lady's maid in the corner.

I suspected most of those men would find their ties to Necros loosened in the coming days, their weakness for a bit of free flesh denoting them as useless to anyone in power. Because everyone knew a prize was worth fighting for, not one you won just by being.

Two lines were formed, eight on each side. I stood near the end, hands tucked into the pockets of my dress pants, bored. Weapons were wheeled out as Necros and his queen took their seats on the outskirts of the ring. She no longer cried or blinked, her skin ashen, her mouth pressed to a fine line.

The harsher Necros was to her, the easier he made my job. She needed a knight, someone willing to help her, and I would prove to be that male. Then destroy everything she'd ever known.

"The rules are simple," Necros said, commanding the room with his deep tenor. "The last six left standing win. All weapons are accepted, including any that were carried in tonight. I've also provided a few items for those who didn't arrive prepared." He relaxed into his throne, his hand clasping Queen Valora's tightly. "Any questions?"

I palmed my blades, my targets in sight.

No one spoke, the anticipation thick in the makeshift arena.

Not even the lady's maid cried now. Or perhaps all sound was drowned out from the rhythmic beating in my ears. I began to count, my instincts taking over and leading my expectations.

Three.

Two.

Necros's hand sliced through the air, igniting chaos throughout the room. "Begin."

Chapter Five

Valora

THUMP.

Thump.

Thump.

The beat of my heart rang in my ears, the noise akin to a bass drum sounding out my death.

Had my husband just made an announcement beyond cruel?

Zaya screamed louder, the noise filled the room and mixed with the sound of men who fought to win me for one night a week. Six unknown males and, on the seventh night, my husband would take me.

Immortality suddenly didn't seem like a gift. A lifetime of hell all because I saved a realm I didn't even know.

Every inch of me wanted to scream and shout, but I knew I had to play the perfect wife.

"Why are you doing this?" I kept my face neutral for everyone in the audience but addressed my husband. "Why do this to me? To Zaya?"

"You don't get it, do you, my dear wife? I do it because I can. You don't seem to understand how to satisfy me, and I want you to learn the art of sex so you will better please me."

His statement caused my composure to slip. "*Bullshit*." The people nearest to me jumped at my words and the venom dripping from them.

Necros waved away their attention with a flick of his wrist. "Remember your place, Valora. You wouldn't want me to have to beat you in front of the assembled guests for disobedience."

My temper spiked and I stood up. "Go to hell."

Necros grabbed my arm and yanked me back into my seat. "Big mistake, little one." He stood and clapped his hands, causing everyone to stop midfight. Even the two men raping Zaya halted, their lustful gazes causing my stomach to churn. I recognized them—they had watched me on my wedding day.

Dampness pricked the corners of my eyes, but I refused to let it fall. I'd not give my "loving" husband the satisfaction of victory over me now. How I thought he had a heart, I didn't know.

"Bring her to me," Necros demanded, his focus on Zaya.

The shorter of the two pulled out of my lady's maid, his cock covered in blood.

Maximus stepped in and pulled Zaya up by her long hair. She was covered in bruises, bites, and unspeakable fluids. Her eyes full of tears, my fun-loving maid was seemingly replaced by a woman longing for death.

"Please," I whimpered, hoping to change my husband's mind from whatever he was going to do even though I knew it was futile.

"It seems my wife hasn't learned enough yet to

believe my intentions are for her benefit," Necros explained to the observing crowd. "Perhaps a demonstration will help?"

Approval radiated through the air, the roughened fighters on the floor gleaming up at the king with deep appreciation. These were the men he'd chosen for me, all of them brutes and covered in warrior wounds. Two of them were already dead. But I couldn't pay them much mind, not with Maximus pushing Zaya to the ground before us.

Oh God… Please no...

Necros removed his member from his pants. Maximus then held Zaya's mouth open while my husband forced his dick inside it.

I fell to my knees next to my maid, the only person in this land who'd ever shown me kindness. I needed to save her from any more suffering.

"Please, she's had enough. I'll do it instead. Here, in front of everyone." I waved my arm around, showing off the assembled crowd.

Necros shoved himself down her throat, suffocating my maid, and paused, calculating his next move.

"All right." He withdrew from Zaya's mouth and shifted in front of me. I opened my mouth wide and shut my eyes. "No, keep your gaze on me."

I opened them again and looked up at him. "My Lord."

Maximus dropped Zaya, half-unconscious, onto the floor of the ballroom and came to stand behind me. Necros thrust into my mouth at the same time as Maximus secured my head. I was nothing but a toy to my husband now, taking everything he gave me.

"Thomas, Demetrius, you can take the maid back and finish what you started," my husband announced at the same time as he thrust deep, halting my ability to breathe. "To the remaining fourteen, continue. Unless you no longer find my errant wife worthy." He withdrew and sheathed himself in my mouth again, causing me to gag as the men chuckled at his crude words.

Zaya yelped and my focus shifted toward her, earning me a slap against my cheek. "Eyes on me, little whore," Necros ordered, and I flicked them back up. I didn't want to watch him, but I knew I had no choice.

He pumped his hips into me like a wild animal. Rough, hard, and with no thought for the fact that every time he pistoned forward, I coughed and choked around him. He was too busy watching the chaos below where the men fought for a chance to fuck me.

Bile rose in my throat, forced back down by the impact of his cock.

I wanted to scream, to bite, to *hurt*.

But I could do nothing other than accept his filthy torment.

It didn't take him long to bury himself deep in the back of my mouth and eject his venomous lust down my throat, spurt after spurt of hot and salty cum that left me retching. Eventually he withdrew and tucked himself back in his pants.

Necros shook his head, disdain coloring his features. "Pitiful and exactly why I require help in your training. You couldn't even swallow properly."

I yelped as he pushed me to the floor, Maximus's

fingers still twined in my hair. Wincing, I glared up at them both, unable to speak beyond the throbbing in my throat.

"Remain there where you belong," Necros demanded, retaking his throne.

My husband was sick.

He was worse than Lucifer himself.

I wanted him dead, and one day I'd be the one to do it. *One does not require power, only the right opportunity to take it.*

Wrapping my skirt around my hand, I used it to wipe my face of saliva and the evidence of my husband's assault.

I would not let them break me.

Ever.

Zaya's shriek sent a chill down my spine. I couldn't see her, but I knew what they were doing to her. All because my husband *could.* I'd try to help her later, return her to her family, *something* to get her out of this hell.

Assuming she survives the night.

Oh, I hated Necros. Loathed him.

Whatever good I tried to see in him was gone, just like my dignity as I sat on the floor, awaiting my fate.

I took in the men fighting, willing them to just kill each other to end this charade so I could return to my room and hide.

The men on the ground were highly skilled, battling fast and hard. All with individual styles that echoed their upbringing. One of the males was twice the size of my husband, with a scar down the center of his face. His crooked nose and beady eyes terrified me just as much as watching him take down opponent after opponent with a weapon that killed immortals. I had to turn away from him, the thought of having him touch me sending shivers down my spine.

How would I manage to do this?

They are going to break me.

My eyes flitted to another man next, one of similar size to my husband but with a hint of coldness to his features. I frowned at him, curious. He possessed the kind of face that would have women throwing themselves at his feet, his dark features and pale skin a contrast most would find desirable. Why was he here? Surely he did not require a fight to bed a woman. And oddly, he didn't have a speck of blood on him. How strange.

Part of me was surprised my husband allowed such a specimen to join the battle.

The other part didn't care. Because what did I know? I was just a woman meant to please her husband.

Fuck them all.

My hand shook, my brow beading with sweat. I gripped my skirts, willing my limbs to cooperate. *Nobody can see my fear. It will only weaken me further in their eyes.*

"One left and then we'll know your men," Necros informed me.

My stomach churned, thinking of the six men who would take me one after the other. Brand me as a whore and destroy the virtue I was brought up to believe in. "Will I be given to the victor tonight?" I wondered quietly, then flinched at the thought of further punishment.

My husband's lips curled into a cruel grin. "No time like the present. I mean, surely you want to reward one of the hardworking victors with your body, right? Or would you prefer all six to share Zaya tonight as a warm-up?" He turned his attention away from the fight and to me, with a questioning eyebrow raised.

I swallowed. *I will kill you.* "I prefer to reward one myself, My Lord," I managed to say, my throat dry.

"Or perhaps all six at once?" He smirked evilly. "Decisions, decisions."

Defeat.

There was no question for me to answer, his attention already drifting. What could I say? Nothing. He owned me. I'd never been my own person. Never controlled my fate. And tonight would be no different.

I refocused on the bloody arena, waiting for the inevitable.

The handsome man wielded his knife with an adept skill, but I was shocked when I saw he focused his attention on the man with the crooked nose. He'd lose, the *fool.*

Arrogance was always a downfall, especially in the Underworld.

I sat stunned when he leaped quickly and soundlessly into action and surprised Crooked Nose with a slice to his throat. I leaned forward, watching every move with awe. I'd never seen a fighter with such skill.

How was that possible?

Crooked Nose grabbed his neck and tried to speak, but no sound came out. The entire room stopped while the giant fell, leaving six victors in his wake.

The handsome male looked down at his knife and wrinkled his nose. Leaning over, he wiped it on the jacket of the dead man before him and then tucked it away like he hadn't just used it to kill someone.

"Excellent. I see some of you came prepared." Necros stood while I remained at his feet, where he'd commanded I stay.

The six men shifted forward, five were covered head to toe in the blood of those they'd defeated, but the man I'd just witnessed kill someone twice his size still remained untouched. He appeared as though he'd been out for a short jog rather than engaging in a bloody battle.

Something about him unsettled me. Perhaps it was the lethal gleam in his gaze or the way he stared stoically at the king. Regardless, Crooked Nose no longer scared me most. This champion did.

"Congratulations." My husband descended the stage like the powerful ruler he was, everyone moving out of his way and bowing in deference to his power. "You've all earned at least one night with my wife, subject to more if I believe you a suitable candidate for her training."

Necros stopped in front of the handsome man.

No. I couldn't call him that.

He continued to scare the hell out of me with his calmness, and he'd just fought a battle for my body.

A person's character was what made them handsome, not the way they looked.

"Hmm, you all fought hard, but one stood out above the rest." Necros's gaze fell to the male I feared most—the lack of blood on his attire likely the reason for my husband's attention. "Prince Adrik of Noxia, I presume?"

Lethality loomed in the male's dark gaze as he gave a subtle bow. Not the full kind as most did in my husband's presence, but a partial bend to imply respect more than servitude. These men were closer to equals. Although, despite Prince Adrik's royal vampire lineage, Necros sat at the top of the throne. Mostly because both kingdoms were allies, with the Queen of Noxia bowing to Necros's will rather than contesting it.

"A pleasure, King of the Dead," Adrik replied, his deep baritone sending a shiver down my spine.

Necros took his measure once more, stroking his bearded chin all the while. "How is Queen Lux?"

"She's well, My Lord, and she sends her warm regards."

"And she approves of your attendance here?" Necros pressed.

Adrik's full lips curled at the side into a devastating smile. *Handsome* had been too tame a term for him. *Sinful* seemed more accurate. *Tempting*, too. "I doubt she will when she finds out, but I desired a challenge." His dark eyes flitted to me, his expression intensifying. "A beautiful one." He returned his focus to Necros. "Your offer was too enticing for me to resist."

Necros chuckled, glancing over his shoulder at me. "Well, a challenge she certainly will be."

"Fortunately, I have experience in that realm." The lewdness in his tone caused my stomach to churn, as did the evil victory radiating from Necros's features.

"So I've heard." My husband shifted back to Adrik. "Would you like to taste her first?"

My breath hitched.

No.

Not him.

A vampire? That was too dangerous. He could kill me. Didn't Necros realize that?

"It would be my honor, My Lord," Adrik replied, licentious energy rolling off him in waves. "I will just need limits addressed."

"No limits." The severity in those words had my heart leaping into my throat.

"You're sure? Because I enjoy sharp elements in the bedroom." Adrik twirled a blade skillfully through his fingers to drive home his point.

My lips parted. No way would Necros allow him to—

"She'll heal," my husband said emotionlessly. "Valora, come say hello to your first trainer." He snapped his fingers behind him as if to beckon me like an animal.

Maximus didn't give me time to process the insanity or make a move on my own. Instead, he fisted my hair and yanked me up off the ground, sending a twinge of pain down my spine. He forced me forward to stand beside my husband, his grip unyielding.

I kept my mouth shut, refusing to say a word.

No, not even that.

I didn't know *what* to say.

All I desired was to scream and *kill.*

"You see what I'm dealing with? Defiance to the

utter end." My husband shook his head in annoyance, raised his hand in the air, and clipped me in the face.

"Hello," I forced out, my head ringing from his assault.

Adrik looked me up and down, his dark eyes bored into my curves displayed prominently in the dress I had chosen.

I inwardly cursed my choice.

I should have worn a black sack.

"That's just how I like them. More fun to break." Adrik tilted his head toward my stomach. "I assume we're to use protection?"

"And spoil the fun for you? No, I believe you'll find me to be far more accommodating. Maximus?"

The guard holding me produced a device from his pocket that looked akin to a gun. He pressed it against my shoulder and fired a button. A pain erupted in my shoulder.

"Ow!" I jerked away from him and glared. I wasn't a toy to be passed around like this. I was a queen! "What the hell was that?"

"Contraception," my husband announced from beside me. "You're very likely barren, if the last six months are any indication, but I can't risk you conceiving a bastard. After you're satisfactorily trained, I'll try for another heir. If that fails, well..."

He allowed the threat to linger between us, his gaze wicked. Then he threw me like a rag doll to Adrik's feet.

"She's all yours."

Chapter Six

Adrik

"Shall I escort you to your room?" Maximus asked. His stature told me he would be a worthy opponent, his ebony eyes warning me not to try.

I smiled. "Not yet."

Valora blinked, her confusion palpable. *What are you thinking, little bird?* I wondered. *Do you think I'm going to go easy on you? Now, in front of all these people? No, sweetheart. No.*

I circled my prey, contemplating what to do to her first. She sat absolutely still on the ground, oblivious to the blood of dead warriors seeping into her gown. Or perhaps immune to it. But her heart gave a slight pang each time I took a step, her breath hitching in her throat as I drew out the dance of her fate.

Necros arched an auburn brow as if to urge me to begin.

And I would.

Soon.

I crouched before her, bringing us to eye level

with one another. "Do you know what your performance lacked earlier, little one?"

Silence swam around us, our audience awaiting her reply. Of which she gave none, her chin jutting out in a stubborn line that intrigued my instincts. It seemed the queen wanted to play. Good.

Her husband raised his fist as if to correct the behavior himself, but I held up a hand. "Allow me, My Lord." I had a show to put on, one I hoped would gain me his favor and allow me some much-needed alone time with his wife. "It's rude to ignore a direct question, Valora."

Gorgeous light blue eyes met my own, her pupils flaring the tiniest bit to display her irritation. Mmm, she didn't like this at all. Not that I blamed her. What would it take to prompt her rebellion? To provoke her enough to kill her own husband?

"Get it over with," she demanded. "Fuck me, if that's your choice. Use me. Do whatever it is you please, *My Prince*."

Such fire and hatred. All for someone she hardly knew. I couldn't help my resulting smile. "Enthusiasm," I informed her softly, tilting my head to the side. "That's the answer, sweetheart."

Her lips flattened. "This game bores me."

I chuckled, adoring this feisty side of her. "Does it? Shall we make it more interesting?" I slid my hand into my pocket, palming the blade I'd just used to take out half a dozen immortal men—*for her.* "Kneel."

The king wanted a demonstration, so I would provide one unlike any he could have anticipated.

Valora did as requested without flinching, her

gaze taking on a distant quality similar to the one she'd given her husband when he forced his seed down her pretty little throat. I went to my knees as well, my height giving me a not-so-subtle advantage over her, and used the hilt of my knife against her chin to force her focus upward.

"Your clear distaste of the moment ruins the experience," I murmured, sliding the weapon between my fingers to press the sharper side to the base of her throat, and glanced up at Necros. "No rules?" He'd stated it once before, but I wanted to hear him say it again. More for those observing the lesson. I knew most of these men. If they thought they could take Valora however they wanted, she wouldn't survive the week.

Necros stroked his beard, his attention falling to the sharp edge resting against Valora's skin. She didn't even flinch as I drew the weapon downward to rest between her cleavage.

Beautifully submissive.

"No permanent damage," Necros finally said. "She might be barren, but I want her alive."

Of course you do, I thought. He wanted her power, same as I did. "So only leave wounds that will heal under immortality?" Again the question was for the benefit of our audience. It would be such a shame to harm someone so gorgeous.

Necros nodded. "Blood is fine. You can even break bone. But only if she can recover without a scar. If I can't breed her, I might as well use her body for other means."

Another benefit of having her trained, I supposed.

Not that I agreed with any of this.

But I had to play along to get what I needed—her heart.

"Understood," I murmured, tracing the tip of my dagger down her corseted top. Her breathing remained steady as she floated in some faraway place, her imagination overtaking her reality. Alas, I couldn't allow her to stay there. I needed her focus and compliance to achieve my goal. "I want to teach you something, Valora," I said, my weapon nearing her belly button. "An important lesson on participation."

She gasped as I sliced through her bodice in one swift flick of my wrist. The fabric parted over her torso, revealing creamy skin and a pair of tits that left our audience growling in approval. Rather than admire my prize, I held her gaze and watched as her pupils engulfed the circumference of her pale irises.

Finally she showed signs of some emotion.

Fear.

Shock.

Confusion.

"Better," I praised, sliding the weapon lower, to her skirts, while ignoring the low murmurs and growls littering the air. Valora commanded me now. Her expression. Her body. The heat wafting up from her exposed skin. "Focus on me. On my touch. On the way I make you feel."

Silky fabrics slipped across my skin as I found a part in her dress that introduced me to her bare thigh. My opposite hand caught her hip to keep her upright, secretly lending her my strength under the guise of control.

No panties.

Just a freshly shaved mound and a feminine heat that wasn't nearly wet enough. "Spread your legs," I encouraged her softly, my hand already pushing them apart as I spoke.

She swallowed.

Her breath hitched.

And another gasp parted her full lips.

"Is it cold?" I asked, the hilt of my blade gliding effortlessly through her slick folds. To those watching, they wouldn't know how I touched her, would likely think the worst, and that was entirely the point. "Answer me, Valora." I needed her cooperation for this to work. If Necros thought for a second that I might go easy on her, he'd take me off this degrading task and I'd have to approach this plan from an entirely different angle.

"It's—"

I pressed the handle upward into her dampening sex, eliciting a yelp from her throat. It was well timed and earned a few chuckles from the audience, but her blown-out pupils captivated my focus.

"Still waiting for a reply," I taunted. "Is it cold?"

"N-no," she stammered, her upper body swaying as my thumb brushed her clit.

"Grab my shoulders," I commanded, not wanting to risk her falling when I had such a lethal object between her thighs. The blade might be pointed downward, but it was sharp and wouldn't take much to damage her tender skin.

Valora didn't hesitate, her nails gripping me for support. I pressed the little bundle of nerves again, eliciting a visible shiver across her exposed skin.

"You're doing so well," I told her, applying more pressure and guiding the handle just a little deeper into her.

She bit her lip, sweat beading her brow. "I don't… What are you…? Why?"

"I'm teaching you how to respond, little one. How to participate and enjoy your purpose." I pressed down on her sensitive nub and set a pace with the weapon, carefully fucking her with the hilt. It took skill on my part, just enough to keep me grounded and in control while Valora lost touch with reality and succumbed to my will.

Sound drowned out around us, my entire existence focused on her reddening cheeks and heavy-lidded gaze. I hadn't expected her to fall beneath the spell of my seduction so easily. But the woman was a natural, her supple form curling into mine, her arousal thickening the air.

"It feels…" The words were hardly audible, a breath against my lips. "I…"

"Give in to it," I urged her, my mouth tracing hers without kissing, my thumb drawing sensuous circles against her, the handle of my knife penetrating her in the most sinful of ways. "Succumb, Valora."

She blinked, her gaze heavy, her tongue snaking out to dampen her plump lower lip.

The bastard king had clearly never introduced Valora to pleasure or ecstasy. That was how I'd so easily managed to enrapture her in this haze of violence. It should have left her cold and unattainable, but she responded beautifully to my blade. I almost wanted to thank Necros for making this so simple.

But Valora held me captive with her soft mewls and lust-flared pupils.

She'd completely forgotten her place.

Lost herself to the sensations.

"Are you going to come for me, Valora?" I whispered, my mouth dropping to her ear. "Fly, little bird. Fly hard and fast."

Her moan sang through my system, her nails gripping me tightly as she fell apart before me in the most beautiful display of pleasure I'd ever witnessed. My mask of indifference almost fell. *Almost.* But I remembered our surroundings at exactly the right moment, my lips curling into the epitome of evil I knew the king would appreciate.

"Mmm, that's how you participate, Valora," I said, my tone just loud enough for others to overhear. "With passion." I slid my palm from her hip to her lower back, catching her as she continued to convulse from the aftershocks of her orgasm. "And you enjoyed it, didn't you?"

Her exhale feathered over my mouth, her mind not yet catching up with the moment. "I… Yes."

I hated what I had to say, hated how I had to shatter such a beautiful moment. But this performance required a finale, one that would win the king's approval and grant me what I required—his tenuous respect.

"Of course you did." I withdrew my knife and brought the handle up to her lips. "Lick."

She didn't hesitate, still lost to the wondrous world of ecstasy that her husband had failed to introduce her to. I coated her tongue and mouth with her juices, allowing everyone to see just how much

Valora enjoyed my brand of fucking.

"Your wife is a beautiful whore," I told the king, despising myself for the role I had to play. "She might pretend not to like it, but we can all see the truth now." I drove my handle into her mouth with those words, forcing her to accept it the way her cunt had and glanced up at her smirking husband. "I think I'll take you up on that room now."

Necros chuckled and waved a hand. "Of course. I think you've more than proven your skill in handling her. And I'll admit, I rather enjoyed the show." His lewd gaze danced over a now-cowering Valora, her shame written across her features and in the horrified glimmer of her eyes.

Yes, she'd completely forgotten our audience.

And my words had snapped her back faster than a bullet piercing the air.

What she didn't know was that the entire show had been for her benefit. I wanted the rules established for those who possessed no regard for humanity, and I required the king's trust with her. His invitation suggested a one-week trial. Hardly good enough for my intentions. Hopefully, tonight's little ruse would earn me more time.

I withdrew my weapon and slid it into the sheath lining my pocket. Then stood and held out my hand. "Shall we, little whore?"

She flinched at the new nickname, while the others guffawed. Pricks. All of them. Not that I felt all that much better from speaking their language.

I consoled myself with images of Caluçon burning to the ground.

Too bad it required harming an innocent in the

process.

Shoving that negative consideration down, I cocked a brow at the still-kneeling queen. "Valora?" I prompted, needing her to comply. The king would expect punishment, and I really didn't want to have to degrade her more than I already had.

She visibly shook herself and stood without accepting my help up off the ground, her pride returning with a vengeance.

I fought a smile, pleased to see that a little public shaming wasn't enough to break her, and grabbed her elbow before she could think to march off without me.

"My Liege," I said, bowing my head in false reverence to the king. "It is an honor to serve."

He grinned. "Trust me, the pleasure is all mine." His gaze shifted to an opening door, where one of his minions stood with a horde of waiting females. "Gentlemen, your gifts for participating in my games have arrived. Adrik, should you require any leftovers when you're done with my wife, you know where to find us."

"Your hospitality is unworldly, King Necros." I allowed my lips to curl. "If your wife performs as poorly as she did earlier, then you will definitely be seeing me again."

He laughed, his attention on an approaching pair of blondes. "Welcome to my daily life, Prince of Noxia." He held open his arms. "There's a reason I don't share a bed with my wife."

Valora was frozen beside me, her arm brittle beneath my palm. I allowed my thumb to graze her inner elbow, just a slight touch of comfort. "I'll take my leave now and provide a report in the morning."

Necros didn't bother with a reply, his lips already otherwise engaged. Valora took in the sight with horror-stricken eyes, something I helped to hide by yanking her into my side.

She said nothing.

Did nothing.

Barely even breathed.

Just followed along at my side like a robot as Maximus led us to a lavish bedroom meant for guests. He explained the furnishings in a few brief sentences, stating it would be my residence while on the property until I desired to leave or the king dismissed us of our duty.

I engaged in the necessary chatter, expressing my gratitude and giving him a fresh smile as he bid us a pleasurable evening. Then I locked the door behind him and turned to find Valora standing as still as a statue beside the colossal bed. Her corset remained ripped in half, her nipples erect in the cold air, her expression one of death.

For someone so powerful, she sure did shut down easily.

My jacket lay over the arm of a nearby chair, causing my lips to twitch. Someone had brought it from the table, which meant it had very likely been inspected. They would have found a standard lighter, a cigar, and a copy of tonight's invitation. All items easily overlooked by the untrained eye.

I flicked the lighter, putting on a show of testing the flames while tinkering with the button on the bottom. The noise cancellation device disguised as a cigar would activate immediately, allowing us to speak freely without interference. But I suspected a camera still lurked in the room, capturing our time together for the king to review later.

I also had a plan for that.

The invitation had been altered, the cardstock thick enough to hide the frequency jammer lined between the paper.

Demon technology. Efficient. Powerful. And so fucking useful.

I slid the card out as if to read it and placed it beside the cigar, then lit another flame to activate the trigger inside the cardstock.

A tiny green light beneath the fire told me I'd accomplished my mission.

The king would be able to watch the film, but the image would be fuzzy and the sound would be in and out. Perfect for my intentions.

Now to heat up the frozen queen.

Chapter Seven

Valora

PRINCE ADRIK WAS DANGEROUS. I already knew that, but his earlier touch drove the point home.

My body felt alien to me. Sensations I'd never experienced swirled beneath my skin, and a slick wetness coated the insides of my thighs. The residual quakes in my lower half were vastly different from the pain I would normally be wishing away right now.

Prince Adrik had willed my body to perform strange things before the assembled audience.

And worse, I had enjoyed it.

An orgasm. At least, that was what I thought had occurred. I'd felt consumed, light-headed, as if floating away on a cloud of utter bliss. Someone once called it the *little death.* I now understood the phrase because, in the moment, I'd almost felt free.

And a twisted part of me desired to experience it again.

No. I shook myself of the thoughts. It couldn't happen again. The vulnerability was something I couldn't afford to feel around one of my husband's allies. Especially one destined to do wicked things to my body.

This whole situation was preposterous. I wasn't a whore but a queen, and I would recover my position and pride and place.

"Remove your clothes," Adrik demanded, cutting into my thoughts.

I turned to face him, defiant. My head held high, although my legs shook like brightly colored autumn leaves dancing in a furious storm.

"I gave you an order," he said, prowling closer.

"I'm queen here. I do not take orders from you."

Adrik's full lips twisted upward into a sinfully decadent smile, one that would have drawn my attention in any other situation apart from this one. While my husband was a decent-looking man, Adrik possessed a beauty that surpassed most, and the dimples flashing deep in his cheeks suggested he knew it.

Power poured from him as he stopped before me, a sinful energy foretelling of disturbing plans to destroy me like the whore he saw me as.

I will not waver.

I will not fall.

"Your gown is covered in blood from those who died tonight. Men I killed for the privilege of your company. Are you sure you want to remain clothed?" Adrik strode over to a wardrobe in his chamber's corner, his strong strides willing my gaze to follow.

Bloody or not, I will not bow to his demands.

"I'm used to being covered in blood. I am married to Necros, after all," I justified out loud. "I would suggest the issue with clothes is more your own. I'm not a fool; I saw the look on your face when you had blood on your weapon. It was one of pure disgust." Which was an odd thing for one of Noxia. They were vampires. They lived for blood.

Adrik appeared directly in front of me, a dressing gown of sheer white silk held in his hand. I jumped like a nervous kitten, not having heard or noticed him moving, and immediately cursed myself for showing weakness.

"On the contrary, My Queen. As a Prince of Noxia, I adore blood, but mostly of the female variety." He waved the dressing gown in my face. "Change. I won't ask you again."

I turned my head away from him, a refusal to entertain or acknowledge him and his demanding ways. The hot space between my legs pulsed in response, enjoying the idea of provoking him. For what purpose, I couldn't say, but it took a valiant effort not to squirm.

What is wrong with me?

I can't enjoy this. Ever.

He was just as bad as Necros.

No, worse. He made me feel...

"Have it your way, then." Adrik whirled me around and up against the bed. In a single strong tug, he ripped the skirt from my body, the sliced corset falling in its wake and leaving me naked before him. The vibrant fuchsia-toned silks were flung across the floor to land in a heap by the only door in the room.

Adrenaline surged through my body. How dare he think he could treat me this way? I was a queen—no, a *person*—not a toy. They couldn't do this to me.

With my own quick movement, I turned to face

the stranger in the room and smacked my hand *hard* across his face. The sound of flesh meeting flesh was so loud it echoed off the cavernous ceilings. My palm stung like I'd just been whipped.

Adrik didn't move, not even a flinch to rub where a red mark had appeared on his strong, stubbled jawline. He just stared at me, his eyes deepening to the hues of the darkest night as mayhem fluttered in them.

I inhaled deeply, sheer terror running through my body and mixing with the aftermath of my recent orgasm. Every nerve ending jumped to attention, stirring a fire within me I couldn't seem to cool.

What is happening to me?

Am I going insane?

"You have so little faith in yourself, yet underneath the shadows is a powerful woman," he advised softly. "Embrace it, use your anger to fuel the fires of your revenge. It's the only way you'll get through this."

I raised my hand again, shock ricocheting through my body at his words. They were in direct contrast to what every man wanted me to be in this palace. Necros wanted me to be docile, a good fuck, and to produce his heirs. Silence was my greatest virtue to everyone.

I didn't understand. Before I had a chance to lash out at him anew, Adrik grabbed me by the neck, his strong hand constricting my breath and pushing me backward onto the bed.

"There are cameras in this room," he advised in that same low tone. "He'll be watching and expecting certain behaviors. I'll need this to appear real."

"What?" None of this made any sense, but as he fumbled with his belt, my confusion flew out the window.

He's going to fuck me now.

Except he only unbuttoned his pants and partially lowered the zipper, his cock remaining hidden behind the silky texture of his suit trousers. He knelt on the bed, pushing me upward with the grip around my throat until my head hit the pillows, and settled between my splayed legs.

"What are you…?" I trailed off as he released my neck to skim his fingers downward between us, his featherlight touch brushing my breastbone and stomach before slipping into the slickness between my thighs.

"Don't let them break you, Valora," he whispered, his lips near mine.

"Adrik," I breathed, conflicted as his thumb unerringly found my already sensitive nub and circled it. This wasn't what I expected, wasn't what we were supposed to do, but the entire time, he kept his ardent gaze on me, drawing me into the danger he possessed inside him.

Who is this man? What does he want from me?

And why am I not fighting him?

His hips circled against me, providing further friction where I needed it.

He wasn't taking me with his cock?

He wasn't taking any pleasure for himself?

"There you are, little bird," he murmured against my jaw, his lips tasting my skin. "Use that fire, that pain, that anger. Memorize it. Cultivate it. Sharpen it. Because it's the fury that will keep you alive."

"Who are you?" I whimpered as my body ignited in another powerful orgasm, this one more intense than the last. "Why me?"

"Because you're everything I need." Adrik pushed himself hard against me and grunted low and feral like he'd just reached his own climax. But it was fake.

For a split second, the mask Prince Adrik wore slipped and the real male beneath gazed down at me. One underlined in an energy unlike any I'd ever felt.

True power.

Too much power for a prince.

I traced my fingers across his face, memorizing the handsome lines and wondering at his true intent. He allowed it, his dark eyes holding mine, granting me that glimpse into his spirit that screamed of the forbidden.

"Sleep," he whispered, an unworldly shadow of strength wrapping around that solitary command that seemed to draw darkness over my vision. "Dream, My Queen."

And I did.

Of a new world, one ruled not by Necros but by Adrik.

With me at his side.

Such a strange turn of events, one I couldn't quite follow, but it seemed accentuated by light and life. Pure vigor—happiness, even—blossoming flowers, and euphoria all around.

A fantasy, one not of my own making but that of a stranger looming in the corner, searching my mind for weaknesses. I *felt* him there, prying into my psyche, using me, exploring my inner sanctuary, learning every nuance of my being.

What are you doing? I wondered. *What's happening to me?*

"Shh," a warm voice murmured, fingers brushing over my jaw, his lips at my neck. "You're safe, little bird."

Safe? I nearly laughed. *I've never been safe.*

"You could be, with me…" Something sharp pierced my skin, washed away into a sea of bliss I didn't understand.

My eyes fought to open, my mind rejecting in disbelief, but still my limbs remained quiet, my naked body encased in a wave of hot, sexy male. I moaned, unsure of his intentions, experiencing sensations I didn't comprehend, ecstasy radiating from my lips.

He was playing my body. Mastering me. Even in my sleep. All for what?

Necros, I thought, recalling what Adrik said about the cameras.

None of it made sense—this tranquility, the groans, the overall feeling of insanity clouding my judgment and vision.

And yet, I found myself floating in the waves of rapture, my soul swimming in a sea of contentment.

You're in my mind, I whispered.

"I am," Adrik replied, his palm against my breast. "But not your body."

I don't understand.

"I'm protecting you." His lips were against my ear, the weight of his strength harsh on top of my own. "I'm giving him what he wants to see."

Who?

"You know who," he replied, his teeth skimming

my throat. "Rest, Valora. You're going to need it to survive."

Wisps of that shadowy energy whirled around me, taking me under into a place of solace. I sighed, content for perhaps the first time in my life while miraculously aware that a foreign presence had put me here. One I shouldn't trust.

I stirred, bewildered, only to be pushed back down by a strength surpassing my own. A cry tore from my throat, frustrated at losing control over my own mind while my body quivered in delightful confusion.

Adrik, I whispered, tasting his name, memorizing it.

"I'm still here, little bird," he vowed, his voice deep and hypnotic. "You can rest."

How? I barely knew him, didn't trust him, couldn't move…

"Shh," he cooed. "It's nearly morning now."

What? How was that even possible?

Warm lips brushed my own, fingers drawing through my hair, my body pressed against hot steel. He'd lost his clothes at some point.

No.

Just his shirt and pants.

His boxers remained.

My mind drifted in and out of comprehension, the world not one I understood. Never in my life had I felt so intimately connected to someone—a man I didn't know.

This is wrong.

"I know," he agreed. "And for that I'm very sorry."

Why are you doing this to me?

"To help you."

I don't understand.

"I know," he repeated, his mouth against my temple. "But one day you will."

Who are you?

"Ah, now you are traveling the right path, little bird. Keep wondering. Keep searching. You'll find me eventually."

That's not helpful.

His chuckle seeped into my skin, rousing my heartbeat and scattering goose bumps down my arms and legs. Dark energy crawled over me, traversing my veins and mingling with my very soul. I sucked in a breath, shocked by the penetration and dulled at the same time.

A tear slid from my eye, one caught by his tongue.

And then I stilled, the warmth slowly leaving a coldness in its wake.

Ice slithered across my skin.

Loneliness blossomed in my heart.

Adrik?

No reply.

My eyes finally opened, the sun peeking through the curtains off to the side. *Morning.*

I blinked, uncertain, only to find myself very alone with no signs of Adrik. Merely the hint of his masculine aftershave, a minty essence that seemed to be ingrained into my skin.

I swallowed and stretched, feeling oddly rejuvenated.

What did you do to me? I wondered, blissed out of my mind. *Was it all just a dream?*

No response.

No sign of life.

Just me lying in my own bed now, wearing the white dressing gown Adrik had selected for me the night before.

A blood-red rose rested on my nightstand, beneath it a note.

See you soon, little bird.

—A

Chapter Eight

Adrik

COFFEE—THE DRINK OF THE GODS.

Or so they said.

I sipped from my mug and waited for Grigory to appear, our meeting place set well in advance of last night's battle. He was late, as per usual.

With a sigh, I closed my eyes and tracked my new quarry through the shadow essence.

Valora.

So beautiful with a spirit underlined in kindness. She'd slept soundly in my arms beneath the sheets while I put on a show for her husband and manipulated his expectations. All the while, I'd twined our souls together on a plane he could never reach, ensuring I could find her at a moment's notice. Even now I sensed her standing in her rooms of the palace, confused and cold, my name at the forefront of her thoughts. She also worried about her broken lady's maid, something about encouraging the family physician to fix her.

So much strength tied to a lifetime of being called weak. It would not be an easy barrier for me to break, but she needed to recognize her inner energy or all of this would be for naught.

Poor darling Valora.

It was oddly difficult leaving her in her own bed this morning, but I had no other choice. My evening was done. Her fate set. All I could do was cloak her in a protective shield, one not even she could feel. It would embolden her for the tasks to come, allow her to lean on my strength in moments of severe need, and call to me if her soul was at risk of leaving hell.

Not part of my original plan.

But it had happened nonetheless.

And fortunately, her husband didn't notice a thing, even commended me for forcing her cooperation. He referred to it as a new approach that he hadn't considered—one underlined in degradation.

"Forcing her to enjoy it is such a beautiful thing," he'd said.

Sick bastard.

I forced myself to swallow more of my coffee and focused on the late afternoon surroundings. One day away and I already missed the place I considered home. Violet hues painted the streets of Noxia, so different from the reds and vibrant colors of Caluçon. I much preferred this, where shadows lurked and allowed me to play.

What would Valora think? I wondered. *Ah, what does it matter? She won't live long enough to ever see this place.*

"You smell of pliant female," Grigory said in greeting as he slid into the empty chair beside me. "Sweet and satisfied."

My lips curled, having sensed his approach just

seconds before he arrived. "That she is. Very satisfied." Valora had called out my name several times throughout the evening, her body succumbing to my touch as I played a role for the camera above. Never once did I seek my own satisfaction, only hers as I led her through the dream world. Necros would assume I fucked her all night, but all I really did was invade her mind.

Which, I supposed, was worse than rape. Except it wouldn't have been possible without her acquiescence. Whether she realized it or not, Valora had granted me access and allowed me to stay. Hell, she'd fucking encouraged me to take over, to push her into a realm of relaxation.

The burden of the world lay across that woman's shoulders.

All I did was carry a bit of it for her while she slept.

"He gave you the first night," Grigory inferred, lifting his hand to signal the waitress. "And you wrapped her in the shadows."

"I may have indulged my stronger half, yes."

He smirked and ordered a blood-laced coffee from the young demoness. She preened at the twinkle in his gaze before flouncing off to fulfill his order.

"It's not even noon and you're flirting," I marveled.

"I didn't spend the night fucking a queen."

I snorted. "Neither did I." Which had been far more difficult than I anticipated. "He doesn't even please her," I added, irritated. "The poor thing thought I was trying to kill her with my touch."

Grigory shrugged. "Necros has always believed

those beneath him are meant to serve, not to be served."

"Yes, well, she deserves better."

"Does she?" He arched an ebony brow. "Don't you plan to use her in a far worse manner than her husband? By destroying her soul?"

The words rolled over me as I finished my cup, Valora's life energy humming through my veins. I'd bitten her last night. Not that she'd remember it or feel it today. But it'd bound us together in an intimate manner, one I planned to exploit later. For now, I would use it to keep her as safe as I could.

"She's never been encouraged to live," I said slowly. "I intend to rectify that."

"By fucking her?"

I shrugged. "By introducing her to a state of existence she's unaccustomed to."

"Only to rip it all away when you take her spirit," he mused, his eyebrows dancing. "How charming."

"Are you here to piss me off?" I wondered flatly. "Because you're doing a fabulous job of it."

"No, I'm here to remind you of your purpose and make sure you don't get caught up in your feelings."

I scoffed at that. "When have I ever allowed emotions to rule my decisions?"

"When you bound yourself to a married queen in the shadows under the guise of getting to know her better?" he suggested.

"I want her alive, jackass." Nothing more. Nothing less.

A taunt lingered in his gaze. "Or perhaps you want her."

"Seriously, you're pissing me off." It was a

warning. One he ignored.

"Good. Because it was a reckless and stupid thing to do."

"It protects her, Grigory," I argued. "You don't know what some of those men have planned for her."

"Oh, I can imagine what they want to do to that delicate little morsel, but you're not her savior. You're her conqueror."

"Tying her to me strengthens my ability to seduce her."

"If you require shadow magic to fuck a woman, then I overestimated you." His scowl twisted into a grin as his drink approached, leaving me glowering at him. When the waitress attempted to flirt with him, I allowed my glare to shift to her and sent her running back to the kitchen. "I can see why you're having difficulties," he murmured, completely unfazed by the lethality simmering beneath my skin.

"Any other insults you'd like to throw my way before I kick your ass?" I asked, my voice deceptively soft.

"Listen to yourself getting all bent out of shape in defending a decision we both know was a mistake." He leaned forward, his forearms on his thick thighs. "What happens when Necros catches wind of the shadow magic thriving in his female's veins?"

"You assume he actually pays enough attention to her to notice."

"And you assume he doesn't."

I shook my head and drew my fingers through my hair. "You weren't there last night, G. He barely notices her, hardly even stands her. And he won't be around her most nights to pick up the trace. All he cares about is having a hole to fuck, not what's beneath the skin. And he's so focused on breaking her that he won't notice the layer of protection thickening her blood. *You* wouldn't even notice if you didn't bait me into revealing it." Because that was what all this had been. He smelled her blood on me and jumped to a conclusion I acknowledged only out of friendship. "No one will notice."

"And if you're wrong?" was all he asked in response.

"Then it's a good thing I've had you as a sparring partner for the last twenty-odd years," I replied, relaxing again. "The link gives me access to her thoughts, her location, and her feelings. Once I obtain a better understanding of her, I can master her."

He busied himself with his drink for a long moment, his black irises disappearing into his widening pupils, the blood satisfying him immensely. The flick of his gaze to the bar in the corner showcased the simpering waitress.

Of course she'd used her own blood to taunt him.

Desperate little demoness.

She wasn't even his type. Grigory preferred badass females who played hard to get, not little pixie toys who would strip on a single command.

He set the mug down, his distaste evident in the downward curl of his lips, but he didn't comment. We both knew he'd either let her down harshly or kill her, depending on his mood. She'd fucked up his drink. Grigory didn't take kindly to that.

"Did you prod her mind last night?" he

prompted. "Dig deep into her conscious to learn her likes and dislikes? Determine how best to manipulate her?"

"No. I fostered a healthy night's rest." Something she had desperately needed. "And put on a show for Necros."

Which had been a hell of a lot harder than I anticipated because all I'd wanted to do was fuck the beauty in my arms, but I refused to defile her in such a way. Pleasuring her in front of the masses had been degrading enough.

"Have you considered why you haven't dug into her mind?"

"Because she's not ready."

He tsked, shaking his head. "A poor excuse and you know it. Think harder, brother. I think you'll find you pity her and wish to play the role of knight, not conqueror." He held up his finger. "Emotions are circling you, Adrik. Specifically, fury. And considering your goal, I'd say it's not your right to be pissed. Not when you plan to destroy her on a level she'll never recover from."

"What is with the pep talk this afternoon?"

"Isn't that why we set up this meeting?" he countered, his tone knowing. "To ensure that I kept you in line? That you wouldn't forget your overall purpose? Bonding to a female as you did fucks with the mind. We both know that. I'm here to keep you grounded and focused."

"By reminding me that I have a job to do," I muttered, glancing upward at the purple-tinted sky of Noxia Kingdom. "I already miss it here," I admitted, palming the back of my neck and blowing out a long breath. "Necros reeks of death."

Grigory chuckled. "Soon it will be lost to the sulfur pits of hell."

"Now *that* I can celebrate," I replied, amused once more.

Until I felt a pang rattle my chest—Valora's panic. I winced beneath the onslaught, my heart racing in time with hers.

Grigory frowned. "Is she all right?"

I pulled on our tenuous tether, searching for the cause of her overwhelming fear, and growled at what I found. "He's just informed her of who she'll be bedding tonight."

"Already?" My best friend glanced at his watch. "It's only five o'clock."

"Apparently, Necros wants her to get a head start."

The bastard planned to give her to one of his most lethal lieutenants.

Lavios.

I'd wanted to kill the sadistic demon last night but knew it would have infuriated Necros to lose such a valuable soldier.

It also would have painted me in a suspicious light, something I desired to avoid.

"He's going to rip her apart," I added.

Grigory sighed. "What can you do?"

"Kill him," I replied immediately.

"And risk everything in the process over a woman you hardly know?" He shook his head. "You've done what you can, protected her in your own way. It's up to Valora now. Maybe she'll surprise you, brother."

Yeah, that was doubtful. I'd watched her shut

down last night and accept her fate without much of a fight. Even the slight show of fury she'd given me died beneath my touch.

"I need to get back," I said, pushing away from the table.

It would take me thirty minutes to traverse the realms via the teleportation network, but at least I would be nearby should she need me to intervene.

Grigory gave me a look. "Don't do anything stupid, Adrik."

"Like kill Necros's favorite lieutenant?"

"Yeah, like that," he replied, his brow coming down sternly. "This girl has gotten into your head, and you barely know her."

"It's not her, just the principle. What Necros is doing to her is wrong."

Grigory stood, his seven-foot frame towering over me by a good eight inches. "And I'll remind you again, brother. You're the one planning to truly break her. Which one of you is worse?"

My fist cut upward of its own accord, only to be caught by his waiting hand.

"Go watch over her, but watch yourself first." He shoved me backward, a warning in his gaze. "And don't make me come over there to rescue your ass, or I'll kill you myself."

"You can try," I taunted, knowing it would be a fairly even fight even if he bested me this time.

"I'll more than try," he vowed. "You owe me a boon, Prince of Shadows."

"And you owe me a blade," I retorted.

He grinned, tossing me the knife he'd taken from my pocket during our minor spat. "There's hope for you yet, brother."

I shook my head and sheathed the dagger. "See you in a week."

"I'll be here."

"I know."

Chapter Nine

Valora

"I DON'T THINK YOUR TIME WITH MY lieutenant will be as much fun as your night with Prince Adrik was." Necros raised the goblet of scarlet liquid to his mouth and took a large gulp. His lips turned up into an evil smirk around the ornate glass. "His tastes are a little more violent."

I ignored my husband's comment and concentrated on my barely touched dinner of raw meat and spices. He designed his words to hurt me, and I refused to allow him to rile me up. It was what he wanted, and he would not win.

"See, Lavios? Unruly." Necros whipped his hand under my plate and flipped it up in the air, the bloody steak hitting me in the face before flopping onto my dress. I didn't move, although in my head I cursed painful murder on my husband.

Why don't you choke on your steak?

Treasonous thoughts but I didn't care.

Lavios merely smiled, his gaze oozing lethal intent. "Don't worry, My Liege. I'll work that out of her."

My stomach churned at the words. "I'll go change," I managed to say, my throat aching with each word.

The wooden legs of my chair screeched across the marbled floors of the banquet room as I pushed myself backward. It was only Necros, me, and Lavios here. My husband's followers were to join him later for continued debauched behavior.

Assholes. All of them.

Thankfully, Zaya wouldn't be a part of it tonight. She'd barely survived the torment inflicted upon her by my husband's orders and now rested in a guest bed within my quarters, lulled into a state of sleep aimed at giving her body time to heal.

Once her parents collected her—which they were on their way to do—my conscience would be clear. And I would be officially alone with no one my husband could hold over my head.

"You don't need to change." Necros grabbed my hand and tugged me hard toward him. I stumbled on my high heels and fell into his side, knocking my leg into the table. I gnawed my lip to stifle the cry of pain. "Lavios doesn't mind a little blood, right?"

"On the contrary, I love it," Lavios replied, his licentious gaze roaming over my cleavage with obvious need.

"Hmm, yes, I believe he wants you now, Valora." My husband's lips twisted into a cruel expression. "And frankly, I would prefer a woman at my side who's more willing to accept my advances and not a frigid, barren bitch."

I hope you die a painful death with rats eating your genitals, I thought at him.

He threw me across the floor to where Lavios stood, the lieutenant's arms folded over his strong chest, the medals of his victories—bones, skin, and hair—decorating his black uniform. Bile rose in my throat, and I was suddenly glad I hadn't eaten much.

"We'll see you in the morning, My King." Lavios bowed to my husband and then threaded his fingers through my hair and yanked me across the marble ground.

I tried to scramble up onto my feet, but he was too quick. He dragged me through the corridors, demons jumping out of his way and gaping at my squirming form behind him. My scalp ached from the torture, my nails begging for purchase on the ground, anything to help me stand. But Lavios had no care for me at all, bumping me into wall after wall and covering my body in soon-to-be bruises.

"Let me go!" I screamed. Several people in the corridor leapt away from us, not one person coming to my aid. I was their fucking queen, but they acted as though seeing me hauled around the palace was a normal occurrence!

The sad truth—it was becoming one.

I longed for the seclusion of my engagement to Necros. At least I didn't have to face anyone and could hide away reading or enjoying time with Zaya.

But she would be gone soon, leaving me alone to my fate. To be raped by men I didn't know. To serve a king I loathed. To perhaps die in this wretched place.

How had I never noticed his true intentions?

Because I'd been hidden away. All this time, I thought it was to protect my virginity, but now I saw the truth. Necros had kept me sheltered from my future, knowing no woman in her right mind would accept such a course.

I hated him even more in that moment, longing to burn this palace to the ground and all the men who resided inside it.

Except maybe Prince Adrik.

I frowned. He hadn't taken me at all but had provided me with foreign pleasure and a unique sleep. Why?

Could he be a friend?

I barely know him.

But maybe?

Lavios brought me out of my reflection when he opened his bedroom door and threw me inside like a doll. I landed on the floor, and my cheek slammed against the cold hardness of the stone. My head swam, painting my vision in black.

Ice hit my face, smothering me in a cool liquid that left me shaking in confusion.

"Get up, you lazy bitch. You won't sleep through this. I want you to feel every moment."

What? He must have knocked me out.

Lavios didn't give me a moment to process, his fingers digging into my shoulders as he lifted me from the ground and tossed me onto the bed. Every part of his countenance terrified me, from the sneer on his lips to the sadistic hunger radiating in his hazel eyes. The light glistened ominously over his bald head, providing him with a false halo where horns should lie.

I'm going to die here, I realized. *This man… I'm just a toy for him, a slave to accept his whims.*

Why would Necros do this to me? A queen? The female he chose to give him heirs? He accused me of being barren. Was it true? Did I hold no value beyond that of my womb?

"How should I fuck you first?" Lavios sucked air into his mouth, making a clicking sound as he mulled over the possibilities. Then he circled me as a predator would its prey, studying me from different angles, his lustful intentions painting his features into an expression that would haunt my nightmares for years to come.

Assuming I survived.

"Do you know what we do to soldiers who don't do as they're told?" he asked silkily.

I kept my mouth shut, fear holding my tongue hostage. I'd heard rumors of this man on the battlefield. He was ruthless, his men ruled out of terror rather than respect. He didn't just kill his opponents; he annihilated them.

My blood went cold as a memory stirred, one where I witnessed Lavios's particular brand of punishment. He'd boiled a demon alive before the entire court for trying to poison King Necros. But due to our immortality, the demon remained alive through the entire demonstration, then writhed on the banquet hall floor while everyone enjoyed a feast around him. Lavios had dined on the male's arm, claiming the demon meat to be tender, if a little crispy.

And finally, after hours of agony, he'd put the man out of his misery. But not in a kind way. No, Lavios did not do kind.

"I asked you a question, slut." The crack across

my cheek sent my vision spiraling once more, the world dimming, only to be stirred again by more of the icy substance. "Necros was right. You're insolent and spoiled and untamed. You don't deserve to be our queen. There's no grace, decorum, or dignity with you. You're nothing more than a whore, and there's only one way to treat them."

His belt slipped from his pants, the hiss of it a taunt to my ears. "You are a lower rank than I," I whispered, trying to find my grounding. He couldn't do this to me. I was his queen. He had a duty to protect me from this insanity, not—

The leather sliced across my cheek, just below my eye. "Whores don't outrank lieutenants, bitch." I raised my palm to my tender skin, only to find my wrist caught in his hand and twisted at an angle that forced me onto my stomach.

His belt met my back, the lash harsher than the one to my face. I lay stunned, unable to make a sound, unable to move, unable to fight.

He's whipping me…

That was unheard of. Unlawful. Punishable by death. Yet this man was the one destined to carry out the sentence.

Did my parents know what fate they'd subjected me to when leaving me here? Would they even care if I told them?

I pictured my mother from my wedding day, the cold calculation in her gaze, the warnings of my purpose to keep Graystall safe.

No. She'd tell me to endure it. To bend over and take it. But who could survive such cruelty? Why me?

The second lash of the belt slammed across my

back. Its sting seeped into my pores, and I bit down hard on my lip to suppress the scream dancing in the back of my throat. I tasted blood where my teeth had penetrated the soft skin.

Another blow followed, forcing me to bite down hard on my lip. Blood pooled in my mouth from how hard I clamped my jaw shut as strike after strike tore through the fabric of my dress to meet my bare skin.

My entire body swam in an agony so painful I lost my sight for a short moment, only to be brought back by the feel of leather against my shoulder blades. It would be so easy to slip away, to fall into an unconscious state, but then what would happen? Would Lavios torment me into awareness? Yes. I knew he would. And then he'd destroy my mind.

"Use that fire, that pain, that anger. Memorize it. Cultivate it. Sharpen it. Because it's the fury that will keep you alive." Adrik's voice played through my mind, his words causing my heart to race.

He's near.

I frowned. *How do I know that?*

Cultivate the fury, I heard him saying. *Fight.*

I shook my head to dispel the thoughts, blaming my predicament for my lapse into dreamland.

"You take punishment well," Lavios praised, drawing me back to the present and the sting against my back.

What's happening to me?

Lavios threw the belt onto the pillow beside my face and yanked on my dress, forcing me closer to him. "A pretty pattern for a pretty whore," he murmured against my abused skin, his tongue lapping at the trails of blood his belt had created. "Delicious, too."

He ripped off the remainder of my dress, exposing my ass. His teeth sank into my globes, causing me to flinch. *This can't continue. I have to do something.*

Fight, Adrik whispered again, confusing me greatly.

How are you in my head?

"I'm so damn hard right now," Lavios groaned. "This first fuck will be quick, but we'll experiment more later. I've got a whole cupboard of toys designed to teach you how to better please Necros. Guns, knives, any weapon I own can be used in a cunt, in my mind. You've just got to know what to do with it. How to make the pussy bleed."

Lavios forced me to my back—the fabric burning as it met my tender flesh. Tears filled my eyes, the need to shriek taunting my throat.

And then he freed his length from his trousers.

Oh… fuck…

The bastard had modified his cock with spike piercings covering his length and giving it the appearance of a morning star mace.

Lavios would rip me apart if he fucked me.

"*No,*" I protested, my thighs squeezing shut.

But it was futile. I had no say. This was my world until Necros grew bored and killed me. All this to save a country I didn't know.

I hated my parents.

I hated Caluçon.

I hated Necros.

But most of all, I hated myself for allowing this to happen to me.

Cultivate the fury, I heard Adrik saying again. *Fight, Valora.*

Fight, I repeated. *Yes.* I couldn't let Lavios tear me apart, couldn't allow anyone to treat me in this manner.

Lavios grabbed my knees, prying them apart with his superior strength. His hardness met my entrance, the first sting of his spiked piercing pushing into my tender flesh.

No!

Use your fury, Valora! Adrik demanded. *Use it now!*

Fire slammed into me and swirled around my body, anger overruling common sense.

He'll not take me this way, I seethed, pouring all my hatred and disgust into the fight for my life.

The fire gathered at my shoulders and surged down my arms.

I won't bend to his will.

My hands ignited into an inferno, landing on his skin.

Die a painful death.

The flames shot from my body and wrapped themselves around Lavios as he pulled back his hips and prepared to thrust inside me. His mouth fell open on a roar I couldn't hear above the sizzle of flesh, his eyes wide with shock.

I scrambled backward, the blaze intensifying around us and sending him to his knees.

Is this a dream? I wondered. *Have I already lost consciousness?*

Because I couldn't be doing this. Not really.

Except his expression told a different story, his skin melting around him in a way I'd never seen before. We were immortal. Fire didn't kill us. But Lavios appeared to be dying.

I did nothing but watch as bones protruded from his body, singeing away into unspeakable ash.

This had to be a figment of my imagination, a way to reconcile the torture he was inflicting on my body. *I'm going insane.*

I supposed it was only a matter of time.

Lavios disappeared into a pile of dust, the smoke-tinged air all that was left of my unbridled flames.

Soon I would wake. Feel the pain. Wish this was all true. And die a little more inside.

"Valora," Adrik's voice came from the shadows, his expression one of pride.

I canted my head, confused. "Why are you here?" Had he sent me into another sleep state to protect me from the horror happening beyond the dream realm?

"Helping you," he said, a smile on his beautiful lips. "You feel it now, right? The power residing inside you? I can teach you how to use it."

I blinked. "What power?"

He glanced pointedly at the ash littering the floor. "That power, little bird. You destroyed him."

My eyes fluttered, my torso wavering beneath the onslaught of exhaustion. I needed to sleep. To cry. To hide. To rule.

So many conflicting desires.

So much… energy. Or lack thereof.

I yawned, lying in the filth of Lavios's bed. One would think my mind could at least teleport me back to my own rooms. But that wasn't how the world worked.

I lived in a true hell.

In Caluçon Kingdom.

Where I served as queen to a monster.

I'll kill you someday, I vowed. *Just wait.*

"And I'll help you," Adrik murmured, sounding closer now.

My heavy lids slid open, my eyes finding his. "Why are you here?" I asked again on a sigh.

"Because I want to kill him, too," he admitted softly.

That only proved this to be a dream. No one wanted Necros dead. No one but me. Yet I allowed the proclamation to lull me into a state of contentment. "We can kill him together." I didn't mean it, of course. Prince Adrik wasn't real. But perhaps in this world of make-believe, we could formulate a plot, one that could provide me with a hint of satisfaction for the months to come.

"It's a date, little bird," he said, his strong arms coming around me to lift me from the sanctuary of sheets. "You can rest. We'll talk more when you wake."

Not likely, but I smiled anyway. "I'd like that."

Even if it was a falsehood.

For I knew that when my eyes opened again, I'd awake to a horror I'd never escape.

Until death.

Chapter Ten

Adrik

GRIGORY IS GOING TO KILL ME.

All my training went out the window over a woman in literal flames. But watching her destroy had been worth every second of reprimand my oldest friend could ever inflict upon me.

Because wow.

Valora coming into her power had been a sight to behold. I'd known for years of her potential. However, seeing it in action provided an entirely different understanding.

I brushed her damp hair away from her face, watching her sleep. It'd been easy to take her back to her quarters. This palace was littered with passageways not even the servants knew about, all old tunnels from a time before Necros's reign. But Lux had access to the original architectural plans, something I'd spent years memorizing.

It was how I knew Lavios's quarters lacked cameras, unlike the guest areas. Necros trusted his lieutenant implicitly, which had made my job easier. Of course, Necros would be wondering what happened to his favorite warrior come morning. But that gave me a few hours to work with Valora on a plan. I just needed her to wake first.

She'd remained unconscious through the bath I'd administered, her supple form putty in my hands. The wounds on her back healed nicely under her display of power, leaving only blood behind—blood I'd carefully scrubbed from her skin.

I could practically hear Grigory growling in my head, berating me for showing kindness to a woman I intended to kill. But I felt compelled to help, and after that display of power, I had something new to consider.

She wanted her husband dead, as did I. What if we worked together to achieve that fate? She certainly possessed the ability, but it needed to be honed—a task I would willingly accept.

I ran my fingers through her luscious brown stands while considering my proposal.

It would require removing the other men from her nightly regimen. Easy enough. We just needed to ensure Necros's distraction, which happened to be working in our favor even now. He had no idea she'd destroyed his lieutenant, too caught up in his debauchery to care.

Oh, I'd been invited to join his brand of fun. But after making a brief appearance to check on the king, I'd returned to Valora.

She snuggled into my side, seeking my warmth, her arm sliding across my lower abdomen. I'd kept my suit on to avoid potential distractions, needing the barrier between us. This only worked if I maintained my focus. Although, her leg inching up my thigh seemed to have other intentions.

"Mmm," she murmured, nuzzling into my pectoral.

"Did I not satisfy you enough last night, little bird?" I wondered aloud, grinning. She wasn't fully awake yet, her lithe form stretching alongside mine. I'd dressed her in a nightgown, but it didn't do much to hide her body. Pretty much everything in her evening wardrobe appeared to be chosen for an audience with the king.

She mumbled something incoherent, the sound decidedly sweet.

So innocent, Valora was.

So beautiful, too.

I'd known all of this, of course. To be presented with it altered some of my earlier bravado regarding this situation. Breaking her heart could prove to be a harder task than killing her husband. If I allowed my emotions to dictate my resolve, anyway.

Which wouldn't happen.

I refused.

Still, we could work together, grant her the opportunity for a little revenge, and strengthen her along the way. "Watching you kill Lavios was, well, arousing." I combed my fingers through her silky strands, adoring the way it clung to my skin as if longing for my touch. "I worried you might have suppressed your inner strength for too many years, but Lux was right. You're finally growing into your power."

I pressed my lips to her forehead, holding her close as she slowly stirred, my voice drawing her from her dreams. Whether she heard me or not, I couldn't say. But she deserved the truth. At least part of it.

"For whatever reason, your parents and husband have chosen to keep you in the dark about what you can do. I think it's fear. Given how you burned Lavios alive, I can understand why. Oh, but I'd like to see more, little bird. And I can help you, too. Together we can destroy them all."

Except for her husband.

No, that bastard was mine. He needed to pay for his sins and the horrible pain he'd inflicted on my kingdom.

I wanted him to live long enough to watch me return the favor.

Then he could die.

Painfully.

Light blue eyes flickered up at me, shrouded in a thick dusting of lashes. "Adrik?"

My lips curled. "That is my name, yes." And I rather adored the way it sounded coming from her alluring mouth. "Do you feel well rested?" It'd been a few hours since her energy outburst. Long enough for her to recover.

"What are you doing here?" she asked sleepily. "Am I dreaming again?"

"Hmm, are you?" I asked, guiding her back into the mattress and hovering over her. "If this was a dream, what would we do?"

"Run," she breathed. "Leave this place."

"Wouldn't it be far more fun to kill them all first? And then run?" I drew my thumb across her cheek as I balanced on my elbows above her. "Paint the city in blood. Destroy everyone in our path. Watch it burn. That would be my dream."

She swallowed, her pupils dilating. "I like that dream."

"You have the power to achieve it, Valora," I said softly. "With the right training."

"Power," she repeated on a wistful sigh. "Power is something I don't have."

"On the contrary, sweetheart. You're brimming with energy. That's how you killed Lavios." I tilted my head, holding her gaze. "You can feel it now, can't you? The fiery energy warming your veins? You incinerated him with it. The heavens above call it angelfire." And it was exquisitely rare in the Underworld.

"I don't…" She frowned, her delicate hands roaming up my arms to my shoulders. "I killed Lavios?"

"You did," I confirmed. "It was a beautiful sight."

"And you were there?"

"Lurking in the shadows, yes. It's where I enjoy playing."

"You watched him…?"

Some of my amusement died. "Beat you? Yes. It was why I urged you to retaliate." For which I was grateful she had. Otherwise, I would have had no choice but to intervene. "You're stronger than you know, Valora. I can help you nurture that strength, help you hone it and use it to take them all down. But only if that's your wish."

Her eyes searched mine, the dazed quality in her icy blue irises fading into understanding. "This isn't a dream."

"No, it's not." I again traced her cheek, my thumb lingering near the edge of her lips. "You killed Lavios, and it was one of the most exquisite deaths I've ever witnessed."

"I killed…" Her nostrils flared, her pulse jumping in her neck. "Necros—"

"Will have no idea what you did," I finished for her. "After tucking you into your bed, I went back to Lavios's quarters to draft a note about taking a week of leave to procure his own toy. Then I compelled two of his men to leave on a false mission. They'll return in a few days with the news that their commander was killed in another realm." Not the best of cover stories, but it beat informing the king that Valora's powers were awakening.

Her mouth worked without sound, her brow crumpling in confusion. "I…" She cleared her throat, trying again. "Who are you? No, *what* are you?"

I smiled. "I'm the one who is going to help you kill them all, little bird."

"That tells me nothing."

"And yet everything at the same time," I mused, cupping her cheek. "Together we can defeat everyone."

Distrust cooled her features. "But I hardly know you."

"True," I agreed, brushing warmth into her skin with my thumb. "What would you like to know?"

She swallowed, her gaze dropping to my lips before slowly lifting back to my eyes. "What did you do to me?"

"Depends on which instance," I murmured, amused. "Last night or tonight?"

"Both."

"I tasted you last night, which granted me access

to your mind and life energy. And tonight, I used that connection to help you recover after your burst of power."

"T-tasted me?" she repeated, her cheeks pinkening.

"Your blood," I clarified. "I'm a Prince of Noxia, remember?" Which was technically only a partial explanation. Yes, my father's side of the family possessed vampire-like tendencies that allowed me to pass as a member of Noxia. But my kind embodied a much darker purpose, one underlined in death.

"Vampire," she breathed. "You can compel?"

"Yes." I caught the flare in her nostrils and cut off her accusation before she could even word it. "I only compelled you to sleep, not to kill Lavios."

She narrowed her gaze, her expression so easy to read. "How would I know the difference?"

"You chose how he died," I said simply. "Had it been up to me, I would have slit his throat with a blade and watched him bleed out. You turned him to ash in a wave of power unlike anything I could control."

"Because I heard you in my head telling me to 'cultivate my fury.' " Fire simmered beneath the surface of those words, her energy swimming around us in a lethal wave of warning. One wrong move and she'd ignite again, her grasp on her gifts too fragile and new for her to understand. "You're commanding me about like a puppet."

I very slowly shifted back to my knees, my legs straddling her hips while my hands hung loose at my side. "My intention is not to demand anything from you, Valora. I only meant to help."

"By forcing me to kill someone?"

"Would you have preferred him to fuck you?" I countered, arching a brow. "I merely meant to embolden your resolve, to encourage you to realize your inner strength. Never once did I recommend killing him. That was *your* choice."

Flames licked across her skin, singeing the air. "You manipulated me. You… you made me kill him."

I shook my head. "No, Valora. I simply encouraged a queen to put her subject in his place."

She blinked. "But you're part of all of this; you're one of *them*."

"Am I?" I asked, placing my palms upward on my thighs. "Do you think I'm like them?"

"You're worse."

"How?"

"You're in my head." She shook it as if that would be enough to force me out. "You… I don't know you."

"But you could," I pointed out. "From what I've observed, you need an ally, Valora. I can be that ally."

She scoffed at that. "And still rape me one night a week? No, thank you."

"Did I rape you last night?" I studied her, watched as a flush painted her porcelain skin, disappearing into the translucent negligee covering her breasts. "Yes, I penetrated your mind, but I also provided you with peace. Then I feigned a show for the camera in my quarters while doing my best to maintain your dignity. And I only did that to appease your bastard of a husband so he would allow me to stay, thereby granting me access to you."

Some of her fire died, not that she seemed to notice. "Access to me? Why?"

"Because you're the key to bringing them all down, Valora." I captured her gaze and held it, needing her to understand. "What you did to Lavios is child's play compared to what I sense inside you."

"But I have no powers."

I gestured to her upper arms with my chin. "Then why are you on fire?"

She glanced down at the embers floating above her skin and gasped. I leapt backward as her body went up in blue flames, her eyes widening in confusion and horror. "What are you doing to me?" she breathed, her pale cheeks a stark contrast to the energy dancing around her.

"Nothing," I said, forcing a calm into my voice that I didn't quite feel. "Your emotions are taking over and creating a defensive layer."

Panic radiated from her, the inferno growing.

"I need you to breathe, Valora." It took serious effort not to dive into her mind and compel her into submission. But she needed to do this on her own, to realize it was *her,* not *me,* driving this force. "Listen to my voice, little bird. Your upbringing smothered your flames, but experience is awakening the storm inside you. Everyone has told you what to do, how to act, who to serve, while your blood qualifies you to be far more than a queen. However, you have to control it, not the other way around."

"How?" she asked, tears streaking down her cheeks. "I don't understand what's happening."

"You're finally allowing yourself to *feel,*" I told her softly.

"I've always felt!" she shouted.

"Yes, but this week more than most, right? What Necros has chosen to do to you is a nightmare, one most women wouldn't survive. But you're not most women, Valora. You're a queen. No, you're a fucking goddess. You have every right to be furious and punish them for thinking they could belittle you in such a way. What's happening now is your emotions taking over and forcing the outlet, but if you're not careful, it'll consume you, Valora. So I need you to listen to me and let me help you."

"Why?" she asked, her voice crackling like the fire circling her being. "Why should I trust you?"

You shouldn't, I wanted to say.

"Because I'm the only one willing to try," I said instead. "I already helped you with Lavios. I can help you with the others, too. All I need is a chance."

It would be so easy to instill a sense of trust inside her, to take advantage of the link between us and force her compliance.

But I needed to earn it, to strengthen the relationship between us to ensure that I obtained her love.

It was the only way to truly win.

And I never lost.

Valora remained quiet for a long time, a battle raging inside her as her skin blazed. That she kept it contained without igniting her nightgown or the bed spoke volumes about her ability.

She didn't realize it yet, but she already commanded her own spirit, ensuring her own safety.

That didn't mean I trusted her not to engulf me in angelfire the same way she did Lavios.

Although, unlike him, I could vanish into smoke, which blended beautifully with fire.

If I desired a mate, Valora would be a fantastic candidate.

Alas, I was not destined for such a future.

Only death.

I didn't move, my eyes unblinking. The flames gradually died, her tears continuing to fall, until the blanket of heat suffocating the air completely diminished, and she collapsed onto the bed on a groan. Exuding that kind of energy took too much out of her.

"Valora," I reached for her, partially afraid I might ignite another maelstrom.

"I don't know what to do," she whispered, broken.

My heart ached for her in that moment, for this female I hardly knew who had been hurt in ways I couldn't even fathom. "I do."

Her vibrant blue eyes lifted to mine, a pleading quality lurking in their depths, her wish for me to give her all the answers. "Tell me."

I smiled and repeated my words from earlier. "We kill them all."

Chapter Eleven

Valora

"WE KILL THEM ALL."

Were those the words I'd really heard from Adrik last night, or were they born of another dream?

I frowned. *I don't like the way he controls me.* It wasn't natural to be so far inside my head whispering thoughts of treason. That had to be why I'd killed Necros's lieutenant. Those flames shot from my body, but I didn't recognize them.

This isn't me.

I was brought up to be a subservient wife, but Prince Adrik had awoken something powerful inside me, and now, well, I didn't know if I wanted to go back. Which meant I needed to control whatever was happening to me, especially around Necros. My heart burned at the thought of my wretched husband, churning my stomach, and when I looked at my hands, I could see where they sparked with red and orange flickering embers.

No, I couldn't allow my anger to take over.

I needed to remain calm.

Just breathe, I coached myself, stealing a few short

breaths. *I need a distraction.* Picking up an old leather-bound book—one I kept hidden in my quarters—I wandered out to the garden to read, a place I adored, for I could see Graystall, the home I never knew.

The hazy mist covering the purple sun swirled around the bracken sculptures littering the grounds. Oddly, the strange structures and black-streaked petals provided a comfort few other places did, allowing me to bask in my own contemplative silence.

Bliss.

Closing my eyes, I soaked in the rays from the strange star above. Rumors claimed Lucifer had created the violet light to shine down upon the realms on this side of the Underworld. Not all the kingdoms were so lucky, and I often wondered if the privilege of illumination was a pact between Lucifer and Necros's ancestors. They'd always seemed close, and to have such a special gift was a sign of affection from the Devil. I dreaded to think what deeds were performed to obtain it.

I settled into a granite chair, striving for comfort. A hardship in my current attire. Alas, my husband possessed a penchant for boned corsets and voluminous skirts. He told me they were regal and that I'd look like a peasant if I wore pants. An excuse, really. He just wanted easy access to what lay beneath the dress for him and his *friends*.

With a sigh, I opened my book, ready to absorb the knowledge it provided about all the kingdoms and the powers within them. Those loyal to Necros had compiled this listing, capturing millions of years of details. I'd found it when I was younger and had spent days studying the section on Graystall to learn more about my own family. It was the only way I could learn about the kingdom I had traded my life for.

However, this time I had another kingdom I wanted to investigate.

Noxia.

As far as I knew, it was a vampire realm, but the way Adrik had vanished from my room last night didn't strike me as vampiric at all. It was something far more sinister and pricked at my ever-present trepidation about the man already pooling in my head.

He was dangerous but kind—a lethal combination in the Underworld.

Trusting him would be a mistake.

Even if he had helped me. Twice.

I found the page I searched for and started my perusal of the words about the Kingdom of Noxia.

Interesting. Queen Lux had ruled for many years on her own since her husband's death. She seemed to be a formidable figure, and I immediately envied her freedom.

What would it be like to rule? To not succumb to the commands of a male? Or be forced into unpleasant *situations?*

I'd likely never know.

Her firstborn son, Prince Grigory, would one day take the throne, and when he did, he would be every inch as powerful as his mother. Hmm, while he bore dark features—same as Adrik—they possessed some distinct differences. Most of which surrounded the gleam in their eyes, the structure of their jaws, and their different noses.

What am I missing?

The book described Adrik as Lux's second child, but not much else was said. Of course, the book predated his adult years. If I were to write about him, I'd include his warrior prowess. And maybe his wicked touch.

Not thinking about that, I chastised myself. Instead, I focused on the description of Noxia, which sounded like a beautiful place. It was full of freedom and choice and ruled under an order that the vampires instilled in themselves rather than by a tyrant-like king.

Maybe one day Adrik can take me there?

Stop. I couldn't entertain thoughts like that. I was Queen of Caluçon and always would be.

"We kill them all." His voice sounded so loud I glanced around for his presence but found myself alone.

Yes, I was definitely going insane with the pressure upon me.

But what if I indulged his idea? What would happen if we killed—

"*Valora?*" My husband's booming voice resonated around the gardens, and I couldn't help but shiver, knowing he wanted me. I tucked the book away under my seat and quickly scrambled to the entrance, where he stood with his hands on his hips and a stern expression on his face.

"I've been looking for you, little whore," he growled, looking me up and down like the piece of meat I was to him.

"Apologies, My Lord." I curtsied, hoping to earn some favor and maybe a reprieve from whatever he desired. "I was getting a breath of fresh air."

He grunted. "*A breath of fresh air.* This is what I've been given as a wife?" He glanced upward, as if speaking to Lucifer himself, and grunted. "When I call for you, I expect you to fall at my feet and ask how you can service me. Not make me work for it. No more hiding outside."

"Of course, My Lord." I reluctantly lowered myself to my knees and bowed my head, needing this to be done. And there was only one way to ensure that he left me alone. "How may I serve you?" The words were forced from my mouth, leaving a bitter aftertaste.

"We kill them all."

I wish.

Necros patted my head. "Good girl." The victory in his voice made me sick to my stomach. "How was your evening yesterday?"

I froze. *Does he know?* Adrik promised he'd taken care of Lavios, provided some sort of story about him leaving the palace on urgent business, but what if—

"I bet Lavios taught you a trick or two," my husband continued, amusement darkening his tone. "Hmm, I should ask for the sheets. I'd love to know how much you bleed."

I shifted uncomfortably on the floor. *All you'll find is a pile of ash,* I thought bitterly. But I couldn't say those words out loud. If Necros discovered the truth… I swallowed. What would he do to me? Kill me? I suspected not, because that would be too easy a punishment. Anything he dreamed up would be designed to degrade me; his intention always leaned toward humiliating those beneath him, and I was little more than dirt on his shoe now.

But I possess the power to burn others alive.

Adrik had awoken it.

And he wanted to help me use it to destroy everyone.

A sharp strike to the side of my head had me nearly falling to the ground. "I'm speaking to you, wife. What did he teach you?"

How to kill. "I'm not sure what he taught me will be of much use to me in pleasing you," I said instead, proud of the steadiness in my tone.

Necros threaded his fingers through my hair and tugged harshly backward to force me to look at him. His eyes sparkled in delight. "Did you enjoy his brand of punishment, pet? Shall I seek the same adornments for my cock? And fuck you so harshly you can't walk the next day?"

My husband was a vile demon with no compassion.

Cultivate the fury.

The phrase popped into my head, and I immediately tried to suppress it.

Not now. I couldn't let Necros know about the power brewing inside me. Tears welled in my eyes as I fought it, causing his lips to curl even more. He thought his words were what hurt. But no, it was the burning sensation threatening to overwhelm me.

"Please," I whimpered, talking more to myself than to Necros.

I felt the sparks igniting in my body.

No.

No.

No.

This can't be happening again.

Adrik? my instincts whispered. *Adrik. Help me suppress it. Please!*

Necros snorted and released me harshly, sending me to the gravel at his feet. "Pathetic. You've only done two nights, and you're already a whimpering mess. I should have had you properly trained before our wedding night. That's what I did wrong, Valora, and I take responsibility for that. So I'm making it up to you the only way I know how."

That was what he felt bad about? That he didn't have me *properly trained* before? And he thought this would make up for it?

What a sick and twisted outlook.

I wasn't *that* unskilled in the bedroom. He only cared about his own pleasure. How the hell was I supposed to enjoy that and wantonly desire to reciprocate?

Bastard.

He snapped his fingers, calling the guards. Two of them approached, one of whom reached down to pull me up to my feet by my hair.

"Well, I suppose at least you'll experience some rest tonight," Necros muttered. "Garul isn't exactly known for his stamina in the bedroom—a sad trait of his demon nature. Still, he's known for his dark preferences, which will no doubt expand your horizons. Even beyond last night." That last part was said with a wicked twinkle in his eye, one that bespoke of his approval regarding his favorite lieutenant's treatment.

I'm glad I killed him, I thought. *I only wish I could do it again.*

Necros took his leave without another word, leaving me to be dragged by the guards up to the room of my partner tonight. My skull ached from the treatment of the one to my right while my arm bruised beneath the cement grip of the guard to my left. I was almost thankful when they dumped me unceremoniously into the new quarters.

The guards bowed at an older demon who sat reading in a comfortable chair in the corner. He finished his page before climbing to his feet, then waved the guards away.

"Valora. It's a pleasure. My name is Garul." He helped me to my feet. A kindness lurked at the forefront of his expression, but behind it lay the lust-filled mask all these men wore when in my presence.

Why wasn't I born ugly?

Garul dropped his trousers and pulled out his cock, not wasting a second.

I stumbled back on instinct alone, trying to escape. *No. Not again. Fuck!*

"Don't move," he snapped, the kindness charade disappearing into an expression of stark need.

My feet wobbled as I forced myself to stand still, my heart beating a chaotic rhythm in my lungs.

I can't do this again, I thought, breaking inside. *I… I can't.*

Take control, Valora, a warm voice whispered. *Exhaust him before he does the same to you.*

Adrik?

Take control, Valora, he repeated.

Are you in here somewhere? I wanted to look around, but that would seem suspicious to the man who bore down on me, stroking his cock to full hardness.

"So pretty," he mused, his licentious gaze roaming over my dress.

I gulped.

"Lower your top. I want to see your breasts."

My hands shook as I lifted them to my shoulders where the material of my dress sat. A small tug and I'd expose my breasts to Garul.

Take control Valora, Adrik growled. *You can do this.*

I-I can't. I don't know how.

Garul glared at me. "I'm waiting, and I should warn you, I'm not a patient man."

You're stronger than the Queen of Noxia herself, Adrik said. *Just give him what he wants. Exhaust him. Trust me.*

"Valora!" Garul shouted, and I jumped backward with fright. He growled in anger.

"I'm s-sorry," I stuttered and lowered myself to my knees before him.

"I'm very disappointed." Garul grabbed my hair and pulled my head back. "This is not how I wanted the evening to go. I know whom you were with yesterday and how sore you must be. I wanted to make it easy for you, but I'm afraid you've given me no choice."

He swiped his palm across my face in a bruising slap, which did the opposite of what he probably intended. It snapped me out of the fear constricting my body. My hand darted out and wrapped around his length. Part of me wanted to rip the offending member from his body, but I knew my strength wouldn't allow it.

So I followed the other instinct.

And stroked him.

Take control.

Exhaust him.

Those were my own words, emboldened by Adrik's approval. This was what he'd meant.

My husband's statement regarding Garul's stamina returned with a vengeance, urging me onward. If I made this demon come, he wouldn't be able to perform. *Right?*

Yes, Adrik whispered, whether in reply to my question or in encouragement to my actions, I didn't know.

"Oh, *fuck*," Garul groaned with desire threaded through his moan. He grabbed my other hand and placed it on his ass. "Fuck punishment. I want this."

I tried to struggle, but he guided one of my fingers into his anus. It was tight and felt so wrong, but within seconds it had Garul thrusting his hips harder into my hand.

"So good. I need this. Harder, whore."

Not a whore, I fought back, refusing to allow his statements to cloud my mind. Otherwise, he might end up as a pile of dust on the floor. Not that he didn't deserve it, but I wouldn't be able to hide *two* murders. It would be too difficult to explain to my husband if all his men disappeared.

With a loud bellow, Garul thrust into my grip and came. I avoided the sticky liquid as best I could, and it pooled on the floor.

"*Yes. Yes. Yes.*"

Eventually, Garul stopped his movements and his essence flow ceased. I didn't move, too afraid of what might happen next. *What if Necros lied about his stamina?* I hadn't considered that before, too focused on *exhausting* the demon.

My throat dried.

Oh—

"What have I done?" Garul's eyes widened as he looked down at me and the mess on the floor. "No, this wasn't how the evening was supposed to go."

He swayed on the spot, and I desperately pulled my hands away from him, itching to wash them.

"*Damn it.*" Garul collapsed to the floor, unmoving.

"Shit." I scrambled to my feet, wondering if I'd killed another one of Necros's men. It would truly be a death sentence if I had. Nobody, not even Adrik, could save me from this.

I tentatively reached forward and felt for a pulse; it beat fast and furious beneath my hand.

Thank Lucifer.

Garul grunted and rolled over onto his side, then started to snore.

He's asleep?

You exhausted him, Adrik said, seemingly amused. *Good job.*

Will he wake up again? I asked, running over to the sink to wash my hands as thoroughly as the water and soap allowed.

Not for another twelve hours. I pictured Adrik leaning against a wall, his hands in his pockets. *Honestly, I'm surprised Necros even allowed his kind to compete. Sure, they can be vicious. But they're so easily subdued.*

Where are you? I demanded.

Waiting for you behind the painting, he drawled. *But don't worry, little bird. We have time. About twelve hours of it.*

Painting? I found an oversized one near the chair Garul had used for his reading.

That's the one.

I washed my hands one more time for good measure, turning the water to scalding and not caring at all that it turned my skin pink. Then I checked my appearance in the mirror. *Not* because I cared what I looked like for Adrik, but because I couldn't stand the idea of carrying any shred of Garul with me anywhere.

Finding myself satisfactory, I moved toward the painting. *Well?*

He pushed it to the side, and sure enough, he stood leaning against a wall with his legs crossed at the ankles.

"Valora," he greeted.

"Adrik."

"Ready to begin?" he asked, gesturing for me to enter.

"Sure," I said, following him inside. "You can start by explaining this telepathic link."

Chapter Twelve

Adrik

"No. Scratch that." Valora whirled around the stone interior. "Explain this to me first. Then the telepathy."

I smiled. "The palace is full of ancient passageways. But very few know about them."

"And how do you?" she demanded, every bit the queen as she stared me down.

I closed the doorway in the wall to hide our location and flipped a switch on my transmitter to bring the cameras back online in Garul's room.

She frowned at the device in my hand. "What's that?"

"You are full of questions tonight, little bird."

She scowled. "And you're not answering any of them."

"Not true." I gestured to the corridor. "I told you the palace is littered with passageways."

"And how do you know about them when I don't? I've lived here for almost my entire life, and you've been here, what, two or three days?" She folded her arms, unwilling to move, apparently.

I sighed. "That, little bird, is a very long story."

"Well, as you pointed out, we have twelve hours. Please begin."

Mmm, I rather liked this new side of her. Feisty with a hint of arrogance. "Power looks good on you, Queen Valora."

Her eyes narrowed, a flame dancing in the pale blue depths. "You know what I can do, so I would suggest you stop teasing me."

"And you know I can help you, so I suggest you not threaten me," I returned, backing her up into the wall as I pocketed my device. She gulped as I placed my palms on either side of her head. "I know about these passages because I've researched these grounds extensively. I know where all the cameras are, how security moves, which hallways lead where, and most importantly, I know how to move around undetected."

The dim lighting did not do justice to her beauty. If anything, it clouded it, creating a murky shadow across her cheek.

No.

Not a shadow.

A mark.

"He hit you," I realized out loud, running my thumb over the bruise while my other palm remained against the stone beside her head. "I can help you, Valora. But only if you allow me to."

"I'm standing here, aren't I?" she countered, arching a brow.

"You are," I agreed, tracing her jaw with my finger before wrapping my hand around the side of her throat. "But you're afraid of me."

"Can you blame me?" she breathed, her eyelashes fluttering.

"No. You should fear me." I squeezed just enough to prove dominance without harming. "I came here to kill everyone, Valora. Including you." I loosened my grip. "But now I see we might be able to form a mutually beneficial arrangement." *At least temporarily,* I thought to myself, careful not to convey that message to her through our telepathic link.

"Who are you?" she marveled, her eyes dancing between my own, back and forth in a hypnotic whirl that drew me closer.

Valora needed more. She required a reason to trust me, some sort of boon to attract her faith.

And there was only one way to accomplish that.

"I'll tell you a story," I murmured. "A true one, but it will be up to you if you want to believe it." I took a step back and held out my hand. "Walk with me. Please."

She glanced down at my palm, then up at my face, and then back at my wiggling fingers. Her brow creased as she considered her options.

Which were simple.

Either she agreed to move deeper into these halls with me…

Or I let her go.

I said as much out loud, causing the lines of her forehead to deepen even more. I leaned against the wall beside her, my hand still hovering between us, awaiting her decision.

"All right," she finally agreed, her delicate palm pressing to mine. "But I want you to tell me about our telepathic link, too."

I nodded. "Deal." I linked our fingers together and guided her down the murky hallway. "If you're attached to that dress, then try not to touch too much." These corridors would more than soil the fine fabrics of her clothes.

Not that I particularly enjoyed the bone adornments.

Those must have been chosen by her betrothed.

"This is why I desire pants," she muttered, causing my lips to curl. "Everyone else has them, even Zaya. But not me."

At the mention of her lady's maid, I asked, "How is she?"

"Still asleep," Valora replied.

"She'll recover." I'd made sure of it on my own, not that Valora would ever know. But I sensed the girl meant something to the queen, and considered it my one good deed for fucking up her life.

Well. Not that I could take all the blame for that. Her husband was doing a fine job of it himself.

"Did you know this palace wasn't always inside Caluçon Kingdom?" I wondered, leading her toward the old part of the estate—the part Necros kept closed off from the public.

She frowned. "No. What did it use to be?"

"One of the Shadow Kingdom palaces." My parents' favorite estate, according to Lux.

"Shadow Kingdom," she repeated. "I've not heard of it."

"No, I imagine not. It was destroyed right before you were born. Graystall was next, but the king and queen traded their valuable daughter to the Caluçon King in return for peace." I looked pointedly at her. "I'm sure you're familiar with that story?"

She grimaced. "Very."

"Well, unfortunately, the Shadow Kingdom didn't have anyone to trade. And further, a prophecy declared that the Shadow King would one day destroy the Caluçon King. So, as you can imagine, Necros very much wanted to destroy the opposing kingdom." I pushed against a wall along the side, revealing a dusty old library with skylights for lighting. The purple glow gave the oval-shaped room an ominous appeal, highlighted by the white sheets covering the old furniture.

Valora stepped through the opening with an expression of awe, her beautiful gaze taking in the room all at once. "Where are we?"

"In the restricted areas," I said, closing the passage behind us. "Have you never wondered why Necros keeps these areas off-limits?"

"He once told me it was old and decrepit and requiring renovation." She ran her fingers along the dusty spines. "But all I see here is a room in need of a good cleaning."

"Oh, I'm sure he plans to renovate someday." Not that he would ever get the chance, as I intended to kill him first. "But for now, the memory of the Shadow Kingdom remains in these walls."

"Why have I never heard about this?" She took an old text from one of the walls, her fingers running over the swirling black ink. She hissed. "Black magic."

I caught the book as it fell from her fingers,

protecting the precious spine.

"No. This is shadow magic." I pressed my palm to the text, allowing the words to rise and settle, the energy pulsing in waves through my being before shuffling into a format she could read. "Here."

Valora studied it but didn't touch it.

I smiled. "Afraid, little bird?"

"H-how did you do that?"

"Mmm." I tucked the item under my arm and studied her. "You read about me today in your old book, but it didn't say much because the words are transcribed by Necros's people. It's exactly why you won't find anything in that text about the Shadow Kingdom. They only write what pleases the king. And as far as they all know, I'm Lux's second child."

She gaped at me. "You saw me in the garden?" Of course she fixated on that and not the very important detail I just dangled before her.

"Yes, and I put your book back before anyone else could find it. Not that they would truly care about you reading it. Now this one?" I held up the item again. "This one they would mind quite a bit. Actually, everything in this library is forbidden. And why? Because these contain the true history of the Underworld, before Necros staked his claim. Because Caluçon never existed."

Valora took the historical text again, her fingers dancing over the engraved lettering. "The Shadow Dynasty," she read out loud.

"Mmm, how appropriate that was the one you selected first. Perhaps give it a read, little bird. You might just learn something." Primarily about my family's legacy. My name was toward the back, the last son born in the Shadow Kingdom. But my identity was kept a secret; not even Necros knew of my existence. Mainly because of the prophecy.

One might say Necros brought it upon himself.

Others would claim it to be destiny.

Regardless, I was here now, ready for my revenge. And the perfect weapon stood eager beside me, her focus falling to the rows and rows of texts. "All of these contain kingdom history?"

"No. Some are about the heavens. Others are artifacts from Earth—both fiction and nonfiction." I steered her toward my mother's favorite shelf, a pang hitting me square in the chest. "These are romance novels, for example. Mostly from human writers." I pointed to one across the room. "And those over there are fighting manuals, which you might find particularly useful."

"How do you know all of this?" she asked, finally looking at me again. "Who are you really, Adrik?"

My lips curled. "As I said, your texts said very little about me. Lux might be my mother, but not by blood. She adopted me when my kingdom fell." I tucked a strand of her hair behind her ear. "I'm the last of my kind, Valora. A Shadow." I purposely left out my true title. *Shadow King.*

Her lips parted. "I don't know what that means. Or what it is."

"Similar to a vampire, but far more powerful," I promised her.

"Then how…?"

"Did Necros manage to destroy us all?" I finished for her. "He harnessed a power that didn't belong to him. One born inside a child from Graystall. A little girl."

Her eyebrows rose. "What?"

"Your people are the harbingers of justice, but how, exactly, do they deliver it?" I studied her, saw the confusion written all over her features. She truly had no idea. "Because Graystall possesses the power of the galaxies within their familial bloodline. *Your* bloodline. They are quite literally the children of the stars. It's what makes your kind so indestructible. But that kind of power comes at a price."

"I've never heard any of this before," she interjected.

"Well, perhaps you'll remember the miracle who was born with unspeakable abilities. So unspeakable that her parents called upon Lucifer himself to help temper the chaotic energy. But bargaining with the Devil always comes at a price, and in this case, it was the manner in which he assisted. He called upon Necros, who absorbed the gift from the stars, providing him with a seat of power unlike any other. And he used his newfound abilities to take down the Shadow Kingdom."

She sputtered, her eyes wide in disbelief.

I sighed. "Unfortunately for Necros, the expunge of energy required to take down my people left him close to death, the power gone in an instant. He went supernova, destroying so much, *too* much, his body not meant to harness such strength. Which left him bereft and the little girl seemingly normal."

For twenty-one years, it seemed.

"But that's the interesting thing about stars," I

continued softly. "They are constantly growing, burning hotter every day. Thus, it's expected that the female—the infant he stole the vitality from—will one day glow hotter than the violet sun above. And not even Lucifer himself will be able to contain her. Unless she finds someone to share that ability with, someone like a husband." I waited for the weight of my claim to settle over her and caught the book she once again dropped. She started to sway, but I caught her hip.

"No," she whispered. "That's… that's not possible."

"Your parents traded their star because they believed Necros still possessed your energy, and they feared for their lives. However, it was the wedding he needed to tie himself to the star he desired to corrupt. And when that didn't work, he chose a new method, one he hopes will shatter the bonds containing her power. *Your* power."

I slid the book back onto the shelf to better hold her upright.

She wanted a story.

I gave her one.

And it seemed she no longer cared about the telepathy, her mind racing over everything I just said.

"You can imagine, perhaps, why I seek to destroy Necros and all that he represents," I whispered, lifting her into my arms. "Because he took everything from me. Yet, he truly stole even more from you."

She shook in my arms, her frail form rejecting the facts I presented to her. But I sensed her mind working through the logic, the foreign heat growing inside, the early memories of her life, and the way

Necros had almost trained his people to degrade her from the beginning of her time here.

"He always saw me as a threat," she whispered, blinking rapidly. "I thought I was a toy, but now…"

"You realize you're a weapon," I replied, brushing her hair from her forehead.

"Why has everyone kept this from me?" But before I could reply, she was already answering. "Because they don't want me to threaten his rule."

"Even more, they want to prevent you from ruling them all." Even Lucifer himself had to fear her power. It was the only reason I could see him bargaining with Necros. They both benefited from keeping her weak.

"You seek to use me, too." Not a question, but a statement.

"I do." I wouldn't lie to her. "To destroy Necros."

"And then?" she asked, her gaze meeting mine as I settled onto one of the clothed couches. "What happens after you defeat him?"

"I go for Lucifer next," I said. "He orchestrated all of this, killed my entire kingdom, and he will pay for his sins."

She considered everything for a long moment. "Let's say I believe you." She swallowed. "What would you have me do next?"

"Learn how to use your power. Sharpen it. Cultivate it. *Control* it." I palmed her cheek, drawing her face closer to mine. "I can feel how volatile you are, how the energy is pressing at the surface, begging for a release. Right now it seems your emotions—

darker ones—unleash the gift. I can help you learn how to harness it, Valora."

"How?"

"By giving you the release you need." I nodded at the center of the room, which I'd purposely cleared to give us ample floor space. "We can train here. Spar. Bounce magic back and forth. *Learn.* But it's up to you. I can't train you if you're unwilling. Because I won't go easy on you."

"What about the other men?"

"We handle them one by one," I said. "Garul was easy. Tomorrow you have Sven." A sadistic dragon breather who would no doubt scorch her skin to a crisp before fucking her nearly to death. "I'll handle him. Then you have Jives. He's a stone giant. Lethal. But I've heard he actually prefers males, which is why he'll go for the back door. Perhaps we can find someone else to entice him with in the interim."

"No," she said, adamant. "I will not subject anyone else to my fate."

While admirable, that wasn't how we could play this game. "Then we find someone willing," I conceded. "Trust me, there are many soldiers in this palace who would happily entertain Jives for a night. Which leaves us with Gareth." I grimaced, not at all a fan of the slimy, three-eyed prick. "We have a few nights to figure him out. I'll work on it."

"And me? What do you want me to do?" she said, sounding a bit miffed that I was handling all of this for her.

"I want you to learn, Valora." I gestured around us. "I want you to come here during the day to read. And meet me here at night to spar. But be prepared to bleed, because it's going to hurt, little bird. As the only way I know how to teach you to fly is to break your already clipped wings."

Chapter Thirteen

Valora

INFORMATION SWIRLED THROUGH MY MIND, all accumulated over the last few days of reading in the library Adrik showed me.

He'd kept his word and helped me avoid torture the last two nights.

Sven hadn't been able to perform—his dick had shriveled and seemingly hid at the thought of attacking me. Then he'd fled Caluçon in horror at his unexplainable reaction. Fortunately, my husband didn't replace his position.

And last night, Adrik sent a male to Jives who was more than willing to entertain the much bigger male. By the time I'd arrived, Jives was already spent and embarrassed, so we struck a bargain. He would pretend we spent the evening together if I didn't mention his proclivities to Necros. An unexpected alliance, but one I accepted.

Tonight, however, I was to go to Gareth.

I shivered.

The male was another of Necros's lieutenants. Not favored like Lavios, but still a sadistic prick of a male who adored torturing others.

This would not—

Necros has called for you, Adrik's voice interjected, flowing through my mind and eliciting a warmth deep inside. *Try to remain calm, little bird. I have this under control.*

What do you—

A pounding at my door jolted me upright.

I hid the banned book I'd been reading between my mattresses and stood as the door flew open.

Two guards forced their way into my room, their gazes falling to Zaya asleep in my bed. I'd moved her from the other room, wanting to look after her myself since her parents had not yet arrived. Strange, really. I expected them days ago.

"Why is she still here?" one of the guards demanded.

I narrowed my eyes. "Because she's my lady's maid. Not that I need to answer to you." I looked toward the door, where it still shook with the force of the violent opening. "Why do you interrupt me in my quarters this way?"

"The king requires your presence." The shorter of the two guards held a spear and used it to motion for me to leave the room.

"I am not properly dressed," I replied, holding my head high. "I'll join him when I'm ready."

"You'll join him *now*," the guard returned, his round face falling into severe lines. "It's your choice on whether I carry you or not."

My eyebrows rose. "I think when addressing *your queen,* you should phrase your words with more sincerity due to my outranking you."

He snorted. "Sweetheart, Necros gave up his claim on you earlier this week. We're free to *address* you however the fuck we want."

"And touch, too," the bigger male beside him drawled, his coffee-colored irises gleaming with malicious intent.

"He gave rights to the victors, not—"

"Do you want a demonstration?" the shorter one demanded, handing his spear to the other and starting around the bed toward me. "Because I'll happily put you in your place, little whore."

"But quickly because Necros requires her presence," the giant warned.

I backed up into the wall as the shorter one approached, his wicked grin one I truly desired to burn off his plump face.

"We'll blame her insolence" was his reasoning as he reached for my arm. "Maybe the king will let us punish her publicly."

"One can dream," his buddy murmured.

Zaya began to stir on the bed, her low groan one that suggested she sensed the shifting of the air in the room.

If she opened her eyes now, she'd scream.

And the men would likely silence her—*harshly*.

Oh, no. If they tried to hurt her, I wouldn't be able to control my reaction. Already I could feel the flames teasing my veins where the brute gripped my flesh. "I'll go," I said quickly. "I'm ready."

"Are you?" he asked, giving me a stern shake. "I'm not certain."

"Please. I'll go right now." It grated to say the words, to force the pleading note into my tone, but I had no other alternative. Not until I understood my power. *Soon,* I promised myself. *Soon, I'll destroy them all.*

Yes, Adrik agreed, his hum of approval enough to straighten my spine and force me to meet the gaze of my captor.

"Take me to Necros," I demanded.

He sighed, releasing me. "Pity. I'd have enjoyed teaching you a lesson."

I bet, I thought, wanting to melt him alive.

I pressed an affectionate kiss to Zaya's forehead, attempting to lull her back into a state of rest, and then left with the guards on either side. Their clipped pace and bruising hold on my arms nearly caused me to stumble in my high-heeled shoes.

"Release me," I ordered as we neared the throne room.

They laughed and threw me in the doorway.

I glowered back at them, livid.

Control your power, Valora, Adrik demanded.

His presence drew my gaze to where he sat in the ornate room's corner, a look of disinterest on his face. *How would you feel to be thrown about like a toy?* I asked him, irritated. I could kill everyone in this room right now, but instead he wanted me to repress my power? *Fuck you.*

Patience, Valora, he whispered. *We have to do this right.*

And what did that mean, anyway?

I knew he wanted revenge. Understood why. But he wasn't the one being degraded like some fuck doll.

"Valora," Necros snapped, his ire sending a chill down my spine.

Adrik wasn't the only one in the room. His court

was present.

Oops.

"Apologies, My Lord." I curtsied to him before taking my seat.

Gareth captured my gaze below, his hunger a palpable presence that had my heart racing. The eye at the top of his triangle-shaped gaze winked at me as one of his three hands stroked the whip laced through the belt of his trousers.

Hell's fire, I hope he doesn't have three… I swallowed, unable to finish.

He doesn't. Adrik almost sounded amused. It was an emotion we did not share.

I really hope you have a plan, I thought at Adrik. *Or that man is going to shred the skin from my body tonight.* I'd witnessed it before during a previous punishment. He was just as sick and twisted as Lavios.

Trust me, Adrik murmured.

I nearly replied, *I do*, but held the words in my heart.

I couldn't trust anyone except Zaya. My only friend. The one I considered family.

"Now that my *queen* has finally arrived," Necros said, his irritation a lash against my spirit.

"Apologies," I whispered, bowing my head slightly in the manner I knew he preferred.

It seemed to work, because he released me of his raven-eyed glare and stood, anger pulsating through his body.

As if he had the right to be angry.

He was the one who fed off my powers like a damn incubus, leaving me powerless at birth.

He was the one who wed me just to access those gifts again once they manifested to completion.

He was the one who married me over a lie—to save a kingdom to which I owed no hint of gratitude to.

Calm down, Valora, Adrik demanded. *Your power is brightening your gaze.*

I narrowed said gaze at him. *Calm down? To what purpose?* I thought back at him.

You're not ready yet, he reminded me.

I nearly growled. As much as I adored the new power humming through my veins, I couldn't control it. And right now, I desired nothing more than to burn this audacious room to the ground.

Do I have enough power for that yet? I mused.

No, Adrik replied. *Not yet.*

Whether he meant to not yet try or that I didn't yet possess the power, I wasn't sure. We were supposed to start sparring and practicing my control soon. I supposed I could endure a few more days of this life. I'd survived the last twenty-one years, after all.

"We have a traitor in our midst," Necros announced, causing my lips to part and a gasp to fall of its own accord.

Oh, sh—

Breathe, Valora, Adrik urged, the words sounding as if he'd forced them between clenched teeth.

I ignored him.

A deep pit of terror crawled over my insides, unleashing a fire through my veins born of the urgent need to protect myself.

He knows.

"Traitor?" I repeated, goose bumps pebbling across the surface of my skin.

Necros ignored me, his focus on Gareth. "Seize

him."

The guards were on him in an instant, divesting the three-eyed demon of his weapons in a swift move before throwing him to the floor below the thrones. A spear pointed hard into his back, another at his head.

"N-Necros?" the shocked demon spluttered.

"*Murderer*," my husband spat, his voice low and menacing. "You will address me as *My Lord*."

"M-my Lord," Gareth whispered. "What am I accused of doing?"

Oh, no…

Just breathe, Valora, Adrik echoed.

Necros stalked down the steps and stepped on Gareth's hand. Bones shifted and cracked as he repositioned the weight of his leather shoe, causing the demon to roar in pain.

"I know you and Lavios had your differences," Necros said conversationally. "But I never expected such treachery among my ranks. Not from those I consider my most loyal." He slammed his boot down on another of Gareth's hands, causing me to flinch at the harsh cacophony of snapping bones.

Valora. Adrik's voice was an unwanted stroke against my senses. *Don't watch.*

My gaze flicked to Adrik's bored expression. He had a knife in his hand and was using it to clean his nails. The picture of nonchalance as Gareth's screams rent the air.

But I killed Lavios, I whispered.

I know.

You framed Gareth. I realized that already, of course, but the words were only now forming. Adrik neither confirmed nor denied it, but he didn't need to. I already knew. *This is wrong.*

I couldn't allow this to happen.

Not to an innocent man.

"Necros, please stop..." The plea left my lips, my mind not catching up with reason.

Necros spun around and glared at me for interrupting his tirade. "Excuse me?"

"Are…" I swallowed, the thick lump in my throat threatening to burst. "A-are you certain he's guilty?"

"Are you questioning my authority, *wife*?" he asked, the lethal softness of his tone holding a whisper of warning.

"N-no, My Lord," I stammered. "I-I'm just… I wondered, is all."

"At the evidence?" he prompted.

I swallowed again. "Y-yes."

His pupils flared, his nostrils following suit. "I am the judge, jury, and executioner in this kingdom. If I say he's guilty, he's guilty."

"Yes, My Lord," I whispered, flinching as he smashed Gareth's third hand without looking at him.

"Does anyone else question my will?" he roared, addressing the crowd.

A chorus of silence served as a reply.

And those sinister eyes fell on me once more. "You'll pay for this interruption later. And I'll make sure you know who is in charge by the end of it before I force you to beg for more."

My throat constricted.

All I could do was nod.

Say no more, Adrik seethed in my mind.

My energy dissipated, no longer able to even reply

to him.

What more could I do? My fate was already sealed. As it seemed Gareth's was as well.

A guard handed Necros the demon's infamous whip. My husband wrapped his large hands around the handle and brought it down hard onto Gareth's back. The former lieutenant writhed in agony as Necros did it again and again and again, ripping the fabric from the male's body and drawing forth rivers of blue blood.

This is my future, I realized, horrified. *When he finds out what I've done, what I'm capable of doing…*

Adrik murmured a reply, but the rushing sound of my own blood blocked him from my mind.

Stop it, stop it, I recited in my head, flooded with guilt.

I couldn't admit what I'd done.

Didn't desire to take Gareth's place, not when I *knew* he deserved this and so much more. He'd destroyed so many, adored raping women, and certainly had a horrible night planned for me. That knowledge was the comfort I had to hold on to.

He deserves this. The voice was my own. Or maybe it belonged to Adrik. At this point, I no longer knew.

Blood had painted my vision a dark shade of blue which didn't match the surroundings.

Lucifer, he's destroying him. And yet Gareth still lived.

Necros threw the whip away and circled his hand around the demon's throat. Gareth was lifted up off the floor, the remainder of his clothes ripped from his body by magic shooting from my husband's other hand.

That was the power everyone feared.

Was it actually my own? I didn't know.

No, Adrik said Necros had consumed and used it all.

Unless… Unless he was wrong.

Necros glanced up at me, his expression cruel. I tried not to give him a reaction, but the tilt of his lips said he caught the misery rioting inside me.

Is this actually meant to be my own punishment? Does he know I killed Lavios?

His gaze gave nothing away, as only darkness existed there—no white sclera, just black all over.

Gareth's screams of anguish grew louder as Necros used his magic to peel small strips of the demon's skin off his body.

Oh, I truly hoped that wasn't a gift he inherited from me. *Please tell me I can't do that.*

Adrik didn't reply.

Or maybe he did.

I was too entranced, too mortified, to focus on anything other than the reveal of Gareth's muscles and bones.

Blue gore dripped onto the marble floor, smearing across the sable-colored tiles.

"*Please.*" I didn't know how much more I could watch. "Just kill him."

Necros growled, and I swore I heard Adrik curse.

My eyes began to blur, the stench of torture too much.

But Necros only continued, two small balls of energy forming on his palm as he sent them into Gareth's body. Somehow the demon remained conscious, a testament to the immortality of his breed.

And oh, that meant I could suffer the same sort of agony…

I shuddered at the thought.

My stomach churned.

Adrik remained unaffected, his expression a mask of boredom.

Jives sat beside him, pale, but watching intently.

And the others all gaped in a mix of awe and excitement.

They're all entertained. This entire kingdom fucking thrived on the torment of others.

Gareth was a former lieutenant, someone who, just earlier this week, carried an esteem revered by his brethren. And now they watched his demise with expressions of enjoyment.

So damn wrong. I stood and made my way to the door, finished with this macabre scene.

"Where do you think you're going, Valora?" Necros demanded as two guards cut off my exit.

"I don't want to watch this," I said, a note of vehemence in my tone. *You are all sick!*

"You think you have a choice?" Necros's lips curled into a menacing smile, and the two guards pushed me back, closer to Gareth. The acrid air of death was suffocating this close, blood mixing with urine and feces. Fuck, his bodily functions were no longer in his control.

Necros flicked his fingers, and Gareth's toes started to separate from his body. His fingers were next. My husband was taking him apart piece by piece. His magic destroying the demon until there was nothing left.

I can't...

Gareth's hands severed at the wrist, sending me running. I formed a fist and sent it flying into the face of the guard holding me and sprinted from the room.

My heels clacked against the marble floor as I forced

myself back to the only place I felt safe in this whole palace.

My quarters.

Tears streamed down my face as I went, my resolve slipping into a puddle at my feet.

I couldn't do this anymore.

I didn't want to feel.

I just wanted to drift through everything happening to me in a bubble of no emotion.

When I reached my bedroom, I found two guards already pulling Zaya from my bed. How they beat me back, I didn't know. But I flung myself toward her, screaming.

No!

Adrik's soul wrapped around my own, halting me midstep.

How?

Why?

"*Let me go*!" I screamed, and the guards looked at me as if I'd gone mad.

You need to calm down, Valora. We can still do this. Necros was just putting on a show; that's all. And we both know Gareth deserved what happened to him. This is all part of your husband's penchant for games.

"*Release me*!" I demanded again, and the guards stepped back from me with their brows furrowed.

Then they dropped Zaya to fall to their knees.

A dark shadow loomed behind me, blocking the doorway.

I knew who it was even though I still couldn't move.

My husband.

He stepped around me, his eyes still fully black, and

his fury exuded from every pore in his body.

"Why is she still here?" he demanded, looking at Zaya. "I thought she was taken care of with her parents?"

My blood ran cold. *Her parents?*

"Sorry, My Lord. I'll follow up to find out why it wasn't done." The guard who spoke blurred in my vision, my mind failing to process what was happening.

"Good. Now leave us. And take that thing with you," he ordered.

That thing was my best friend.

The only one in this palace I could trust.

And still I couldn't move, Adrik's will holding my own.

He whispered something important, but Necros's fist against my temple destroyed my ability to hear.

And another hit to my head snapped Adrik's hold and sent me to the ground.

My vision faded into shades of black as a nightmarish realization rolled through my thoughts...

There's no defeating Necros.

He's too strong.

He'll rule forever.

Chapter Fourteen

Adrik

VALORA HAD CUT ME OFF FOR *three* fucking days. Every time I tried to peek into her head, I sensed nothing. Just a shade of black, barely blinking with life.

It took all manner of discipline not to do something about it.

But it was too soon. I couldn't take on Necros yet, especially with her in what felt like a comatose state.

Whatever depraved insanity Necros has done to her... My hands fisted with my desire to punch the wall. Again.

"Fuck," I growled, pacing my guest quarters.

I'd already slipped through the passageways to her rooms, but grunts from Necros kept me from entering.

Because I would have killed him.

Or tried to, anyway.

I palmed the back of my neck and blew out a breath. Necros was a lot of things, but weak, unfortunately, was not among those traits.

Taking him on while emotionally enraged would

backfire.

I'd lose.

And Valora, well, she'd suffer, too. More than whatever he was doing to her right now.

I needed a sparring partner to work out some of this pent-up aggression with before I did something stupid. If only Grigory had stayed after—

The door to my chambers flew open, Necros standing on the threshold. He didn't even knock. Nor did he seem unrepentant as he tossed Valora into my room. "Sorry for the leftovers, Adrik. You can have her for the next few days. Maybe even the week. Just let me know if you tire of her, because Lucifer knows I have." He glowered at her mop of dark hair, hiding a face I knew would be covered in bruises.

A myriad of replies taunted my tongue. Most of them curt. A few threats. Instead, I shrugged and forced a nonchalant tone. "I'll find a way to amuse myself."

"Attaboy," the king replied, grinning. "I like you."

Feeling isn't mutual, asshole. "And I appreciate your hospitality," I returned, somewhat meaning that. I had enjoyed wandering the palace I considered to be mine.

"Good." He gave a nod and left as abruptly as he'd arrived.

I supposed it was a compliment that he'd dropped her off here himself.

But I suspected it was more him wanting to catch me off guard. It implied that he *knew* I was in my room, which could be perceived as a reminder that this was his domain. Little did he realize I *allowed* him to know my whereabouts, especially the last two days as I awaited my time with Valora.

"Get up," I said harshly, aware that Necros stood just outside the door. His dark aura always left a residual stain on my senses, and it blasted heavily at me now.

The sick bastard wanted to hear what I intended to do.

I'd altered the cameras in this room and the surrounding hallways over the last week, slowly changing the areas they surveyed and putting them on loops that his security team failed to notice. The audio recorders had all been altered with white noise, and I'd set a variety of traps throughout the room to alert me if anyone messed with my things.

So far, so good.

Which didn't surprise me. Necros's guards suffered from the misconception that no one in their right mind would challenge their king.

I crouched before Valora's still form, longing for the connection to her mind, and threaded my fingers through her hair to gently tug her head back.

Her eyes, while open, stared at nothing.

"I see." I sighed loudly for our audience outside the door. "Well, you're worthless to me for the night." I shifted out of my jacket, wrapped it around my hand, and drove my fist into the floor, creating a dull thud the king would assume was a kick to her soft body. "Don't even think of pissing all over my floor." I spat to the side, stood, put my jacket back on, and made a show of stomping off toward the exit.

When I flung the door open, it was to the sound of Necros's departing chuckle, his back disappearing around the corner.

I leaned against the frame, waiting to see if he returned.

After five minutes of silence, I quietly slid back inside and twisted the new deadbolts I'd installed over the weekend.

No one would disturb us without warning.

This time when I crouched before Valora, I ran my fingers through her hair and examined the blemishes marring her beautiful face. She'd retreated into the deepest recesses of her mind to avoid whatever wickedness Necros had inflicted upon her.

"Oh, little bird," I murmured, gathering her into my arms and carrying her to my bathroom. "Let's repair those broken wings, shall we?"

She didn't reply, didn't even blink, so lost inside her head.

I sat her on the counter by the sink, assured she wouldn't fall, and fixed her a bath. "Yes, Necros, I do enjoy your accommodations," I murmured, finding the ingredients I needed to create a healing aroma of sorts. Then I gathered a handful of ointments I'd brought from Noxia, most of which were infused with vampire blood.

My shadow essence would cure her as well, but I needed her to function enough to swallow for that to work. And she was nowhere near that level.

Valora remained catatonic as I undressed her, and she didn't flinch beneath my examination of her wounds. Necros had bitten her, sliced her, *beaten* her, likely all in an effort to garner a reaction that she clearly didn't give.

I was almost proud of her for that. It showed

strength on her part for not shattering beneath his ministrations.

Unless, of course, he'd destroyed her mind.

In which case, we had a serious problem.

I spread her thighs and grimaced at the destruction, shaking my head. "I'm going to enjoy killing that bastard."

Still no sign of life from the woman I knew possessed more vivacious energy than anyone in the Underworld. I cupped her cheek, tracing my thumb over her bottom lip.

"By the time I'm finished, you'll be as good as new, sweet star."

I removed my clothes, folding them and placing them on the opposite counter. Then I threw her poor excuse of a wardrobe into the bin. She'd never have to look at those offending blood-soaked fabrics again.

Guiding her back into my arms, I carried her to the large oval-shaped bathtub and climbed inside, situating her on my lap. Sponges sat waiting for me on the solid stone rim, as did a variety of healing ointments. I used them carefully, massaging the essences into her skin while encouraging the magical properties of the ingredients to take root.

Come back to me, little bird, I whispered. *Please.*

Nothing.

But I didn't expect it to work right away.

No, healing like this would take time.

So I gave her as much of it as she required, bathing her continuously, draining the bathtub, filling it with warm water again, and repeating the motions over and over. All the while, I hummed, urging her body to recover, begging her mind to hear mine, and watching as her wounds slowly began to mend into smooth, satiny skin beneath my touch. While intimate, it was also clinical, the famous Noxia remedies working wonders for her essence.

You're safe, I whispered, hearing nothing in response.

The sun disappeared, denoting the midnight hour, the only indication of how many hours had passed us by.

But I refused to stop until I had her back.

I should have killed him, I thought, not for the first time.

Allowing her to go through this under the guise of not being ready no longer felt adequate. Surely I could kill Necros if I caught him off guard. Yes, he still possessed some supernatural energy—as he'd demonstrated on Gareth the other day—but I was the Shadow King.

I sighed. It would be a fair fight. I knew that. But what if I lost?

Lux was adamant that I needed Valora to defeat Necros. *The prophecy says*, I parroted, thinking of her teaching tone.

What if you're wrong? I wondered. *What if I can do this on my own?*

Do what? a soft voice whispered.

It took me a moment to realize the source. I tugged Valora's head back to find her gorgeous eyes focused and very much alive. "How long have you been awake?" I demanded, alarmed that I hadn't felt her stir.

"Since you refilled the bathtub," she replied, the strength in her voice proving her words. No raspy quality like she'd just woken up, but the tone of a woman mostly healed. "I don't know how long ago that was, but it's getting cold again."

I reached around her to pull the drain, then held her as the water began to gurgle in its descent.

How do you feel? I asked, drawing my thumb up and down her now-smooth arm.

Hungry, she replied. *And cold.*

As soon as the last of the water disappeared, I refilled the tub with warmer water than before, which caused her to sigh back against me.

If she noticed we were both naked, she didn't react.

Instead, she seemed almost content.

Until some thought reached her mind and she jolted, jumping straight out of the tub and out the bathroom door.

"Valora!" I called, chasing after her as she bolted toward the exit of the room. She frantically tried to unfasten the bolts, her movements and eyes wild. "You're safe, Valora. You're safe. Calm down. I'm not going—"

"Zaya!" she yelled, her nails breaking as she futilely tried to fight the locks on the door.

Oh. Understanding smacked me in the face.

No, that was her fist.

She fought me in earnest, demanding I open the door, then turned and bolted toward the corner chair in search of what she knew was a secret passageway behind it.

I caught her by the hips and yanked her backward. If she ran now, we'd both be fucked. Because Necros would know immediately that I'd healed her even though she clearly had a long way to go.

I allowed her to scream as I pulled her toward the bed, knowing that if anyone heard her, they would just assume I was doing my job.

"Let go of me!" she demanded as I pinned her to the mattress, my lips falling to her ear as she fought for dear life beneath me.

"Zaya is safe," I whispered.

She didn't hear me, too caught up in her need to fight and flee.

The water clinging to our skin had us slipping against each other, which placed my hardening cock at a very precarious point of her as I pinned her yet again with my hips.

"*Valora,*" I growled, needing her to focus.

But she was wild in her need. Her limbs wrapped around my waist, her heels trying to kick me in one of the worst places.

Then fire flickered across her skin, only to die on a harsh scream.

She couldn't access her energy.

But she wanted to.

She saw me as the enemy and I couldn't blame her, but I needed her to fucking hear me.

Zaya is safe! I roared into her mind. *I sent her to Noxia. All right? She's fine.*

Valora's fight slowed, my words finally breaking through.

"I intercepted her the other night." The words were a breath against her ear. "I gave her some of my blood to heal her enough to walk. And then I gave her to Grigory, who assured me he would nurse her back to health." He wasn't thrilled about it, seeing the halfling demon as well beneath his station, but one look at the woman's face had him rethinking his position.

Valora had gone completely still. "Prince Grigory?"

"Yes." I loosened my hold on her wrists, lifting onto my elbows on either side of her face.

She stared up at me with an odd mix of wonder and distrust. "Prove it." The dare in her tone had me narrowing my eyes.

"You don't believe me?" After bathing her for hours? Healing her back to health? Giving her access to all the information she needed to destroy this kingdom?

"No." A flat response.

I nodded. "I see." Well, that was one way to kill my erection.

I rolled off her and walked over to the painting hiding the old passageways and pushed it aside.

"Where are you going?" Valora demanded, not following me.

I didn't reply, already inside and searching for the bag I'd hidden nearby. The communication device I needed sat in an exterior pocket, making it easy to find, and by the time I returned, it was to find Valora sitting up in the middle of the bed with her brown locks tousled over one shoulder.

A beautiful sight.

Naked.

Wet.

Angry.

Mmm. Too bad we couldn't channel that emotion into something more worthwhile.

I tossed her a shirt from my wardrobe. "Put it on." Harsh words because I hated saying them, but I wasn't about to let Grigory see her naked. I dialed the code I knew would force his response and waited for the device to ring.

Humans called them phones.

But in the Underworld, our tech was a little more advanced.

Grigory's face appeared above the console, a pillow outlining his head. "What's wrong?"

A feminine voice complained as my friend shifted, clearly having been in bed *entertaining*.

"I need you to put Zaya on," I said flatly.

"What?" He shook a manicured hand off his shoulder. "Hold on." The scenery changed as he shifted from the bed, the angle telling me he was putting on a pair of drawers.

A female whine had him growling an apology. "Go play. I'll be back."

Ah, he had more than one woman in bed.

Typical Grigory.

"What did you tell me to do?" he asked, the dark tones of his bedroom flashing as he exited the room and entered a familiar corridor.

"You heard me. Zaya."

"You dialed the urgency code to talk to a woman?" he demanded. "No, wait, *for* a woman."

I didn't reply. Because nothing I could say would resolve the severe lines in his expression.

"Fuck, Adrik." He muttered a slew of ancient words, most of them curses, as he moved through the familiar halls of the palace. My gut ached at the sight. *Home.*

How long had it been? Only ten or eleven days? Fuck, it felt like a lifetime ago. And while I didn't regret my mission, I did miss my life.

Valora met my gaze, her ire lessening by the second as a new emotion brewed in the azure depths of her eyes. She still had a long road to recovery, as was evidenced by the lack of a glimmer in her pupils. If I didn't know better, I'd say Necros stole more of her power.

But he would have flaunted it earlier if that were the case.

A pounding sounded, Grigory being as delicate as always. "Zaya!"

"Go away!" a sharp voice replied.

Valora was on her feet in an instant, grabbing the device from my hand. "Put her on."

Grigory did a double take at his screen. "Lucifer's nutsack," he muttered, pounding again. "I have a call for you, damn it!"

"Tell her it's Valora."

"Yes, let me broadcast that the motherfucking Queen of Caluçon is on the console," Grigory drawled. "That won't attract attention at all."

"Stop being a dick," I told him.

"I'll stop being a dick when you stop thinking with yours," he retorted, banging a third time. "If you don't open this damn—"

The door flew open with a livid-looking little

pixie on the other side. "You'll *what*?"

For a woman who'd just been nearly raped to death, she seemed to be up and moving just fine. "Your charm is clearly rubbing off on her, Grigory," I said, surprised.

"Valora?" she whispered, seizing the device.

"Oh, Lucifer, you're all right." Valora pressed her free palm to her heart, her eyes glistening at the edges. "I thought… I thought Necros…"

Zaya's face clouded over, her body swaying over the monitor, ending in Grigory cursing. He caught the little halfling with one arm and looked at the phone. "Yeah, thanks for that, *Your Highness*." His gaze flicked toward mine. "Next time you use the urgency code? Make it a real emergency, jackass."

The device went silent.

Valora whimpered, nearly dropping the very expensive piece of tech. I plucked it from her fingertips and stored it temporarily in one of my drawers, then faced her. "Satisfied?"

"She's alive."

"And safe," I added, folding my arms.

She nodded slowly. "And her parents?"

Ah, that I couldn't stop. "They were killed at the borders on Necros's orders."

Valora cleared her throat, her gaze falling to the ground. "Because I'd called them here."

"Which was a logical decision on your part. Necros killed them because he's a cruel bastard. That's on him. Not you."

"But they wouldn't—"

"Don't go down that path, Valora. Don't blame yourself for *what-ifs* or potential outcomes. You called them to retrieve their daughter after he had her violently raped to the point of near death. Then he killed them because he could. All of that is *his* fault. Not yours."

She said nothing for so long that I worried I'd lost her again, that she'd fallen into a pit of self-despair I'd have to pull her out of, but when her gaze met mine, all I found was rage.

And something else.

Something… heated.

"You saved Zaya's life." Not a question now, just a statement. "Why?"

"For you." I wouldn't lie to her. If I hadn't seen how much she cared for the girl, I wouldn't have interfered. But I knew Zaya meant something to her, and I refused to allow Necros to take anything else from her.

Valora took a step forward.

Then another.

Until her breasts pressed against my folded arms through the thin shirt she wore. "I'm going to kiss you now," she declared, shocking the hell out of me.

But not nearly as much as when she gripped my elbows to go up onto her toes and pressed her mouth to mine.

Chapter Fifteen

Valora

NECROS WAS THE ONLY MAN I'D EVER kissed, and he never reciprocated.

I expected Adrik to be the same, only his lips softened beneath mine, accepting and returning the motion as I clung to his arms for balance.

My heart skipped a beat, my stomach tightening as foreign sensations warmed my bloodstream.

This was my first *real* kiss.

And I wanted more.

I'd meant this to be a gesture of gratitude, a way of thanking him for helping the only real friend I'd ever known. But with each tender brush of my lips against his, my desire for something dark unfolded.

My fingers danced up his hard biceps to his shoulders, gripping him tightly as I tried to kiss him harder.

But his forearms remained crossed.

His body stiff.

Yet his lips parted for mine.

The conflicting signals left me growling against him, confused. Was he denying my exploration or accepting it?

I pulled back, meeting his obsidian gaze. His dilated pupils unveiled his interest while his expression remained studiously blank. "Am I…?" I trailed off, swallowing. "Is this all right? Because I want to do that again."

He dipped his head, the manner oddly subservient. "You can do whatever you want, Valora," he replied, his voice deeper than before. "Whatever you need."

His words tightened my core, causing me to desire things I shouldn't.

Like exploring every inch of him with my tongue.

Because he was still very naked.

And aroused, I realized, my gaze falling to his groin. I'd felt him against me a few times, knew he was well-endowed, but seeing it stirred something new to the surface. A longing I never would have anticipated.

Adrik didn't try to cover himself, his arms still folded, his eyes on me.

He's giving me control.

No man had ever allowed that. Not that my experience was vast, but Necros had trained me to expect dominance in the bedroom. He always chose what we did, how we did it, with no care as to what *I* desired. And the last week—or however long it'd been—hadn't been much different.

I honestly couldn't remember most of it, having found a place to hide inside my mind while Necros defiled me in unspeakable ways.

The last thing I remembered was him telling me the cruelty his men had planned for Zaya, how it would be a dream compared to what he intended to do to me. Despair had driven me to the edge of my thoughts, where I buried myself in agony and retreated from the world. Then I'd awoken in Adrik's arms feeling oddly safe, and incredibly numb. It had taken me far too long to understand what had happened. To recall Zaya.

But Adrik had already saved her. For me.

I knew he wanted to use me, had heard it in his mind while lounging in the bath. He'd left himself wide open in his efforts to connect with me, and I'd swum through his thoughts with abandon.

He'd never lied to me.

He wanted to kill Necros, to punish him for what he'd done to the Shadow Kingdom, and he needed my power to do it. The Queen of Noxia told him that, but he'd been questioning whether or not she was right before. Wondering if he could take Necros down now, to stop him from harming me for another second.

No one had considered me in such a way, desiring to *protect* me. I wasn't sure how to interpret that.

And now, with Zaya… I swallowed. My mind was a mess, my body still bruised, while my heart beat wildly against my ribs. Emotions were a fickle notion. They drove others to do absurd things, and right now, mine desired for me to kiss Adrik again.

So I did.

This time with my palm wrapped securely around the back of his neck. I used my other hand for balance as I remained on my toes, my breasts pressed into those still-folded arms.

My tongue parted his lips. Exploring. Tasting.

And he responded in kind, his touch soft and hesitant against my own as I indulged in my first proper embrace.

His arms eventually fell, his hands loose at his sides as if debating whether or not to touch me. I took the option away by pressing my chest to his, wrapping my arms around his neck, and driving our kiss to the next level.

He groaned, his arousal hot and heavy against my flat belly, as he finally pressed a palm to my lower back. Necros would be harsh, ripping at the shirt covering my torso. But Adrik wasn't. He merely held me close while I devoured his mouth.

I learned how to nip, lick, and kiss, using his tongue and lips as my guide. Each stroke set my blood on fire, until I felt I might burst. So hot. So intense. So *right.*

"More," I whispered, my voice unrecognizable to my own ears.

"Take whatever you need," he breathed, his fingers flexing against my spine.

My thighs clenched at the permission in those words and the very real yearning underlining his tone.

This was wrong.

I shouldn't want any of this.

But I'd also never been given such an opportunity.

And I *wanted* to feel. To be in charge. To make decisions for myself. To experience pleasure on my own terms. To make a man bow to me for once.

I started backward toward the bed, my hands on his biceps, tugging him with me.

"Lie down," I said, my tone a husky feminine sound that somehow intensified the moment even more.

Adrik slid onto the comforter, his strong body taking up a good portion of the mattress as he relaxed onto his back with his hands tucked behind his head.

Another concession.

He wouldn't touch me unless I asked. Wouldn't kiss me unless I kissed him. Wouldn't push me to do anything I didn't want while allowing me to do whatever I desired to him in return.

A heady sensation settled over me, intoxicating in its lust.

Adrik was helping me to heal in the only way I knew how—by taking back control of my own life.

I knelt beside him on the bed, admiring the cut lines of his abdomen and how they tapered to a perfect V at his waist.

Every inch of him was immaculately outlined, even the little dark hairs trailing down from his belly button. I bent to trace the path with my tongue, earning me a groan from the virile male beneath me.

Mmm, I liked that sound very much.

I wanted to hear it again.

Straddling one muscular thigh, I leaned over to lick him once more, this time to the heart of his groin. The heat of his cock brushed my cheek, the allure of his perfection calling to my mouth. I took him deep, the way Necros always demanded.

A chill swept across my skin at the thought, my neck tensing as I waited for a hand to clamp onto my scalp and force me further.

"*Valora*," Adrik said, my name resembling a curse

on his tongue and pulling me expertly back to him when my mind threatened to drift. His muscles were tense, his jaw tightened in apparent agony, but he held himself still.

I'm in control.

This is my choice.

Not his.

I can do whatever I want.

Each potent thought heated my blood all the more, eliciting a craving from deep within. Adrik was mine to explore, to touch, to fuck, to *enjoy*.

He was the toy now.

A very willing one, if the substance coating my tongue was any indication.

And oh, he tasted different in the best way. I sucked him harder, desiring more, and moaned as he indulged me with another hint of his cum. So decadent, salty, and all Adrik.

I released him from my mouth with a pop and crawled over him, kissing and licking and nipping his muscular flesh all the way up to his mouth. "Can I…?" I swallowed, uncertain of how to voice my cravings. But I wanted to know this was okay. To feel him come on my terms, not his.

"You have my permission to do whatever you want, little bird," he murmured, his voice rough and sexy and tantalizing my senses. I squeezed my thighs around his hips, a new yearning stirring between my legs.

I'm on top.

I'd never been in this position before, and I wanted—no, *needed*—to explore it.

I moved slightly downward, feeling his stiff length between my damp folds, and groaned in both pain and yearning. Whatever Necros had done, it'd hurt. Badly.

And now I wanted Adrik to heal me. But in my own way.

He hissed as I shifted my hips, his abdomen clenching beneath me. The manner in which he bit his lip told me he was trying to hold back, to not reach out and take over.

I couldn't imagine how difficult this was for him, almost wanted to give in and let him claim me, except I needed this. Something he seemed to understand as I sat up and lifted myself to position him at my entrance.

His eyes met mine, reminding me of smoldering obsidian. An intense hunger lurked there, one barely tempered that leaked into the harsh lines of his body.

I slowly guided him inside, biting my lip to keep from crying out at the odd mixture of pleasure and pain.

It hurt, my insides abused and aching, but still I took him, deeper and deeper, until I couldn't take another inch.

Adrik never broke eye contact, his arms still tucked behind his head even as a tear rolled down my cheek. We stayed like that for what felt like hours, staring at one another, absorbing the moment, his hard cock filling me to completion as I worked to accept the agony thriving throughout my core.

Until, finally, I could move again.

Slowly. Steadily. Purposefully.

Each shift tingled more and more, pushing away

the discomfort and yielding to pleasure. I hummed in appreciation, my limbs shaking beneath the onslaught of pain-filled ecstasy growing between my legs.

Adrik's lips parted, his breaths coming faster as I picked up speed, following the path oblivion had carved out for me and searching for the bliss I knew existed at the end.

"Fly," he whispered. "Fly for me."

Oh, I wanted to.

I really, really wanted to.

And I was so close. So very, very close.

An inferno built deep in my soul, curling, churning, and threatening to take us both. The intensity of it scared me, sent me falling forward onto his slick chest, where I shuddered. His fingers threaded through my hair, combing out the tangled wet strands, making me think of our bath together. How he'd touched me. Healed me. *Cared* for me.

My walls clenched down around him, reminding me of his cock still locked deep inside and the hunger that thrived between us like a live beast that required taming.

No. Not taming.

Release.

I whimpered, unsure of what I needed. Confused by the dueling sentiments of lust and fear. My heart began to race as Adrik lifted, my nails clinging to his shoulders.

No, no.

He couldn't take control now.

Not yet.

I wasn't ready.

"Valora," he breathed, his lips against my cheek as he slowed his movements, stopping as he sat up completely, my thighs on either side of his. "Try this."

I couldn't. Too afraid. Too bewildered by his guidance.

"You're still in charge," he whispered, kissing my neck softly. "You move however fast or slow you want. But this position will help you. Trust me."

I shivered, those last two words a resounding promise to my very soul.

Trust me.

Could I? Could I trust him?

We barely knew each other. Yet, I felt as if I knew him better than anyone else. Maybe it was the glimpse inside his head when his walls were completely down. I experienced so much with him. His memories. His desires. His goals.

And most importantly, I saw his guilt for leaving me with Necros. Not at missing the opportunity to hurt the monster, but for allowing such cruelty to befall me. Even though he *knew* there wasn't anything he could do.

Because I'd felt his power inside. And while it rivaled Necros's, it wasn't enough. Not with the marital ties binding me to the King of Caluçon, and the history between us.

I might not be at full strength yet—nowhere near it—but Necros could still potentially use me. And that little energy would be enough to defeat Adrik.

Neither of us was ready.

But we would be.

Together.

I kissed him, sealing the unspoken vow while allowing my hips freedom to move once more. He was right. This position intensified everything, brushed my swollen nub against his pelvis, and heightened the passion burning through my veins.

"Adrik," I breathed, picking up the pace and finding the rhythm I needed. Pushing that hot boundary, seeking the rapture I felt building beyond. I threaded my fingers through his hair, holding him to me as our mouths hovered over one another, panting, licking, and nipping.

He seemed to be losing his fight not to take over, his hands gently grasping my hips to encourage me onward.

I allowed it, needing his touch to ground me, to remind me it was Adrik inside me and no one else.

This was my choice.

My desire leading us both.

I sat on top. I took him into my body. I set the limits. *Me.*

A volcano erupted in my core, shooting me to the stars on a scream that shook my very spirit. It was so intense. So unexpected. So *amazing.* I truly flew, just as Adrik had desired, and I took him over the edge with me into a whirlpool of sensation. He groaned against my neck, his body shuddering beneath mine as his seed warmed my insides.

Time seemed to still.

My inhales and exhales an echo around us.

He remained taut beneath me, his palms soft as he stroked up and down my sides. A warming touch meant to soothe, to memorize, to cherish.

I kissed his cheek, his jaw, and then his lips, and sighed as he returned the embrace. His tongue was my new addiction. This feeling my new favorite sensation. I hugged him close, my breasts to his chest, startled to realize the shirt still clung to my curves.

The experience seemed almost more intimate now, knowing that he'd allowed me to remain covered while our bodies met in an erotic dance below.

Everything had been for me.

To heal my spirit.

To teach me to trust.

To open my eyes to a way of existence I never could have anticipated.

And I only wanted more.

My hips began to move, guided by my newfound resolve. Adrik shuddered in response, his hand stilling against my ribs. He'd not even gone under the fabric to feel me, yet his touch burned my skin, branding my flesh as his. I pulled back to meet his gaze before removing the barrier between us. Black pools of admiration fell to my breasts, his palms returning to my sides, lightly grazing upward.

"You're healing beautifully, Valora," he said, his tone a deep, masculine purr that caused my thighs to clench.

"Because of you." The sultry quality of my voice shocked me. So improper and not like the woman I was raised to be, which made it all the more welcome.

I pressed my lips to his, indulging myself and taking advantage of his willingness to kiss me back. His touch grew bolder, sliding over my back, his fingers teasing the hairs at my nape and trailing a light caress down my spine.

This wasn't the way I expected to recover, but I wouldn't have chosen any other way. Not as his hips met mine in a slow thrust. Not as his tongue slid deep into my mouth. Not as his hands explored my breasts. Not as my body began to overheat all over again.

I didn't regret a second.

Memorized each one as if this were a dream that might shatter in the next moment.

Screamed his name as I came once again.

And cried softly against his shoulder as the emotions of the last few days came bearing down upon me.

He held me through it all. Acting as my foundation. And for the night, I allowed it.

In the morning, everything would be different.

But for now, I succumbed to the desire to feel comforted.

To be cared for, adored, and protected.

As I fell into my dreams, I imagined an alternate life where this was my reality.

My every day.

My being.

Knowing full well that when I finally awoke, the nightmare would truly begin.

For Adrik had chipped at the barrier securing my heart, and a sliver of him had been allowed inside. Just enough to cause superficial damage.

If I wasn't careful, the results of whatever this was that brewed between us could lead to catastrophe.

And the worst part was, I'd welcome it.

Because at least then I would know what it meant to truly feel something other than exquisite pain.

Chapter Sixteen

Adrik

I FOLDED MY ARMS, UNAMUSED. "Again."

Valora growled, the sound sexy as fuck, and stirred a cluster of embers in the air. Sweat beaded across her brow in a sign of exertion, but nothing more than a faint flicker graced her beautiful skin.

I shook my head. "You're thinking too much."

"I'm thinking about killing you," she snarled.

I smirked. "Then do it." We'd been at this for days, trying to provoke her power to come out and play so she could learn how to tame it. Yet, it seemed regardless of what I said to her, I couldn't piss her off enough to want to kill me.

I supposed that served as a positive sign in regard to our relationship.

But I couldn't train her if I didn't know the extent of energy we were dealing with.

"We're running out of time, Valora," I said, glancing at the skylights over the old library. "Necros will want to fuck you again soon." He'd dropped her off a week ago, having sent guards only twice to see if she'd regained consciousness. Both times, I'd claimed she'd been hardly coherent and feigned disappointment in her performance.

I'd wondered each time if they'd checked on me in person because of the faulty cameras, but they never said a word. And during a recent shadow visit to the security lounge, I found that the feeds weren't even being recorded.

It seemed Necros trusted me.

Or maybe he just didn't care what happened to Valora so long as she remained breathing.

A flicker of light sailed over my shoulder, smoldering to ash before it hit anything of import, and Valora cursed, falling to her knees. "I *hate* this."

"Oh, good. A pity party," I drawled, walking over to lean against the bookshelf. "Okay, little bird. Show me your tears. I'm ready to feign some sympathy for you."

Her eyes narrowed. "Are you trying to piss me off?"

Yes. "Are you trying to fail?" I countered. "Because that's what you're doing. And we both know you're stronger than this."

"We don't know anything," she countered, standing once again. "That's the problem. *I don't know how to do this.*"

I pushed away from the shelving unit and stalked toward her. "Then let's spar instead." I'd taught her a few moves over the last several days. Mostly ways to defend herself and incapacitate an attacker. She was, surprisingly, a quick study, her movements agile and lithe, as if she were born to fight. But a week paled in comparison to my experience, as well as everyone else's in this palace. Which was why I needed her powers to come out and play.

Valora braced her feet in the stance I'd shown her, bending her legs at the knees. "Now you're speaking my language."

"Oh?" I circled her with my hands behind my back, purposely keeping a nonthreatening pose. "You like our little sparring matches, do you?"

"Gives me a chance to hit you," she returned, grinning.

"You mean it gives you cause to touch me." Something she'd done every night since Necros left her in my guest quarters. I let her lead each time, recognizing her need to heal and feel in charge.

But fuck, it was growing harder and harder not to give in to my own needs.

She wasn't the only one who craved control.

And I also desired her blood.

Valora came at me when all I did was continue to pace, her leg trying to sweep mine out from under me. I jumped deftly with a chuckle and shook my head. "Trying to put me on my back already? And here I thought we had at least another hour before fucking time."

"You're becoming quite arrogant." She put her hands on her hips. "Maybe I don't want to fuck tonight."

I smiled and darted behind her back, clamping one arm around her waist and the other around her throat. "Distractions are deadly," I whispered against her ear. "Remember that the enemy will always look for an opening, even when you perceive them as innocent."

She squirmed, trying to drop the way I'd taught her earlier this week, but my grasp was too tight.

"What are you going to do, little bird?" I licked the throbbing pulse against her neck. "How are you going to fly again with your wings trapped?"

Her resulting snarl had my lips curling.

"You're adorable when frustrated," I continued, knowing my words both excited and enraged her. "Mmm, it's too bad you can't best me, sweetheart." I dropped my voice to a teasing hum. "Shall I take my prize? You weren't interested in fucking, so maybe I'll just use your mouth."

She began to fight in earnest, my cruel words igniting something inside her.

Valora couldn't *see* me. And my voice had lowered so much it became ambiguous, bringing back memories of pain—ones she wanted to remain buried.

But I couldn't allow her to continue to hide.

She needed her wings to fly, and those wings were born of pain and anguish.

I drew my teeth across her pulse, threatening her tender skin. "I want to make you bleed," I admitted, knowing she would take the proclamation negatively, but needing that inferno to rise. "You're okay with a little pain, right?"

I couldn't bring myself to call her degrading names even though I knew it would push her over the edge faster. And the way her heart thudded in her chest told me we were almost there without it.

She'd gone still. Her skin ice cold.

Either I'd knocked her back into that hiding place with my callousness or she—

Flames erupted over her skin, forcing me to release her and jump backward. My shadow energy rolled over my clothes, putting out the flickers that remained before they caused damage.

Valora turned, her lips curled back into a snarl, until her eyes found mine.

I maintained a loose position, ready to move if she decided to make a lethal example of my taunts.

But the flames cooled to a simmer when she realized it was just me behind her, and a shudder shook her small frame.

"Don't lose it," I said softly. "Channel it into your palm. See what you can create."

Some of the heat intensified as she focused, her eyes falling closed. "Keep talking to me."

"Harshly? Or coaching?" While I suspected what she needed, I wanted her to say it.

"Pretend you're Necros."

Right. That was what I'd anticipated.

I rolled my neck, taking in the surroundings, and channeled my rage for the male who took all this away from me and my family. A monster. A predator. A dictator who deserved to die.

She wanted me to be him.

I'd practiced that.

Because to kill thine enemy, one needed to understand him.

"What the hell are you wearing?" I demanded, taking in Valora's attire. She wore my boxers and an undershirt from my wardrobe. She looked sexy as fuck. But Necros would hate it. "Why aren't you kneeling? Have I not made it clear that your place is at my feet?" I dared to take a step forward, even as the flames grew. "Do you need another lesson? Shall I orchestrate a new battle? Bring in fourteen men to train you? Give you to them all at once? Watch them shred you apart? Fuck you until you can't breathe?"

Her chest heaved, as did mine.

I loathed this game. But I understood it. She needed to learn control. Needed to be able to hear these words and *not* react. Not until she was ready.

"More?" I asked her softly.

She nodded. "Yes."

Clearing my mind, I started again, saying everything I could think of that Necros would use to belittle her. Everything except calling her a whore. Some part of me couldn't do that, couldn't allow that word to cross my lips. Yet all manner of vile statements littered the air, including ones about what Necros had done to her physically. Threatening to defile her again in a similar manner, to fuck her so absolutely that she begged for death.

She grew hotter with each word, until sweat poured off my skin from the proximity. But she maintained it, maybe because she knew it was me speaking. I paused after every tirade to check in, and each time, she told me to continue.

And I did.

Until a ball of blue angelfire curled around her wrist, crawling up her arm.

I took several steps back, the energy hypnotic in its lethality. One touch and she'd incinerate me.

"Valora," I whispered.

She didn't reply, the power swimming in vines across her skin and singeing the fabric covering her torso, then her legs.

I swallowed. *You're glowing violet,* I warned.

"I'm okay," she replied, gritting her teeth.

I remained absolutely still. *Tell me what you need.*

You, she whispered. *Talk.*

"You look beautiful." I spoke softly, understanding that she wanted *my* words now. Not those of Necros. "This is your destiny, Valora. To be a true queen, one of the most powerful and revered in the Underworld. And you wear it well." I went to my knees, placing myself in an inferior position. "Open your eyes. See where you are, remember *who* you are, and observe the glory you've created."

Because she was truly magnificent, radiating an energy so pure I nearly wept looking at her.

And what's more, she *controlled* it.

Even in a library filled with books—a location I now regretted choosing for this sort of training—she managed to contain the inferno to her skin alone.

Of course, the clothes she wore were gone. Something I would have liked a hell of a lot more without all the flames. Still, this was the goal. And she'd finally started to achieve it.

Her irises glowed with liquid blue fire as she finally looked at me, a note of concentration in their depths. "Adrik…"

"I'm here, sweet star." *Little bird* no longer seemed like an adequate name. Valora's clipped wings kept her from flying, but the light inside her rivaled the galaxies above. "How do you feel?"

"Powerful," she marveled, looking at her arms and rolling the rope of bluish-purple flames across her skin. She smiled. "I can't wield it yet, but it's responding to my desire to stay close. To not harm *you*."

A good sign that she was starting to truly trust me, which meant I was one step closer in my plan for her heart. I swallowed as my own ached at the thought. But I shoved the emotion away and focused on *her*. She needed help to come down from the high; I could see it in the power radiating from her eyes.

"Can you harness it?" I phrased it as a curious question, not a demand. "Or does it feel too good to be free?"

"Necros won't touch me in this form," she said, almost to herself. "No one would."

"You'd incinerate anyone who came too close," I agreed. "It's why I'm over here."

She frowned, glancing up at me. "I would never hurt you."

"Not on purpose, no." Yet I had every intention of harming her. How was that fair? And why did that suddenly feel like the worst idea in the world?

Fuck, Grigory was going to slaughter me.

Not only had I missed one of our meetings—something that resulted in a disgruntled call—but I almost regretted what I had to do.

"Adrik?" She took a step forward. "Are you all right?"

I flinched a little at the singeing heat radiating from her form. "Just getting a little warm," I joked, my damp skin a testament to the truth. "I'm going to need an ice bath after this."

Her lips curled. "A bath? Can I join you?"

"I thought you didn't want to fuck tonight?" I

teased, happy to see her flames going down a little as we spoke. If she noticed, she didn't comment.

"Maybe I've changed my mind."

"Maybe I want to be on top," I returned, meaning it despite the playful note in my voice. The woman was *killing* me.

"Hmm." She eyed the angelfire, watching as it shifted back to a safer orange-red flicker. "Maybe I'd like that." The fire continued to cool until only embers danced over her naked form. "I did it," she breathed, her expression a mixture of awe and pride. The heat left her gaze, returning her irises to a pale blue as she looked at me. "Adrik, *I did it.*"

I stood just in time to catch her in a hug. Her skin lacked the warmth I expected, her limbs almost icy as she clung to my neck and buried her head against my chest. "You were magnificent," I whispered, pressing my lips to her temple and lifting her into the air.

Her legs wrapped around my waist, placing the hottest part of her against my growing cock.

Naked.

Powerful.

Beautiful.

Woman.

I groaned against her neck. "Valora, I—" My wrist buzzed with an alarm that had my head shooting up. "*Fuck.*" I'd rigged the area outside my quarters to warn me if anyone disturbed the proximity of my door. It gave me a two-minute warning, tops. Which was usually more than enough. But not tonight. "We need to get back. Now."

The hours had escaped me.

It was well past evening on our seventh night together.

Necros probably wanted his wife back.

Chapter Seventeen

Valora

Adrik pulled me through the tunnels at a rapid speed, telling me the plan as we went.

I didn't like one word of it. Especially now that I knew how to awaken my power. And I told him as much.

"Valora," he said, grasping my shoulders just outside of his quarters. "You just burned through hours of energy. Yes, you're powerful. But we need to be smart about this. Play submissive. Buy me time to be located elsewhere. Or this will all implode tonight, and we're not ready."

He pushed me into his rooms, where the door rattled beneath Necros's fists, his fury palpable.

Adrik ruffled my hair, pulling it over my shoulders, giving me a horrid appearance.

"Act groggy. Then beg him to take you back, apologize profusely, tell him you missed him. Do whatever he asks." Adrik cupped my cheek as a resounding bang hit the wood, shaking the walls. "Go to him," he whispered. "Trust me."

And with that, he left me alone with the raging

lion in the hallway.

"*Adrik*!" my husband roared. Another slam rattled the fixtures throughout the room.

Oh, he was livid. And yet, what did he suspect by giving his wife away to another man? I blew out a long breath and wandered over to the door. "Necros?" I called in as weak a voice as I could muster.

The pounding stopped.

"Open the door," he ordered.

"Yes," I replied, forcing a note of fear into my tone.

Adrik had showed me how to unbolt the door earlier this week, not wanting me to feel trapped in his quarters. I slid them across slowly, pretending to struggle, and collapsed against the wall beside the entrance when done, doing my best to feign exhaustion.

Necros threw the door open, the wood crashing into the stone interior, and stormed inside with two guards behind him. Good thing I'd chosen the opposite wall or that heavy oak would have slammed right into my face.

"Where's the prince?" he snarled, searching the dark room, noting the crisply folded sheets and the thin blankets on the floor near the bottom of the bed. Adrik had thrown those there several days ago, stating it would show Necros a level of detachment if he thought that was where I slept.

It seemed to work, because my husband's shoulders slightly loosened as he found me sliding down the wall. I put my head in my hands as if trying to rouse myself. "Forgive me, My Lord. I'm… I've not been well."

"He's not here, My King," one of the guards announced after having checked the bathroom and side room.

"He left my wife alone?" He sounded quite angry with that fact, which I found humorous considering all the days and nights he left me alone in my own rooms. "Find him. Now."

"Of course, My Lord," they said in unison, bowing.

The door remained opened as they left, giving me a false sense of security that soon dissipated beneath the boots of Necros's approach. "You're pathetic," he spat. "It's been a week, and you're still recovering?"

"I-I'm sorry," I spluttered, making a show of forcing myself onto my knees.

He grunted. "I thought Adrik was training you. But all you've been doing is sleeping. What a fucking waste."

Shit. I couldn't let him blame Adrik for my behavior—something that was Necros's fault more than anyone else's. But he would never see it that way. He'd accuse Adrik of not upholding his side of the bargain, may even force him to leave. *That can't happen.*

"Please, Necros. Please. I'm trying. I… I…" I grabbed his belt to keep him from stepping away, not knowing another way to make him hear me. "I'm l-learning. I-I promise." I slid the leather through the buckle, hating myself for what I had to do.

No, I hated *Necros.*

He put me in this position.

He made me do these things.

But knowing that gave me power, put me back in charge. It gave me a way to manipulate him, to beat him at his own game.

And I saw it now, felt it in the way he froze, mystified by my show of submission before him. His hands hung loose at his sides, his cock growing beneath the zipper I pulled down.

"Can I please you, My Lord?" I asked, peeking up at him through my mess of curls. "I-I want to please you." Wrong. I wanted to bite him and flay him alive with my angelfire, but Adrik was right. I wasn't ready yet. We needed to lull Necros into a state of comfort. Make him think he'd won and broken my resolve. Then hit him at the height of his arrogance, when he felt the most confident in his superiority.

It would make his fall all the better.

I didn't wait for his permission, taking his member into my mouth and sucking him deep, the way I knew he preferred. That he hadn't touched me yet denoted his shock at my willingness, the act one I'd initiated rather than him.

It gave me power over him.

Put me on top.

Made this my act to command.

I held his green gaze and imagined they were ebony, dark, the picture of midnight. *Adrik*, I thought, forcing his image into my mind, and pretended this was him. *My prince.*

The fingers combing through my tangled hair didn't belong to Necros.

The groan of appreciation didn't come from my

husband.

And the tug against my scalp as the fingers turned into a fist, guiding my motions, wasn't that of a king.

But my prince.

My Adrik.

The taste was wrong. The size, too. Yet, I lost myself to the fantasy, allowed myself to feel hunger, pretending this was the man I preferred. We did this only last night, Adrik coming down my throat while I straddled his face. A new experience, one underlined in rapture. These feelings and sensations were dangerous, the way I was able to picture him so perfectly now, while in the grasp of another, an indication of how deep I'd fallen.

I expected regret.

Waited for a hint of annoyance.

Except all I felt was utter bliss.

"Yes," Necros groaned, his voice not deep enough, not sexy enough, to be my Adrik. So I listened for his words instead, recalling them from last night, how he'd cursed and growled my name. How his entire body was lined in tension as he forced himself not to take command.

It had to be killing him to allow me complete control.

Which made me wonder what it would be like when he finally dictated a session. Would I feel afraid? Or would it turn me on even more?

"Your Highness," a low voice said, his throat clearing. "We, uh, found him in the communications room talking to his brother."

I started to slip away, returning to the moment,

the disgust inside my mouth, but the hand at the back of my head urged me onward even as Necros addressed his minions. "Why did you leave my wife alone?" he asked, his voice a low growl of sound, all hints of his anger gone.

"This is the most lively I've seen her all week," Adrik replied, causing my heart to skip a beat. It felt wrong for him to watch this, to see me on my knees before another man. Even if that man was my husband.

But as I tried to pull back, I was forced down again, taking even more of Necros into my throat. I fought a gag, knowing it would infuriate him, and tried to find my focus again, to remember the one I truly wanted between my lips.

"She's been asleep, My Lord," Adrik continued, sounding bored. "I locked her inside and went to catch up with my brother."

"Locked her inside?" one of the guards repeated, snorting. "More like locked us out."

"Of course," Adrik replied. "Because the king entrusted me with her care and I didn't want to risk his wrath should anything happen to her while she slept. Did I misunderstand my charge?"

"You're supposed to be training her," Necros cut in, his grip tightening against my scalp as he picked up his pace with bruising thrusts.

"Hard to train a corpse, Your Highness," Adrik returned. "But I've done what I can, and given the way she's eagerly sucking your cock, I'd say I've had at least a small impact on her skill."

Eagerly, I repeated with a snort. I tried again not to gag at the harsh penetration into my throat, adding, *Hardly.*

Trust me, I'm not enjoying this, either.

It's not your mouth he's fucking, I pointed out, doing my best to again fall into my dream of this being Adrik, not Necros, and failing because of the conversation flowing around me.

"It is different to have her beg to suck me off," Necros agreed, his eyes finding mine and smiling. "I do like you in this position, Valora. It's so befitting of a whore."

Fire ignited in my soul, but I forced it down and drew my teeth along his length instead, which earned me a growl of approval from deep in his throat.

Pretend it's Adrik, I coached myself. *Pretend it's Adrik.*

Green eyes melted to black once more, the smirk belonging to a pair of full lips I longed to kiss and the hand in my hair turning to a caress down my neck.

Think of my tongue between your thighs, Adrik whispered, causing my legs to clench. *Of your sweet, swollen clit between my teeth as I nibble and lick and suck until you shatter.*

Oh God.

Mmm, that's it, sweet star. Imagine my cock filling your mouth, my seed pouring down your throat, and swallow for me. Take me deep inside. Keep me where I belong.

I did. I swallowed every salty, thick drop, knowing all the while it tasted *wrong,* that it lacked Adrik's smoky notes, yet pretending it was him all the same. I even licked my lips for more as the thick length left my mouth, my heated gaze staring longingly into a pair of eyes that were the wrong color.

"Fuck," Necros breathed, his hand still on my head, stroking me as one would a pet. "Well, that's an improvement."

Adrik stood in the hallway, leaning against the wall, his focus on Necros. He lifted a shoulder. "It's a work in progress."

A flash of hurt seared my heart. It was all part of the charade. I knew that. But a part of me worried he meant it.

I hadn't allowed him to be himself in the bedroom yet.

I hadn't been able to.

Was I not satisfying enough for him?

I lowered my gaze, falling back to my heels, and bowed my head.

"Hmm, I see," Necros murmured. "Well. How about a night with my whores? That should help."

"I would enjoy that," Adrik replied, sending another arrow to my chest.

Why do I feel this way? It wasn't like he belonged to me. We owed each other nothing. And these worries were frivolous, unfounded, and not relevant.

"Good." Necros finished buckling his pants, then turned to clap Adrik on the shoulder. "Then let's go." He started to lead the way, then paused to glance over his shoulder to where I still sat on the floor. "Clean yourself up, Valora. You look like shit."

The door slammed.

I shuddered.

What just happened? I'd felt so in control a few moments ago. And now… *now* I didn't know what to expect.

Why had Adrik agreed to go visit with Necros's

whores? Would he fuck one of them?

Adrik? I whispered.

No reply.

He'd blocked me from his mind.

Which could only mean one thing—he intended to fulfill his needs.

With someone other than me.

Chapter Eighteen

Adrik

SHUTTING VALORA OUT PHYSICALLY pained me, but I needed to concentrate. This was a test, not a show of camaraderie. Necros suspected my behavior, as he should. While I'd done my best to cover my tracks, tonight's time lapse put me in a precarious position. As well as the clear healing of his wife.

Oh, Valora had done a fantastic job of feigning exhaustion and distracting the monster, but Necros had noticed the clean lines of her skin. The lack of blemishes. The clear countenance of her gaze.

It would be abundantly clear to him that I'd been going easy on her. Another negative mark against me in his eyes.

And now he wanted to know why. However, rather than come out and ask me about it, he'd chosen this little game of kiss and tell.

I sipped my wine while twirling a finger idly around a piece of blonde hair that had fallen over my chest from the little seductress on my lap. She nibbled on my ear, played her nails over my chest and down my abs, all with the intent of enticing a reaction from me.

Had she been Valora, she might have succeeded.

"You look bored," Necros sighed. A female sat between his legs, her head bobbing up and down as she tried to please him, while another sat on the arm of the chair—naked. Valora's earlier attentions had clearly left him depleted, because the two females were struggling to make him come, despite alternating their mouths on him for the last thirty minutes. Or perhaps it was a testament to his plotting because he'd yet to get to the point of our little impromptu meeting, and I highly doubted the purpose was to watch him indulge his harem.

"Not bored," I finally said, replying to his comment. "I'm thinking." I wrapped my fist around the woman's hair as she drew too close to my belt again, and tsked in her ear. "When I'm ready, I'll ask."

She whimpered, her full bottom lip disappearing between little white teeth.

I almost pitied her. Except I knew she enjoyed this. Almost all succubi did. But if anyone would be feeding tonight, it would be me.

"Thinking," Necros repeated, closing his eyes in the epitome of bliss. "Mmm, that's a dangerous move in this room."

Says the man trying to distract me with eager pussy, I thought. "My brother is eager for me to return to Noxia," I said, deciding to provoke the conversation I knew he desired. "I'm not sure I feel the same way."

"Oh?" He didn't look at me, his expression one of euphoria. However, I sensed his astute awareness.

It was written all over his tense form. He tried to act like a male lost to the passion of his females, even went so far as to lace his fingers through the woman's hair to drive her downward, but I saw through the charade.

Because I was playing one, too.

"We didn't talk for long, as I'd literally just dialed him when your guards approached." No sense in trying to pretend I'd been in that communications room for longer than a few seconds before they'd arrived. There were cameras everywhere. "Alas, his first words were in regard to my return. And I have no doubt his final ones would have been the same. Apparently, my family misses me."

"And you don't miss them?" he prompted, his curiosity piqued.

Good. Yes. Let's focus on my history, remind you who you think I am.

"I do. But not Noxia. Not my place, anyway. I mean, Grigory's the heir apparent. And who am I? Just the second child." I drew my finger across the succubus's mouth, pretending to be enthralled with the way her tongue peeked out to lick me. "There's not much left for me there, other than a comfortable life. I'm thinking of exploring the other kingdoms, see what mischief I can find for myself." I winked at the blonde. She giggled in reply.

"Is that what you're doing here?" Necros mused, lifting his head to look at me. "Looking for mischief?"

There it is—the distrust. I smiled. "Always." Ignoring him, I nipped at the woman's neck, hard enough to bleed. She jolted, then sighed as I ran my tongue across the superficial wound, absorbing her tangy essence. I preferred Valora's, but I needed to do this to gain control of the female on my lap.

Riian, I thought, finally learning her name with a brief prod into her mind.

Another lap at the wound gave me access to her emotions: her intrinsic fear of Necros and her gratitude for my presence. Mmm, it seemed not even his harem enjoyed his company. Well, lucky for Riian, I'd be saving her for the evening.

I took a real bite, drinking from her pulse with a thick pull that satisfied the growing hunger inside me. It also provided me with the depth I required in her mind, one that would allow me to control her with a quick command of a thought.

She sighed against me, her body succumbing to my vampiric kiss.

I wasn't a Son of Noxia but a Son of Shadows. And we were very closely related, both possessing the need for blood to satiate our appetites. Only, my kind required significantly less, and we tended to temporarily inherit the powers of our victims. As Riian wasn't the first succubus of my acquaintance, I was prepared for her seductive energy and knew exactly how to tame it. But I might just bring it out later for fun with Valora.

Necros chuckled. "I like you, Adrik."

My lips curled against Riian's and licked the bite marks marring her pale skin. "Does that mean I can stay for a while longer? Continue my brand of mischief?" It was meant as a challenge—did he want to demand I leave, or allow me to stay and determine my motives?

"Depends on what you've been up to."

I shrugged. "Training your wife, mostly." I met his gaze. "She has a problem with authority. Seems to think her title of *queen* grants her some sort of right over me. We're still working through it."

He regarded me curiously as the women on his lap switched places, the darker-skinned female going to her knees between his splayed thighs. The poor girls were going to be doing this all night at this rate. No wonder Riian felt thankful to be seated on my lap, even if her throat hurt a little from my not-so-pleasant bite.

"I'm surprised you feel that way, what with your mother being the supreme authority in your kingdom." He wrapped his arm around the female, pulling her to sit astride his lap and on top of the woman's head below. "Please yourself for me, whore."

"Yes, My Lord," she whispered, her hand disappearing between her thighs.

A real man would take care of her himself. But Necros knew nothing about feminine pleasure, as was evidenced by his wife.

He leaned to the side to better see me, ignoring the show going on before him.

What a prick.

"Does Lux know you feel queens are beneath your station?" he asked, arching one bushy auburn brow.

I smirked. "Not all queens," I corrected. "Just yours."

Both his eyebrows lifted at that proclamation.

"Should I be offended?"

"Hardly," I scoffed. "I mean, surely you've noticed there's nothing special about her. Aside from her beauty, of course. But it seems the galaxies only gifted her with looks, no real power. She's as ordinary as a gremlin demon." I tilted my head. "Isn't that why you opted to have her trained? A woman of her stature and appeal is meant for the bedroom, but only if she knows how to behave."

Fuck, I hated myself a little. But I needed him to believe me ignorant as to her true nature.

And from the glimmer in his irises, he did.

"I think there's more to her than she allows us to see," he admitted, surprising me. "It's why I thought these games would, perhaps, *awaken* her."

"Like a dormant power?" I asked, scratching the stubble dotting my jaw. I'd forgotten to shave earlier before sparring with Valora.

He lifted a shoulder. "I mean, it's just a theory. But I thought if I scared her enough, she might, I don't know, unlock an ability and fight for herself."

I snorted. "Oh, she tries to fight—with words."

"Which are useless."

"Indeed," I agreed. *Unless she pairs them with angelfire, in which case, good luck to you.* "She never feels afraid to me. Just pissed off."

His responding grin radiated evil. "She felt fear last week."

"Perhaps, but was it for her life?" I asked, idly wondering how far he'd take this conversation, how much he would reveal. "I mean, the men you chose to train her are harming her, yes. But it's all for sexual gratification. She knows that. So while she might fear the pain, does she truly fear for her life? Enough to fight?"

He rubbed his chin, considering, while the female atop him began to mewl. Necros knocked her to the ground with a flick of his wrist, causing her to cry out. "Shut up," he snapped. Then looked at me again as if he hadn't just assaulted a female on the edge of an orgasm.

And this was what Valora had lived with all these years? *Fuck*.

"You bring up an intriguing point, one I hadn't considered." He sounded quite pleased, if a bit mystified. "She doesn't feel the need to fight because she knows she's not in danger."

Oh, she wants to fight, I thought. *She wants to kill you all.* "I'm still not convinced she harbors a power beyond that of her mouth around a cock," I said, feigning disinterest. "Just my observation."

"Mmm," he murmured, not listening to me at all. And not because of the female trying tirelessly to suck him off.

I pretended to ignore him, my focus shifting to Riian. A trickle of blood from my bite had trailed down to her collarbone. I lapped it up, earning me a purr from the succubus. Her desire blossomed in my senses, telling me how starved she was for attention. Necros didn't know how to treat any of his females, it seemed.

Or perhaps he just didn't care.

"You will keep my wife occupied for a few more days," Necros decided, shocking me for the first time tonight. "While I orchestrate something—a surprise of sorts—for next week." He finally looked at me again. "I'd lock her in her rooms, but she wanders into the gardens from there, and I'd prefer her to remain broken on your floor. It'll keep her weak."

"Of course," I replied. "Shall I continue training her?"

He lifted a shoulder. "Fuck her all you want. It's not like I'm getting much joy from her these days." He glanced at the female curled on the floor. "Why have you stopped pleasing yourself?" he demanded.

She immediately continued her ministrations, her posture stiff and unyielding.

Necros sighed, shaking his head. "All of you are fucking useless." He tugged the female off his cock and tossed her to the side. "I need a walk." He stood, fixed his pants, and made to leave, then turned back to me. "Feel free to use them as you like. I won't be back tonight."

"Can I take them to my rooms?" I asked, not wanting to stay here where cameras would capture my every move. "Perhaps Valora will learn a thing or two from watching us all?"

The king seemed to consider, then smiled. "Yes. I think she'd enjoy that very much."

"Your hospitality is astoundingly gracious, My Lord," I said, bowing my head. "Thank you."

"Of course." He was already lost to his own thoughts again, his face clouding over in contemplation. "Enjoy your evening, Prince of Noxia."

"Oh, I will." I took in the females before me and allowed my vampiric senses to take over, just in case he studied my face later in the films.

He left us then.

Not caring at all that I might feed and kill one of his harem members.

I made a show of tasting each of them for the cameras, taking their blood into my system to better control their minds. It would make the rest of the evening so much easier.

"Come, ladies," I cooed, leading the trio with a thick strand of lust looped around their essences. "Let's retire, shall we?"

CHAPTER NINETEEN

VALORA

I PACED THE ROOM FOR THE THOUSANDTH time, debating if I should just return to my own rooms or wait for Adrik to return.

From what? I thought with a laugh. *A fuck party with my husband?*

Ugh, Adrik still hadn't opened our link. I had no idea what to think. What if Necros realized we'd been working together? What if we hadn't gotten away with this at all and Necros had led Adrik away to his slaughter?

No. He's stronger than that.

And he'd reach out to me then.

Right?

I shook my head on a growl, irritated with myself just as much as with Adrik. It was ludicrous, really, to be upset. We were not promised to one another. Had never once discussed a relationship.

Because we couldn't have one.

Because I was already married.

"This is insane," I whispered, dragging my fingers through my freshly washed hair. "Absolute madness."

I couldn't be upset with Adrik. Not when we owed each other nothing. Not when I'd just sucked my husband off in front of him only hours ago. Who was I to be upset with Adrik for engaging in similar activities, under Necros's command, with another female?

And even without my husband's order, Adrik could do whomever and whatever he wanted.

I had no claims on him.

I just, well, sort of *wanted* to.

Which was wrong.

Very, very wrong.

Giggles came from the hallway, causing me to still midstep. And then the door opened to reveal Adrik with not one, not two, but *three* naked demonesses. He laughed as he ushered them inside, his expression one I wanted to slap off his handsome face and also see once more.

He shut the door and locked it without looking at me, cooing something to the triad of females.

They started toward the bed, only to change course toward the sitting area after a few steps. One appeared to be limping, her arm cradled against her belly.

"There," Adrik murmured, situating two of them on the couch together. "Indulge in each other as I know you crave." The limping one he took into his arms and placed on the chair beside them, his palm running over her side. "Rest, Lithiana. You'll feel better in the morning."

"Yes, My Prince," she replied, drawing her nail across his lips before closing her eyes in a deep slumber.

I watched in a mixture of shock and horror.

But rather than join the two females on the couch—who were now eagerly making out with one another—he backed away slowly and slid the doors closed between the rooms.

Then he finally looked at me. "Necros thinks I'm giving you a lesson in sex with other women."

My lips opened, closed, and opened again, but no sound escaped. What was I to say to that?

I missed you, he whispered into my mind, the caress of words a stroke against my senses that snapped me out of my stupor.

"You cut me off!" I snapped, not meaning to yell, but damn it, I didn't approve. "To what? Fuck another woman?" Oh, that was not supposed to fly out of my mouth, either. But now that we were here… "Or did she just suck you off? No, wait, there's three of them. Maybe they took turns?" I clapped my hand over my mouth, needing to stop this idiocy from escaping.

Except Adrik's response was to laugh.

Which had my palm leaving my face and cracking across his.

"Oh!" I jumped backward, holding my wrist, mortified. "I… I…" *What is wrong with me?* He'd done nothing wrong. Just brought three willing females back to his nest.

Where I waited for him.

"I should go." Maybe I'd ruined his plans for the night. I didn't know. Couldn't allow myself to consider it. I just needed to—

Adrik grabbed my hip and tugged me forward, his lips landing on mine. I flinched at the stench of female perfume all over his face and skin but sighed as his tongue slid into my mouth.

Because he tasted like my Adrik.

Not of another woman.

And I loved the way he kissed me.

My arms wrapped around his neck as he lifted me into the air and walked me backward to the bed. *I put on a show, but other than bite them, I did nothing,* he whispered into my mind, laying me down on the mattress. "I like you jealous, Valora," he mused, crawling over me.

"Jealous?" I repeated. "I'm not jealous."

"You are very jealous," he teased, nipping at my jaw. "But it's okay. Because I felt the same about you and Necros. It took everything inside me not to rip his head off while he…" The words were cut off on a growl as he kissed me again, this time harder, with a hint of possession underlying his touch.

I liked it.

Especially the way his palm circled my throat, holding me in place as he devoured my mouth. His other hand remained on my hip, pushing me into the bed as he settled between my splayed thighs.

"I love you in my clothes," he said, running his lips across my cheek to my neck. "It's so fucking sexy."

I warmed beneath him, pleased at the compliment, then stilled as his lips brushed my pulse. "Adrik…" He'd never really bitten me before, not while I was coherent.

"Do you know how I'm controlling them?" His

voice whispered across my skin, making my heart race. "Because I bit them, Valora. It's how I access and control the minds of others. But you're different."

"How?" I breathed, hypnotized by his words and his touch. "Why am I different?"

"I let you inside my mind. I let you *hear* me." His canines skimmed my throat, sending shivers down my arms. "It's a very intimate experience, having you in my head. I had to block you out to concentrate earlier. And it hurt to do so."

His lips closed around my throbbing pulse, sucking lightly, his tongue tracing the rhythm pounding beneath my skin.

My fingers threaded through his hair, urging him to taste me again. To bite me. To allow me to *feel* his power.

"I need to replace them," he murmured. "Their blood still coats my throat when all I desire is yours."

"Then do it," I replied. "Bite me."

His teeth pierced my neck, the puncture deep and true. I groaned beneath the strange sensation, my blood heating and cooling simultaneously as he took a harsh pull from my vein.

If the stars had a taste, it would be you, Valora. His words were sharp in my mind, his hunger palpable.

It should have terrified me, but the moment felt so right. So erotic. Even while screams of pleasure came from the other room as the women on the couch reached a crescendo in their passion.

One is a succubus who hasn't fed in a month, he advised. *And the other is a demon who prefers females to men. Your husband is a sick fuck.*

I know.

We will kill him.

I know, I repeated, arching into him as he sucked once more, guiding my life essence into his mouth and down his own throat. My thighs tightened around his legs, my core beginning to ache with a need only Adrik could satisfy. But he sighed into my neck instead, his teeth replaced by his tongue as he sealed the wounds with some sort of shadow magic.

"Necros is planning something," he said, going to his elbows on either side of my head. "I think he means to hurt you, Valora. Badly."

I gazed up at him. "What do you mean?" *And why is he bringing this up now?*

"Because we need to discuss it before I grow distracted," he replied, hearing my thought and punctuating his words with a soft thrust of his hardness against my dampening center. "Necros orchestrated this sick and twisted game to break you, thinking that you might respond to the torment with your gifts."

My blood began to cool. "I did."

"I know, but he doesn't know that. And I rather stupidly pointed out that while sexual games may evoke fear, it's not the same kind of fear as a near-death situation. I'd meant it as a deterrent, to try to end his erotic insanity, but I think I awoke a new idea instead." He had the good grace to grimace. "I just don't know what."

"So he intends to… do something else to me… instead of the sharing?"

He nodded. "Garul and Jives were relieved last

week, but I wondered if he might bring in more. Now, I think he's planning something far worse."

"To provoke my power to rise," I translated. "So he can steal it again."

"Yes. Or rather, so he can try." He cleared his throat, his fingers combing through my curls. "Your energy is bubbling beneath the surface of your skin like molten lava waiting to erupt. But Necros seems oblivious, which leads me to believe Lucifer has to be present to assist. Otherwise, your husband would have sensed your growing energy these last few days and already tried to absorb it."

"But you said the purpose of the wedding was to create a link."

"It was, but what if that link isn't duty-bound to the vows, but to the heart?" he asked softly. "Lucifer had to help before. What about now? Do you feel any obligation or connection to Necros? Anything that gives him a right to your energy?"

I considered and shook my head. "I feel nothing." Not even a sense of loyalty like I once did. I wanted nothing to do with Necros other than to be the one to drive a blade through his heart. "So what you're saying is, even if I displayed my ability, he won't be able to steal it. Not immediately, anyway." *Not without Lucifer.*

"Yes. Which, I think, gives us an opportunity."

"You want me to demonstrate my ability during his next test." I didn't ask, because I already knew. It made sense. "He'll think he's won, that I'm finally giving him what he needs."

"And that's when we'll strike," Adrik agreed,

drawing his thumb across my cheek. "But it will have to be a weak display of power, to make him think it's just finally coming to life."

"Which will make him want to provoke even more from me."

Adrik dipped his chin in agreement. "It will also put you in a position of power that he'll have to respect. At least until he can take it."

"But we won't let him get that far."

"No, we won't." He lowered his mouth to mine, whispering a kiss across my mouth. "Fortunately, we still have a few days of practice ahead of us. But I'll do everything I can to help you prepare, sweet star."

"I'll be ready," I vowed. "I don't have a choice."

"And I'll be with you for whatever you need," he murmured, kissing me again. "I've put the demonesses to sleep. Which means I'm officially all yours."

"Won't they wake if you forget about them?" I asked, curious about his ability and how it worked.

"No. I compelled them to dream for twelve hours. Their minds will comply without my continued influence."

"That's what you did to me the first night," I realized out loud, my eyes widening.

"Yes, but as I said, you were different." His midnight gaze sparkled with desire, his lips curling suggestively. "I let you into my mind, Valora. I've never granted that privilege to anyone, not even Grigory."

I ran my fingers down his back, tracing the fabric of his jacket. "Why me?" I wondered aloud. "Why did you let me in?"

"Because I knew you were different." He canted his head, his obsidian pupils flaring with the truth of his words. "I've always known who you were, Valora. My beautiful star. I've always wanted you to awaken. It's our destiny, yours and mine, to take down this kingdom. It's written in the galaxies."

"To kill them all," I breathed. He'd promised me that from early on, but only recently did I understand why. "Everyone knows you as a Prince of Noxia, but that's not who you are at all."

"No. I'm the King of Shadows, and one day soon, the Underworld will know how I earned that name." He kissed me again, his mouth insistent against mine. "Will you take me, Valora? Will you lead us both into a sea of bliss?"

"I thought you wanted control tonight," I reminded him.

"I'm always in control, sweet star." He rolled us, placing me on top, his hands supporting my hips as I found my balance. "Ride me."

I smiled. "Only if you promise to bite me again afterward."

"Oh, I'll do more than bite you, My Queen." He wrapped his palm around my neck, pulling me flat against him as his lips brushed mine. "Now fuck me, Valora. Fuck me like I'm yours."

Chapter Twenty

Valora

I KICKED MY LEGS AGAINST MY BED, BORED.

After another week of beautiful bliss in Adrik's arms, I'd been forced to return to my quarters with no explanation as to why. I'd half expected Necros to demand entry last night and fuck me, but he'd left me alone to dwell in my own nerves.

Sleep had turned to nightmares as violent visions of doom invaded my dreams. I'd woken up sweating with sparks flying from my hands that threatened to ignite my bedsheets. Adrik's name had been the first to enter my thoughts, my need for him a scary realization. And then he'd been there, his presence warming me to my core from afar while never setting foot inside my physical rooms.

I would never understand how he was able to elicit such bliss from my body. How his mere thoughts dismantled my tension and calmed my chaotic mind.

Adrik? I called, curious as to why I hadn't heard from him yet today.

I'd bathed and dressed in clothes to appease

Necros, assuming he had a need for me beyond just lounging in my rooms. My dark teal dress was embroidered with jewels and bones along the bodice, something I knew would please my husband. The gory details weren't my favorite, but it did seem a shame that such a beautiful garment would probably be ruined by the end of the day.

Hmm, although, maybe if I destroyed all my dresses, Necros would allow me to wear pants.

My lips curled at the thought. Then flattened as I realized Adrik had never replied.

Are you in the library? I wondered. *Shall I meet you there?* I knew the way by heart, having memorized the palace's intricate maze of hidden hallways over the last few weeks.

It felt like months since I used the normal corridors.

Adrik? I tried again, frowning in earnest now. *Where are you?*

I could sense he was near but otherwise occupied.

Maybe Necros had him doing something. I'd learned my lesson after their last meeting not to grow concerned. Adrik wasn't truly mine, but he'd remained faithful in his own way. Something I appreciated in a strangely warm way.

Shaking myself of my thoughts, I decided a walk through the gardens would clear my mind and help me focus on the pending tasks of whatever Necros had planned. Perhaps my defying his recent rules would prompt him to act faster.

"No more hiding outside," he'd decreed all those weeks ago.

Well, it was time to see if he meant it.

Guards swept out of my way as I stepped outside through the glass doors bordering my sitting area. Neither of the males made snide comments, one even bowed. It took me aback, and I stopped to stare at the curly-haired brute.

The skin on the back of my neck prickled with goose bumps. *Something isn't right.*

"Where's my husband?" I asked the bowing male.

He rose, no expression on his round face. "King Necros is busy with court matters."

A polite response.

How… strange.

I waved my hand to dismiss him, then remembered his job was to stand sentry at my doors.

The guards exchanged glances, small smiles curving at the edges of their mouths. They were full of the promise of darkness.

Would they tell Necros I'd opted for a stroll against his wishes? I sort of hoped so. I'd enjoy getting to the bottom of whatever was happening around here.

Adrik. I tried again, venturing farther into the gardens. *Something's happening. Whatever Necros planned, it's coming to fruition now. Where are you? I don't know if I can do this alone. Please.*

Still no response.

Worry knotted heavily in my body, my shoulders tensing as the calmness of the last week disintegrated. I needed fresher air, untainted by the demons at my back.

Running down the path, I passed my usual reading nook and sprinted toward the cliffs of the gardens. The purple sun was high in the sky, its rays cascading down into eerie patterns on the ground.

Adrik, I tried once more, true anxiety spilling into my mental voice. *Where are you?*

I still felt him near, but closed off.

What's happening? I wondered.

Maybe Necros suspected?

My heart crashed against my ribs at the thought, my vision blurring with the violet haze around me. I stole a deep breath, forcing myself to calm down, needing to focus.

It didn't work.

I fled to the right, running through the black statues forming my wicked tangle of a garden to a place I revered for silence—a notch in the cliffside with views of Caluçon. I sometimes sat here with Zaya, discussing my ideas and thoughts for growth. It was here that we finalized our plans for the women and children bordering the city without aid.

I miss you, I thought at her now. *I wish you were here.*

A breeze was the only response, the kingdom's warmth washing over my skin.

I collapsed onto a slab of granite, sighing as the boned section of my corset dug into my ribs.

Adrik. It came out as a plea now.

A plea he left unanswered.

My chest ached with a loneliness I despised. I was a queen, not some smitten female who needed her lover to provide purpose. I'd just come to rely on him over the last few weeks, his presence a security blanket I craved.

I needed to do this alone. I possessed the power to do so; I just required the confidence to believe in myself.

The majestic landscape danced before me, a picturesque scene that soothed some of my inner turmoil. The other night, Adrik mentioned that in the human world, real stars sparkled in the night. I wondered if I would one day experience them, as well as the notorious golden sun that shone throughout the day. The purple hues of Caluçon's sky didn't allow for bright skies or nights filled with millions of twinkling lights.

I closed my eyes, daydreaming about what it might look like based on Adrik's description.

Heavy leather boots stomped on the grounds below, vibrating the cliffside and jarring me out of my stupor. I sat up, dazed, and watched as a troop of royal warriors descended toward the outskirts of the palace grounds.

Toward the group of women and children I knew required aid.

"What are you doing?" I called down to them.

They ignored me. Or perhaps didn't hear me over the chaos ensuing.

Screams in the distance pierced my ears, causing me to flinch.

What in Lucifer's name is happening?

I ran along the cliffside to a staircase built into the wall and began my descent as more guards flooded the grassy plains below, all of them heading toward the women Zaya and I met that fateful day all those weeks—or was it months?—ago.

"What's happening?" I called as I reached the bottom, trying to grab one of the guards. He pushed me off him, and I fell hard onto the ground.

"How dare you!" I jumped up and slapped him

hard across the face.

He didn't flinch, but I sensed a hint of hesitation. He'd stopped moving with the others, not just because of my strike, but because of something else.

"Talk to me," I ordered, but he remained mute, his eyes hard.

The others halted several yards away, aiming their spears.

"What…?" I didn't understand.

Until the fire poured from the ends, the aim unfathomable and *wrong*.

"No!" I screamed, watching in horror as the first of the flames hit the grounds by the women and children.

I couldn't see them, but I *felt* their pain, their agony, their fear. Like a live wire directly to my heart. I fell to my knees, horrified by the sight of these men attacking innocents.

"King said they're using up resources and have to be dealt with," the guard finally said beside me, his spear still at his side. He was the only one not glorifying in the chaos, as if my smack across his face had knocked sense into him.

The cruel laughs littering the air told me the others did not share his sense of morality.

That they *enjoyed* hurting others.

This entire kingdom needed expunging, my husband's influence tainting them all beyond rehabilitation.

"You're all insane," I breathed, the heat of their weapons singeing my senses as pleas for help carved a hole into my heart.

My fingers dug into the fresh soil, my mind

snapping beneath a million thoughts of murder and *pain.*

The hatred within me swirled and ignited into pools of angelfire beneath my palms, stirring beautiful flames that inched across the blades, seeking to destroy.

My eyes closed.

My breathing evened.

And I focused on my power, giving the strands a target for their impending destruction.

Shrieks from the guards made my lips curl.

Their bodies ignited beneath the wave of my tremendous energy. I captured them all in twisting tendrils of liquid blue fire and sighed as it melted their skin and demolished them to piles of ash. I didn't stop until they were all dead. All one hundred and seventeen souls.

I only saved the one beside me, the one who didn't point a spear at the village.

And then I used the remains of my control to absorb the shock of fire from the outskirts, saving what was left of the women's huts.

Valora, a breath whispered against my ear, tugging me back to my reality in a slow blink of time. Adrik's scent wrapped around me, intoxicating in its familiarity, his soul a hum against my heart.

Then it was gone.

Leaving me in a still field littered with death.

No whispers of gratitude followed my power.

No screams.

Only a slow clap of sound from behind me. To where Necros stood applauding my display. "Well done, little wife," he cooed.

The soldier at my side had fallen to his knee, his head bowed in reverence. Not to the king, but to me.

Necros tossed a flame in his direction as if to incinerate his insolence, but I caught it and smothered it into the grass.

Mine, I thought. *This guard is now mine.*

The smile on my husband's lips said he approved. "About bloody time," he murmured, his eyes lighting up at the promise of my power. "You know, I wondered if this would work. I heard you talking about those women with your slut of a friend some time ago, and had a good laugh over your thoughts on the subject. But then it occurred to me that those worthless females might actually have value after all. And look at this—they do."

A chill slithered down my spine. He'd *spied* on me with Zaya. Laughed at my ideas. Then thought to use those innocents against me. "How can you be so cruel? So vile? So evil?"

He chuckled. "My darling whore, you've known who I am for years, just chose not to acknowledge it. Just to enjoy the riches I gave you instead. Truly, you're no better than I am. In fact, I'd say you're worse for being so ignorant all this time." He stepped closer, his lips curling deviously.

"Don't touch me," I growled, warning him with a ring of angelfire around my wrists.

He tsked. "Now, now, Valora. I think you'll find the vows protect me. What were Lucifer's words that you repeated? Ah, yes, to never harm me—in any capacity." His grin was cruel. "Try, little whore. Try and see what happens."

This was his test.

I knew that deep down.

But I took the bait anyway and sent a flame directly at his heart.

He flicked it away as one would a bug, his mouth broadcasting his victory. "Beautiful," he marveled, sending a blast of power into my shoulder that knocked me sideways. "And what I adore most is that Lucifer didn't require the same pledge from me. Something you would do well to remember."

"You're a monster," I whispered, somehow hating him even more.

"A monster who owns you," he agreed. "You're going to be my greatest weapon, Valora. I can't wait to properly use you." He turned as Adrik approached with a hint of dark amusement in his handsome features. "Ah, there you are. Enjoy the show?"

"I did, yes," the prince replied. "She's magnificent."

"Isn't she?" Necros smiled. "I owe you thanks for steering me in the right direction." He clapped Adrik on the shoulder, causing my lips to curl down.

He couldn't mean…

"Anytime," Adrik murmured, his dark eyes meeting mine.

No flicker of regret.

Only pride.

Was this all a setup? Another cruel, wicked game? One where Adrik feigned an interest to ignite my power?

"Shall we celebrate?" Necros asked.

Adrik turned with him, oblivious to the turmoil destroying my mind and piercing my heart. "Indeed. A toast to the future?"

"As we dine on the blood of our enemies," Necros agreed, guiding Adrik away.

I knelt in the grass, stunned, feeling even more alone.

I trusted you, I whispered. *I trusted you to help me…*

And I have, Adrik replied. *Don't give up on me yet, sweet star.*

His mental caress drew a tear to my eye, confusion fluttering inside my cracking chest.

And before I could ask what he meant, he was gone. Again.

Chapter Twenty-One

Adrik

IF NECROS HIT THE FEMALE on his lap one more time, I'd have no choice but to punch him in the jaw.

The king was deep into his cups, sloshing demon blood–infused wine across the table as he guffawed over the words of one of his pompous nobles. All I wanted was to go to Valora, but I was stuck dining with a horde of imbeciles.

Today had gone as planned.

She'd demonstrated her power—and her control—in a brilliant sweep of flames. Then proved something I had suspected about her ties to Necros. He couldn't absorb her energy, but he was immune to it. Which made his comfort all the more important. It wouldn't be easy to destroy him, not when the strongest among us couldn't hurt him.

Except, something else had happened out on that field. I'd conducted a little test of my own by seeking out her power during her rage. And she'd given me part of her flame.

The key to her power is through her heart, Lux had repeatedly said.

It seemed she was right. But she also always told me I'd have to use and abuse Valora's love to absorb enough energy to finish off Necros.

And I wasn't sure I could do that. Not anymore. Not after the last few weeks with her.

She deserves better, my soul whispered. *She deserves to be a proper queen.*

Although, it would be so easy. Because even now, I felt her energy humming through my veins. I had access to her heart, to the very power I required to fulfill my life's quest for revenge.

Alas, I couldn't do it.

I couldn't chance hurting her.

I sighed, sipping my wine, and again pushed the female beside me off my thigh. She kept trying to touch me, to play, and I had no interest in her or any of the other naked women in attendance.

The only one I wanted was locked up in her rooms. Her presence a live wire electrifying my insides, calling for me, begging me to come to her.

Not talking to Valora today had been one of the hardest tasks of my life, but she needed to know that she could do this on her own. Because I might not always be here to help her.

Raucous laughter rent the air as one of the women choked and sputtered on whatever Necros had forced her to swallow.

My stomach churned as she fell to the floor writhing in exquisite pain.

Part of me wanted to leave her, to let her die. It would be better than living in this hell.

But this woman lived in what I considered to be

my kingdom.

I stood and kicked her hard in the back, dislodging the item from her throat. It shot across the room, a cock ring far too large for her feminine throat.

The chuckles died, Necros arching a brow in question.

I shrugged. "She's the one I want to play with tonight, which I can't do if she's dead. Unless I'm not allowed a treat? In which case, continue."

If he denied me the female, I'd have no choice but to leave her to her fate. However, the faint twitch of his lips said he found my choice amusing. "You're a fan of succubi."

"Aren't we all?" I countered, a forced smile in my voice.

"They're very durable," Necros agreed, waving his hand. "You can take her. I've gotten what I needed from the slut."

"Excellent. Then you don't mind if I retire with her?" I held my hand out for the wheezing female, her body still working to heal from the injury caused to her throat. And, well, her back. Which I'd be apologizing for soon.

Necros gestured happily. "Do as you please, Prince Adrik. My home is your home."

You have no idea how true that is, I thought, nodding in my version of a bow. "Congratulations again on your victory, My Lord."

"Cheers," several of the nobles proclaimed, pleasing Necros greatly.

I left them to their debauchery, the wounded succubus following with a snap of my fingers.

Knowing cameras watched our every move, I didn't turn or acknowledge her, just expected her to follow. It wasn't until we entered my chambers that I finally addressed her.

She was a petite little waif of a female with tangled red hair, pearly white skin, and bones that protruded in places they shouldn't. She didn't look at me, her head bowed, her hands already inching closer to my belt as if she expected me to shove her to her knees immediately.

Instead, I swept her messy locks away from her face, cupped her cheek, and forced her glazed eyes to meet mine. "You will eat. You will rest. You will recover." Each statement was laced in compulsion, something I hated to do, but I didn't have time to perfect my approach. And I refused to bite what was clearly a drug-enslaved succubus.

She collapsed into one of the chairs in my sitting area. I retrieved some water and snacks from the en-suite bar. "Eat these and drink this," I said, holding her gaze once more. "When you feel more comfortable, sleep. I'll bring you better food in the morning."

It was all I could do for her.

She lost herself to the chocolate bar I left in her lap, her hum of approval one that would haunt my dreams for days to come.

Necros would pay for this sin and all the others. In time.

Sweet star, I murmured, entering the passageway behind the painting in my room and heading toward her quarters. *Are you awake?*

Her mind told me she was alert, but her mental voice didn't reply, a hint of anger and hurt lurking in the thread between us.

I'm sorry for cutting you off, I whispered, knowing that to be the cause. *But I needed you to perform on your own today, to prove to yourself how powerful you truly are. And you were amazing, Valora. The brightest star I've ever seen.*

Women and children died, she replied, her tone holding a mixture of annoyance and despair. *Because you didn't warn me.*

I frowned. *I didn't know what he planned to do. He invited me out to watch as the chaos unfolded. But I did warn you something was coming.* I drew closer to her rooms, the hallways all too familiar now that I'd made this trek so many times.

She didn't know, but I'd spent last night here, keeping her company in her dreams. Several weeks of sharing a bed with her had unexpectedly changed me and caused me to crave her presence. She wasn't the first female I'd experienced such an intimate act with, but she was the first I wanted to continuously bed. Perhaps because I'd yet to take her the way I craved.

That was going to change tonight.

If she allowed it.

If she forgave me for what I had come here to say.

Valora. I'm here.

I waited in the dark for her reply, hoping she would grant me entry.

Light peeked at me from the interior of her room as she slowly revealed the entry, her wary gaze meeting mine.

"What's wrong?" I asked softly, moving inside to

cup her cheek. She had no reason to be mad at me yet, as we hadn't even begun our conversation.

Valora stepped away from me. "Are you working with Necros?"

"*What*?" I nearly laughed, but the look on her face said she was serious. "Why the fuck would you think that?" And how was this the beginning of our discussion? I'd expected to at least have a chance to warm her up a little before we started down a dangerous path.

"He thanked you for your help in guiding me, then asked if you wanted to celebrate." She folded her arms. "Are you working with him? Is all of this just another fucked-up game? One where you tame my powers for the king?"

My jaw actually hit the floor.

After weeks of being everything she needed and more, she questioned my loyalty over a few exchanged words with Necros? If only she knew how accurate her suspicion proved to be, but she suspected me for the wrong reasons entirely.

"What a tortured life you've led to have to be so distrusting of those around you," I marveled.

But I also understood.

If I'd been raised by someone like Necros, I wouldn't have a shred of faith left in anyone. And the fact of the matter was, I hadn't sought her out with the purest intentions. I had wanted to use her for myself, to seek justice for my loved ones.

Except, at some point, my loyalties had shifted. So much so that I couldn't stop the words that came next.

"Your husband believes the vows grant him rights to your natural gifts, but he couldn't absorb them today. I watched him try and fail. The only thing your marriage has done is protect him against your power." Rather than touch her again, I leaned against the wall, hands in the pockets of my suit pants. "Create a flame, Valora."

Her brows pulled down. "Excuse me?"

"Please?" I pressed. "Can you create a flame for me?"

Over the last few days, she'd been able to call the energy to her with a thought rather than being pressured or bullied into it.

She blew out a breath and held out her hand, a ball of blue fire spinning in a hypnotic pattern across her pale skin.

I smiled. "Beautiful."

"And not an answer to my question," she added, irritation heavy in her voice. "Your avoidance only proves that you're hiding something from me."

"I am hiding something from you," I admitted, pushing away from the wall. "I've been hiding something all along, but it's not what you think."

It was a risk to confess this to her.

A risk to both my future and hers.

But it felt wrong to allow the truth to fester and burn between us like a dark fog threatening to destroy the foundation of our fates.

"Tell me," she demanded, the angelfire glowing against her fair complexion.

"The prophecy claims that your betrothed can claim your power," I said slowly. "That's why Necros wed you. However, he didn't understand that it's not just about the forced vows but also about your heart."

I tugged on the tenuous link between us, mentally calling upon her fire, begging for a taste. It was pure instinct. Her eyes widened as a flicker of blue flame graced my fingertips.

Valora's lips parted in awe. "How are you…?"

"Lux always told me that the key to your power resides in your heart, and it seems she's right." I curled my fingers into a wave, diminishing the energy into embers and releasing my yearning for her power. "You've let me inside and I could take it all, if I so desired. At least, that's what the prophecy says."

Her cheeks whitened, her own flames dying on her palm. "You took some of it earlier. While in the fields."

"When you were done, yes. I tested the theory, then briefly wondered if I could use your power to kill Necros. Because while you can't harm him, I hold no such vow." Which meant, in theory, I could do whatever I wanted to him, including using the fire of his betrothed to kill him. "But the problem is, sweet star, if I take too much, it'll hurt you. And though that may not have been a concern when we first met, it's become one."

And there was the truth.

The words I had kept from her since the beginning.

The real reason I was here.

"You've known all this time…" She trailed off, her emotions swimming through her features, each one sending an arrow into my chest. But I couldn't stop now. I had to be honest with her. It was the realization I came to earlier today when her power infused my spirit.

If I didn't tell her, I risked losing far more than my rightful kingdom.

I risked losing her.

And I didn't want to lose her.

"Yes. I came here to win your heart and use your powers to destroy Necros." The admission hurt, but not nearly as much as the tear that fell from her eye.

"So it was all a lie," she whispered. "This was always about your revenge."

"Until it wasn't," I replied, taking a step toward her.

She took several back, holding up a palm. "Don't."

I never knew a word could pain me so much, but it was nothing compared to the agony I felt inside her mind.

"Valora, I've spent my entire life preparing for this. Twenty-five years of pent-up hatred and plotting, all aimed at the man who dares to call himself king of this kingdom. Who renamed my lands *Caluçon* because he stole the powers of an infant to wipe out shadowkind." Just saying the words stirred a rage inside me—a rage that desired the powers within her. It would be so easy, her life energy mine for the taking. I could feel it throbbing in time with mine, waiting for me to act, to steal her very breath.

But my heart held me back.

A fickle organ I never thought much about other than its importance in keeping me alive.

Until this moment.

Now I knew with every ounce of my being that if I chose revenge over the emotions building inside me, I'd crave my own death. Because hurting this woman was a destiny I couldn't endure.

Valora trembled, her spirit fracturing before my eyes. "And now you wish to steal those powers from a full-grown woman. From me."

My shoulders fell, my head shaking slowly in the negative. "I've wanted nothing more than to kill Necros for longer than I can remember. Yet, a few weeks with you has changed all my priorities. Here I am, able to take exactly what I've desired… and I can't. Because I can't hurt you." I slid to my knees before her, needing her to hear me, to understand. "Whatever this is, whoever you are to me now, it means more to me than his death. I cannot—*will* not—use you to kill him. I will find another way."

Her glassy eyes met mine, the lashes blinking rapidly, her lips parting without sound.

"I could have taken your power earlier, finished him once and for all, but I didn't," I whispered. "I also could have absorbed them while attending his idiotic celebration, killed him right there in his drunken state, but I didn't."

"Why?" she breathed, her entire demeanor brittle, on the verge of breaking completely. "Why didn't you?"

I'd already told her that, but I would try again. For her. For us.

"Because I won't risk hurting you, Valora," I said softly. "I'm telling you all of this now because you deserve to know. Because I refuse to hide this from you. Because I still believe we can work together and take him down, but we need to be united for that to happen. We need to have total faith in each other. And that can't exist while I'm keeping this truth from you. So here I am, on my knees, telling you everything and begging you to forgive me. To believe me. To accept me once more. To make me yours."

Chapter Twenty-Two

Valora

I'D SPENT THE EVENING THINKING ADRIK was working with Necros, that everything between us had been a lie, a manipulation, a wicked trick.

And now…

Now I didn't know what to think. What to say. How to react.

Adrik admitted to wanting to use my power.

Admitted that he could take it right now to use against Necros.

But didn't.

And why? Because he refused to hurt me.

Everyone in my life used me for one purpose or another. Necros stole my power. My parents gave me up to secure their kingdom. The men who won Necros's fucked-up game wanted to take pleasure from me without asking. The guards treated me as a peasant, not a queen.

While Adrik had treated me as a person. An equal. A lover. All because he wanted something from me, too.

But unlike the others, he didn't take it. Instead, he

confessed his sins, put himself in a vulnerable position, and begged me for forgiveness. Pleaded with me to keep him. To make him mine once more.

"Is that what you are?" I wondered out loud. "Mine?"

"If you'll have me," he replied, swallowing. "I don't deserve it—don't deserve *you*—but I want you just the same. I want to be yours. I want you to be mine. I want this, whatever it is, that's growing between us. I want it more than a lifetime of revenge."

"So if I asked you to run with me, you would?" I asked, considering the option.

He didn't hesitate. "I would go anywhere you wanted to go."

"Even if it meant allowing Necros to live?"

Adrik swallowed, the motion drawing my gaze to the thick column of his neck. "We both know he deserves to die. But if you wanted to run, I'd help you run. And I'd never look back."

"While regretting your lost chance at revenge for the rest of time," I finished for him, drawing my gaze back up to his. "You could live with that?"

"It wouldn't be easy, but sacrificing you…" He trailed off, shaking his head. "I can't, Valora. I can't hurt you."

"Then why not kill him together?" I asked, confused. "Why is it an either-or scenario? I want him dead, too, Adrik."

He remained quiet for so long I thought he might not reply. But his sigh was heavy with sorrow. "It's not an either-or situation. I think we can defeat him together, but you needed the truth first so nothing could come between us. Because if we're going to do this, we need to trust each other. Implicitly."

Right. He'd said that. In my confusion to wrap my head around this madness, I'd warped his statements with the lost ones inside my mind. The foreign pang his admission had caused. Followed by the seductive heat stirred by his emotional confession.

It wasn't love.

Not quite.

But something pure. Something honorable. Something extraordinary.

"I want to work together," I whispered. "I want to work with you." He was the only one to concede his nefarious intentions and regret them. The only one *not* to use me without a regard.

Adrik cared.

I felt it in the bond we had created. Read it in his mind that he left open to me even now, his thoughts honest and tangible. No more secrets. No more lies. Just the truth. His adoration. His tangible lust. His regret. His pride. His confusion. His warmth for me. His yearning for my forgiveness.

It all swam through our connection, so raw and real that it took my breath away.

He'd said something. An affirmation of sorts. But I wasn't listening. I no longer cared to talk. I wanted to experience him—the *real* him. Without a veil. Without him holding back. Without him worrying about my sensibilities.

I wanted him to fuck me the way he truly desired, the manner in which I observed inside his mind.

Harsh. Hard. All-consuming. Bliss.

"Take me to bed, Adrik," I said, interrupting whatever he'd just said.

I took a step back, releasing the silk robe I wore, revealing my nakedness underneath. I had expected Necros. But I never wanted that foul creature to touch me again. Only Adrik. And if Necros interrupted us, I'd light this entire palace on fire. Maybe I couldn't hurt him, but the falling structure could.

And Adrik could absorb enough to fight him off.

Together.

Together we could do this.

But first… first I needed to embrace the chemistry thriving between us. The lethal heat swirling in the air. The predator lurking in the shadows. I wanted it all. I wanted *him*, and I said as much again, as I led him backward toward the bed.

He didn't crawl; he stood.

And he didn't run; he walked.

Slowly.

His fingers deftly removing his jacket and allowing it to fall to the floor before working over the buttons of his shirt. His mouth moved. Words I didn't care to understand.

"Now, Adrik," I said, cutting him off.

Primal instinct had taken over.

This wasn't the land of conversation anymore. Not verbal communication, anyway.

No. I let my body speak for me. I lay on the bed, spreading my legs, showing him how much I desired him. Watched as his pupils dilated, his nostrils flaring at the scent of my need.

His dress shirt fell.

His abdomen rippling as he unfastened his pants.

Mmm, I wanted this. So, so badly. I dipped my hand between my thighs, eliciting a feral growl from the male in the room. This wasn't normal. This intrinsic *need.* But I no longer cared to think. I wanted to feel, to fuck, to *fly.*

"Adrik," I groaned, my finger disappearing into my wet channel the way I wished his cock would.

He kicked off his pants and his shoes, leaving him just the way I wanted him—naked. Primed. Ready. *Hard.*

"Valora." My name was a rumble in his chest, a warning of sorts.

I responded to it with a command. "Fuck me, Adrik."

The animalistic sound from his throat had me moaning in need, my thighs clenching, my finger working, only to be torn from my body and replaced with the instrument I craved more. So thick. So perfect. So *mine.*

Adrik slid inside me in a quick thrust, his palm wrapping around my throat, his hips settling between mine. He didn't wait for me to accommodate, didn't ask how I wanted it; he just moved.

And oh, it was perfect.

Almost savage.

A coupling between beasts being driven by the need to mate, our souls taking over and driving us into the stars, where our destinies intertwined.

This was fate personified.

A prophecy coming to life.

The future unfolding in the bed of a queen.

My breaths came in pants, my heart racing against my chest, as Adrik fucked me into oblivion and back. Neither of us caring who heard. Neither of us *thinking*. Just feeling. Experiencing. Being.

My toes curled, my legs tightening, my core thundering.

It hurt so beautifully that tears streamed from my eyes, Adrik's tongue licking them as he continued to move.

Skin slapped skin.

Sweat slicked our bodies.

Groans and growls flooded the room.

A ferocious claiming, culminating in Adrik's teeth sinking into my neck.

I screamed his name and threaded my fingers through his hair, forcing him to drink his fill. Taking me into him, sealing our lives together in a forbidden embrace, mating me despite my marital ties.

"Mine," I whispered, my world shattering over and over again, the galaxies rejoicing with my cries.

This was meant to be.

Adrik and me.

Forever and always.

A king and queen finally united.

CHAPTER TWENTY-THREE

ADRIK

FIRE LICKED ACROSS MY KNUCKLES, the embers a kiss against my skin. One I returned with my lips against Valora's mouth. She hummed in approval, her tongue dancing with mine as I slid into her slick channel once more. Her hips rose to meet mine, her lithe form perfectly keeping pace with my movements, earning her a low growl of approval from my throat.

Hours.

We'd been doing this for *hours*.

And had hardly spoken a word.

It was as if something had snapped. Some sort of cautionary barrier that had been holding us in limbo, away from one another. But now nothing could keep us apart.

I bit her.

I fucked her.

I kissed her.

I repeated it all again.

And again.

Her mewls of satisfaction were music to my ears.

She came again on a scream, her nails ripping down my back and igniting my flesh in more of her delicious flames. If she noticed the power exchange, she didn't comment. I wasn't trying to tap into her energy; she was pushing it into me. As if she had too much to contain and needed someone to bear the weight of her fire.

Her lip bled beneath my tongue, exciting my instincts. I lapped at the wound, closing it and creating another beside it. She hissed in response, then arched into my driving cock and demanded more.

It was a whirlwind of sensation unlike any I'd ever experienced.

I never wanted it to stop.

Could do this forever.

Lost in the world of oblivion.

With my Valora.

"My Adrik," she whispered, so deep into my thoughts that we were thinking as one. Whatever had happened, whatever caused that wall to fall, was the best and worst thing to ever happen to us.

Valora agreed with a groan, her mouth taking mine as I shifted our positions. She straddled my lap, sitting with me, riding me, taking her pleasure again and again before I pressed her into the headboard and nearly fucked the life out of her.

More fire.

More scratches.

So much blood.

She bit me, too. Her blunt little teeth marking my skin as hers while I repaid the favor against her breasts. Then I feasted between her legs, loving the echo of embers that teased my tongue after her explosive orgasm.

And lay in bliss as she took me in her mouth to return the favor.

The purple horizon was the only indication of just how much time had passed, how lost we'd been in this new rapturous world.

I'd spent nights with succubi that paled in comparison to this.

Fuck, *everything* paled in comparison to this.

Valora curled into my chest, her blue eyes drowsy with pleasure as she stared at me. I lost myself to that beautiful gaze, falling deep into the rivers of adoration as I swam in her addictive aura.

She giggled, drawing a line of fire down my abdomen to my finally depleted cock. "You've been holding out on me," she accused, her voice a sultry sound that stroked my senses.

"I could say the same about you." I caught her wrist and brought her finger to my mouth, nibbling the pad before sucking the digit deep. She groaned in reply, her eyelids drooping. "Still not satisfied?" I teased.

"I'm pretty sure I won't be able to walk today," she replied, eyes still closed. "And I don't regret a second of it."

"Neither do I." I angled her chin upward to kiss her softly, my tongue tracing the seam of her mouth. "I'm not sure what happened between us last night, but I've never felt better."

"We fucked. A lot."

"I don't know about you, sweet star, but I don't

usually enjoy being burned." I glanced pointedly at the pattern she was sketching with her fire-laced fingers. "We did a lot more than fuck, sweetheart."

She smiled lazily. "I'm too tired to worry about it."

"Mmm, you should sleep," I agreed. "But I need to return to my rooms before someone notices I'm missing." The lack of warning on my watch was a good sign. But I didn't want to push my luck.

"Okay," she whispered. "Meet me later today?"

"Just name the place and time," I replied, kissing her forehead before rolling out of the sex-saturated sheets. If Necros visited her today, he would not be pleased. When I said as much, she merely shrugged.

Not arrogance, just confidence.

She no longer feared the king.

And oddly, neither did I.

Together we would kill him. I felt the truth of it all the way to my very soul.

Don't tune me out today, Valora whispered, her eyes already closed.

I'll never block you again, I vowed, dressing myself in last night's clothes.

Good.

I kissed her once more, smiling as she barely returned the motions, her body already succumbing to sleep. *Sweet dreams, my beautiful star.*

Only of you, she replied softly.

Those words carried me back to my quarters, the warmth in them putting me at ease. Confessing had been the best decision of my life. Followed closely by giving in to my urges last night and fucking Valora senseless. I smiled as I slipped back into my room.

Then paused as I sensed something not right.

Death.

I blinked. The stench of it hung heavy in the air, coming from the sitting area.

The succubus.

I vaulted over the couch and gagged at the torturous sight before me. Blood. Innards. Tears. And semen.

That was when I noticed the other presence in the room.

The demons lying in wait.

I'd let my guard down, too consumed with thoughts of Valora to notice their appearance.

And when I spun around, it was too late.

A bullet sailed through the air.

Hitting me right between the eyes.

Val—

Darkness.

CHAPTER TWENTY-FOUR

VALORA

MY BODY STILL HUMMED from the way Adrik had taken me all night, leaving me sore in a way I'd yet to experience. Usually, I ached from hours of torture. But this was different. Oh, Adrik hadn't been gentle, and my muscles screamed at me for recovery, but his attentions had left me in a dreamlike state of pure bliss. So I didn't mind the subtle ache between my thighs or the bite-shaped bruises on my flesh.

I felt alive.

Exuberant.

Like a new woman.

It was a strange thing to no longer fear my husband, but it provided me with a fresh perspective. My power was the key to defeating Necros, and while Adrik could access it, he chose not to abuse it. Instead, he wanted to work together, to *rule* together. I'd seen it in his mind, heard it in his words, and sensed it in his heart.

We would end this.

I slid from the bed and yawned, exhausted yet

invigorated. My skin carried Adrik's scent, comforting me and warming my insides. The entire room smelled of hours upon hours of fucking, blood dotted the tangled sheets, and ash covered the bed. I never thought I could be so wild, but now that I'd found the inner goddess hiding within me, I would never suppress her again.

Necros no longer controlled me in any way, and that included my body. All his years of torment and torture were about to backfire on him.

He would die. Perhaps even today.

I pulled the top cover over the bed to hide the soiled sheets. I would change them later, but first, I needed to dress and find Adrik. My heart yearned to be near him again, the vital organ wrapped in his dark shadows. I felt him with me as I showered the sex from my body, eased my aching muscles beneath the spray, and washed the ash—caused by my power—from my hair.

Bliss.

Happiness.

Rightness.

I searched through my wardrobe, looking for the right dress. Despite my pleasant mood, innocent women and children had died yesterday. Wearing color would be a disgrace to their memory. And Necros also preferred color.

Hmm, black it is, I thought, fondling the sable fabric of a gown. No jewels on the bodice. Just a simple crisscross pattern of black ribbons weaved around the front and back to hold me into the dress. It wasn't easy to put on without a lady's maid, but I managed it.

Oh, how I missed Zaya. How was she now? Recovering? Adrik told me Grigory had helped to heal her physical wounds by use of his blood, but I could only imagine her mental state. She'd shown a hint of it during the one and only call we'd shared since her departure. Maybe Adrik would allow me to call her again today.

Adrik, do you think I could speak to Zaya again later?

No answer.

I frowned. *Adrik?*

Silence.

Is this a joke? Because I didn't find it very funny. He'd vowed to keep his mind open to me. Yet while I could feel him nearby, he remained decidedly closed off.

I scowled.

We just spoke about this earlier today, and already he'd locked me out. Unacceptable. I trusted him, I did, but this picking and choosing when to talk to me had to stop. What was the point of the link if he could just turn it off with an instant thought? That made things one-way, giving him all the control, and I didn't appreciate it.

I grabbed my hairbrush and tugged it roughly through my hair to remove the tangles from our lovemaking. I didn't doubt what Adrik felt for me. He had my heart, and I had his. But I did want to know his reason.

I finished my hair with a twist of the long tendrils into a knot at the back of my head and secured it with an opulent clip. That would be the only evidence of jewels on my person today, except for my wedding band, of course. The gaudy gold-and-ruby ring had to always remain in place to show I was Necros's possession.

For now.

I dared to call Adrik once more and again received no answer. Not that it shocked me.

Men were all the same, really. Adrik had broken a promise, just like many others in my short history. I wouldn't let him off lightly when I found him.

I checked the clock on my bedside table and decided there was only one place he could be—exploring.

Finding the hidden lever on the wall, I pulled it and stepped into the secret passageways of the castle. I wished I'd known about these years ago. I would have loved to explore them while growing up, to find all the secrets hidden within them. Perhaps even illicit love affairs just like the one Adrik and I were indulging in.

I neared our usual meeting place but stopped when voices grew loud in the tunnels.

Guards.

They were searching for something in the darkness.

Adrik? I half whispered inside my head but also into the surrounding air.

He didn't show himself or reply.

This couldn't be good. The guards shouldn't know about these pathways. No one but Adrik and I knew, unless they somehow stumbled upon a door somewhere. Had we accidentally left one open?

It didn't matter. I could think about it later.

I needed to get out of here. If anyone caught me in these tunnels, Necros would punish me, and given his immunity to my powers, I wouldn't be able to fight back. Not without Adrik.

I hid my shoes in the darkness so I could flee on silent feet and tiptoed through the passageway toward my room. Ugh, but my skirts kept swishing despite my holding them off the ground.

This was where pants would be useful. I longed for—

Voices.

The guards were gaining on me.

I needed somewhere to hide.

Adrik, I tried again, starting to worry. *What's happening?*

Finding a small alcove, I bent down into a tiny ball, thanking my lucky stars I wore a black dress and not a bright-colored one.

Adrik, they're in the tunnels.

No reply.

Something's very wrong, I realized. Adrik wouldn't cut me off without a reason. I knew that. But I'd felt so betrayed that I hadn't considered the obvious, that something had happened to him.

Footsteps approached. Loud. Penetrating. Demanding.

I held my breath, praying to be invisible, as a trio of guards walked past chatting together.

I listened to their words but captured nothing of importance in them. Just that they were searching the tunnels following their discovery to ensure they didn't pose a threat to the king.

When they disappeared around a corner, I emerged as quietly as possible and fled down the corridors to the entrance of my rooms.

I jumped inside and closed the door quietly behind me. My heart was beating so fast I thought it might leap right out of my chest.

I needed to get out of my room and find out what had happened with Adrik.

If they've discovered him—

No. I couldn't think those thoughts.

My hand covered my mouth.

But if he had been caught, then he was wrapped up somewhere in one of my husband's schemes, unable to talk to me. Where he couldn't use my powers to defend himself because he refused to risk killing me.

Fuck!

A whimper flowed into my palm, and I swallowed it back down.

Think, Valora!

Crying solves nothing.

Use your power.

You're a star.

All the words were mine, but underlined in Adrik's influence. It was time I owned my birthright. Time I *fought.*

The door to my rooms rattled beneath my palms, refusing to budge. I narrowed my gaze. *Then I'll burn you down.*

It was wood, after all.

Flickers of blue embers emerged from the tips of my fingers and curled around my hands.

I stepped back, ready to unleash a firestorm, when the door slammed open, almost flying off its hinges as my husband strode inside.

I hid my hands behind my back, willing the flames to subside.

"Wife." Necros scowled at me. "I've been looking for you."

"Shouldn't have been very hard, *husband.* After all, you locked me in here. Remember?" I replied, taunting him.

His gaze narrowed. "I think I need a stronger armory for my new weapon."

I supposed *weapon* was more of a compliment than him calling me a *whore.*

Ignoring him, I turned to go into my bathroom, but he strode across the room in a few quick paces and grabbed me around the waist.

"Missing Graystall today, are you?" he breathed into my ear and forced me to face him. "You know I despise black on you."

"That's too bad," I drawled. "Maybe you shouldn't have killed all those innocents yesterday."

His brow furrowed.

And then he laughed, the sound so loud I expected the glass in the windows to smash from the vibrations of it resonating around the room. "You mourn for the rats of Caluçon?"

"They were people, Necros. Women and children."

"Ah, yes, the ones you desired to save. What was it you said? You wanted to *educate* them." He chuckled again, shaking his head. "It's a good thing you're useful, or I'd grant your wish and leave you with them to die."

I hated the reminder of him spying on me.

Hated more his cruelty and disregard for others.

And truly hated the way he pulled me against him to force me to feel his thickening cock.

He grasped my chin with his opposite hand, his touch deceptively gentle.

"My naïve little wife," he cooed, his lips lowering to mine.

I couldn't bear his touch anymore. The feel of his hand against my skin. His breath on my mouth.

Before, I'd let him touch me because it was my duty, but he no longer possessed a hold over me.

I *loathed* him.

"Get off me," I demanded, trying to shove him away.

But he held me with ease, my power useless against him, and slid his hand up into my hair, where he picked something from the strands.

He grinned as he held it before my eyes.

A spider web.

Oh, Lucifer.

It must have been from the tunnels.

"I think I have every right to touch you, Valora," he said, his voice lethally quiet. "You're my wife. I *own* you. And I think it's about time I showed you what happens to people who forget their place."

I didn't have time to answer as he snatched my hand and hauled me from my bedroom.

Adrik, I whispered in my head, knowing it was futile.

Because I knew where we were heading.

And it without a doubt involved Adrik.

Our secrets were about to be revealed to the entire kingdom.

Chapter Twenty-Five

Valora

I WANTED TO THROW NECROS away from me. To burn this palace to the ground. But I needed to find Adrik first.

"Necros." I struggled against my husband as he dragged me toward the throne room with his hand around my throat.

"You've completely lost your place," he sighed, noting my choice of using his name rather than his formal address.

"Necros," I spat again.

He curled his fist in response, blocking off my airway.

I tried to dig my bare feet into the ground, but they skated over the smooth marbled floors. My vision began to blacken as he threw me inside the throne room, causing me to land hard against the ground. I coughed, my throat burning as I inhaled greedily. Tears streamed down my face, eliciting even more hatred from my chest.

A hatred that expanded into concern and horror as I found Adrik's unconscious form a few steps away.

Blood smeared over his forehead where a gunshot wound indented his skull.

Dead.

He was gone.

I was too late.

"What have you done?" My anger fueled my veins, sending me to my feet and directly into Necros's chest. My tiny fists bashed hard at his torso, but he pushed me away from him like I was nothing.

To him, I supposed I was.

I landed harshly again on the floor and skidded across it.

"I can smell him on you," Necros growled. "It's disgusting."

I couldn't help the hysterical laugh that bubbled from my lips. "You gave me to him, Necros. So of course you smell him on me. You asked him to rape me!"

"Yes, I did. But that's not what happened, is it? My whore of a wife *enjoyed* it. Didn't you?"

"Can you blame me?" I retorted, fury getting the best of my tongue. "He at least knows how to touch a woman. You're just a sick excuse for your gender, too consumed with yourself to think of anyone else. And your cock leaves a lot to be desired."

Necros laughed, his amusement harsh, and bent to rip the fabric of my bodice with his fist. His gaze dropped to the bites on my breasts, his smile falling. "*Whore.*"

"Weapon," I corrected, my skin going up in flames.

Necros's fist slammed into my face, sending my

skull into the marble below. I swore the stone cracked. Or maybe that was my head.

My power curled inside me, hiding, waiting.

"What has he told you?" he demanded. "Why's he really here? Because I know it's not just to fuck my whore of a wife." Necros leaned over me and cuffed his hands around my throat. He pushed me back until I hit Adrik's body, my hand falling into the blood that had flowed from his body onto the floor.

"He's a man; why would he talk to me?" I wheezed, playing into his own games. "Squeeze harder, husband. Why don't you kill me?" I taunted him because I knew he couldn't murder me until he'd taken my powers. Unfortunately for him, that would never happen. They belonged to Adrik.

Which meant Adrik was still alive, just healing. The bullet wound was a temporary measure.

Necros clasped his hand tighter, making my chest burn from the lack of oxygen.

Dark specks dotted my vision.

Valora? a warm voice whispered, groggy with sleep.

Adrik. I smiled, which only enraged my husband further.

What's happening? Adrik asked. *I can't move.*

They shot you. Necros knows about us. He's after your secrets.

Secrets? he repeated, a hint of confused exhaustion in his mind's voice.

Who you are and why you're here.

Necros shook me, his words a rumble I refused to hear. Not with the bliss of Adrik's voice in my head.

I need to wake up, Adrik said.

No. Stay asleep. Rest for as long as you can. Trust me this time.

Valora? he asked as if he couldn't hear me. And maybe he couldn't over the roaring beast above me.

Play dead, Adrik. Trust me.

With those parting words, I shut him out of my mind and kicked out against my husband. I hit him in the most painful place for a man—between his thighs. He crumpled to the ground, releasing my neck. I gasped fresh air into my lungs once more and tried to scramble away.

Only to be surrounded by guards.

I recognized one of them as the man who'd bowed to me in the garden yesterday. His face was covered in bruises, no doubt a punishment for his betrayal. The man was lucky to still be alive.

"Take a seat on the throne, Your Majesty," he said flatly. "The king hasn't finished his discussion yet."

I laughed with a choked sound and shook my head. "Never," I rasped.

The guard knelt, his eyes meeting mine with some sort of secret question. "Please," he breathed, the word for my ears alone. Then he glanced over his shoulder to where Necros had pulled a knife out of an intricately woven box.

I recognized the blade immediately.

It was one of Adrik's daggers. Like the ones he'd used to kill the others during my husband's fucked-up games.

"I think it's about time we woke him up, don't you?" Necros said, his green gaze melting into cruel pools of black. "I'll ask him the questions myself before I kill him."

Those blades would cause irreparable damage, the magic in them meant to wound immortals permanently.

Necros must have seen the knowledge in my face, the very real fear that he could kill Adrik, because he swirled the knife around in his hand and lowered it toward Adrik's leg. "I'll ask you one final time, Valora. Who is he?"

The guard beside me growled, startling me from my shock.

He stood and ran for my husband, his spear pointed forward and flames erupting from it. Necros dropped the knife and easily disarmed the male with a flick of his hand.

"I should have killed you yesterday." My husband raised his hand, lifting the guard from the floor with a magical hold around the male's neck. "Nobody dares to defy me. I'm the power here, and each and every one of you needs to remember that. My wife is merely a vessel whose riches I will plunder and control until the day I kill her."

"Leave him alone," I demanded, pushing my way to my feet.

Necros ignored me, squeezing the noose of energy tighter, causing the guard to choke and sputter, his eyes bulging in his skull.

"*Enough*! I shouted. I'd claimed the guard as mine yesterday, and *no one* threatened what was mine. That included this male I didn't know. Adrik. Zaya. All of Graystall. The innocents of Caluçon. And anyone else I decided to protect. "*Release him.*"

The bastard ignored me, his lips curling as the guard turned blue.

Flames rippled across my flesh, down my arms and legs, destroying my gown and singeing the air with rising heat.

I focused on the faces of all the other guards in the room, found their souls within, and flooded their bodies with my power, incinerating them to ash. The energy coiled through the room, the palace, the grounds, searching and seething, desiring anyone and everyone who had wronged me.

The attendees at our wedding.

The males who raped Zaya.

The members of society who sat by and *watched* my degradation and destruction.

Anyone and everyone with loyalties to my husband.

I found them all. Wrapped them in my vise. *Squeezed.*

"Valora!" Necros grabbed my shoulders. "*Stop.*"

Oh, but I'd only just begun. I smiled at him, noted his immunity to my flames, and continued my destruction of everything he held dear.

His kingdom.

His palace.

All the monsters. The loyalists. The blackened spirits who littered this realm.

The tendrils of my flames twisted and turned, wrapping around my husband's limbs to keep him in place, to force him to watch my glory. A newfound strength surged through my body, one born of pride and relief. Because my husband no longer had control. He would bow to me now.

And I forced him to, sending him to his knees with a blow of power.

I shot a lightning bolt from my left hand, latching onto his precious throne, and threw it out the windows of the throne room. The stained glass bubbled and boiled in its wake, forming a mucky, brown-colored substance that flowed over the stone walls.

It was time.

Necros would die here today. Whether by my hand or Adrik's.

I felt my lover stirring as my husband broke the energy binding his ankles and wrists. His own gifts were coming to the forefront, his fury over the devastation I'd caused fueling his steps toward me.

I wasn't done yet, not by a long shot, my power still seeking and destroying, but his energy coiled around mine, crushing me beneath his iron fist.

"You caught me off guard," he said, the promise of death swirling in his tone. "But I'm still stronger."

A lie.

The only reason he bested me now was a result of the insidious vows I'd murmured all those months ago. Without the restrictions, I'd slay him.

As he would soon find out, with Adrik stirring behind him.

Because Adrik could absorb my powers, could use them where I couldn't.

It might kill me, or deplete my energy for life, but both were sacrifices I was willing to make. For the betterment of the Underworld. To destroy the vile presence that was Necros.

"You'll lose," I whispered, smiling through the

onslaught of his magical assault.

Life or death.

Love or fear.

Adrik or Necros.

There was only one choice in each.

I had made my decisions.

"You want to know who Adrik is? Then why don't you ask him yourself?"

Chapter Twenty-Six

Adrik

I ROLLED MY NECK, cracking it sharply in the cold room.

Ash swept across the marble floor, the bodies of former guards diminished beneath Valora's impressive display of power. Only one remained—the one at my side. He'd helped me stand, his head bowed in reverence not to me but to his queen.

To the goddess rippling in flames.

Fuck, she was beautiful.

Even losing to Necros's will, she resembled a being of pure light and power. Her husband's hands were circling her neck, his biceps bulging as he tried to choke her out. I wondered if Valora even realized it. She hadn't taken a breath in minutes, yet seemed to be overflowing with life.

I felt it humming through my veins, warming my skin, begging me to take over, to pull her energy into myself and use it to finish the King of Caluçon.

No, not her power… but Valora.

Her words were on repeat in my mind, telling me to absorb her gifts and finish him. She knew the costs, had accepted them, and was trying to convince me to take charge.

No.

We would find another way.

I picked up my knives from the casing on the floor, thankful to Necros for bringing them to me, and twirled the familiar weight between my fingers.

"Twenty-five years ago, you stole my kingdom," I said, my voice deep and clear and filled with renewed life. "A prophecy told you the King of Shadows would take your life. I'm here today to see that destiny fulfilled."

I threw a blade toward his back, only to watch a wave of power brush it aside. He tossed Valora to the side, knocking her into the sole remaining throne, and turned. "I killed the King of Shadows with my bare hands," he seethed, coiling his dark energy around me in thick ropes of pain.

"You killed the former King of Shadows," I corrected, using another knife to cut through the invisible strands. He hissed at the burn, then growled as I disappeared into smoke to return on his other side. "My father," I whispered, directly into his ear, before shifting again to the corner of the room.

He spun, searching. "Impossible."

"Is it?" I breathed, sending the words through the air on a wisp of smoke, curling it around his skin. "Lux raised me as her own, as a favor to King Maverick and Queen Soren. My parents. The ones you killed in this very palace before claiming it as your own."

I whispered around him in a cloud, slicing out with my blade across his bare arm, then ghosting back to my place before he could grab me. He whirled again, his growl vibrating the walls.

"Some might say you brought this on yourself," I continued softly. "That destroying my kingdom was what breathed rebellion into my blood, and the dark need to carve my name into your burning flesh." I slithered by him once more, adding another mark, followed swiftly by a third to complete the *A* in his arm.

His energy shot out, wrapping around me again and halting my retreating steps. I sliced through the bands with my blade, spinning and dodging as he sent more blasts my way.

Use my power! Valora demanded, trying to push her essence into me.

It came too suddenly, causing my feet to trip beneath me and sending me to the floor. I rolled to avoid a deadly blast from Necros, then fought to mist to the shadows but found my ankle trapped in one of his sticky webs.

Valora's warmth burned through my veins, her gift an addiction that called to my instincts. But I couldn't use it, not when I knew what would happen to her.

Stop forcing it, I growled.

Take it, she pleaded. *Please.*

She seemed to think Necros was winning, perhaps because of the purple smog climbing ominously over my prone form.

"You're weak," the king spat, walking toward me. "I can't believe I ever feared you."

Adrik! she screamed, her fire engulfing me from head to foot, but Necros's energy penetrated it, his power immune to hers.

Unless I wielded it.

This was what I desired all my life.

What I'd been bred and trained to do.

But hurting Valora…

I can't.

Her agony pierced my heart, her resolve crumbling into ash around me as Necros overruled her. His essence wrapped around my throat, squeezing, threatening to end me. I used my knife against it, but another developed in its wake, like Medusa's snakelike hair but in the form of lethal claws from the beast hovering over me.

"When I'm finished with you, I'm going to destroy her," Necros seethed. "Her power is mine. The vows she spoke promised that whatever she owned, she would share. With me. And I will take what's mine, demolish Noxia for raising you, and make sure your name is a rumor of the past. A forgotten promise that everyone will only remember as a failure."

I narrowed my gaze.

Not at his pledge to harm me.

But to those I cared about.

No. He would not win. I refused. My knife sliced through yet another branch and the one that came after it, all while he laughed at my plight.

Valora was right.

I had to use her power to stop him.

I was weakened by the unexpected bullet his minions had fired into my brain, my body not yet at full strength despite the desire in my heart to slay this maleficent creature.

I needed just a little more strength.

From Valora.

I closed my eyes, seeking our connection and finding it wide open, her heart mine for the taking. And I broke off a piece that I swore to return.

Flames erupted across my skin, forming in my hands, granting me an electrical current that I used against Necros. He screamed as I drove the spark into his chest, my precision resolute.

Violet waves erupted from him, encasing him in a sea of protection.

I growled, irritated at being cut off. Annoyed that he still possessed so much of his own aura to create such a shield.

And then he shouted to the skies above, demanding the Almighty's presence to give him his due. "*Lucifer!*" he bellowed over and over again.

The floor shook.

Marble pillars cracked.

The sky above cackled with resounding explosions.

Valora grabbed my arm, forcing me back, her palms caressing my cheeks, my head, my neck. She'd created some sort of perimeter, the fire burning brightly. But I knew it was no match for what was coming.

Necros had called upon the Supreme Being. The fallen angel who dictated all of the Underworld. And the rumble beneath our feet said he was responding to the call.

We were doomed.

Killing Necros, we could accomplish together.

But neither of us was ready to face Lucifer.

"So we go down fighting," Valora whispered, her lips close to mine. "I'm with you to the end, Adrik. Even if it means giving you my inner star. I'll give it all if it means remaining by your side."

I kissed her, accepting the vow, the promise, the pledge for eternity. Even if it was short-lived, we were in this together now.

My sweet star.

My Valora.

My queen.

My heart.

An overwhelming blindness sent us both to our knees, but her perimeter remained, glowing harshly and preventing entry.

Until a sweep of a stern hand dissolved the power to ash.

Lucifer had arrived, his expression one of esteemed boredom. "Well." He glanced around, taking in the damage of the once great throne room and gazing out at the grounds beyond. "I see you've been busy, daughter of mine."

Chapter Twenty-Seven

Valora

"DAUGHTER?" I repeated, wondering if I'd heard him right.

"Mmm," the Devil replied, his hands clasped behind his back as he wandered the room. "Interesting redecorating choice," he commented, his gaze on the bronze-covered walls. "Might I suggest something a little more ornate for the future throne room? Perhaps a sparkle of light?"

Necros stirred on the floor, his feet sliding beneath him as he stood to his full height. "Gold," he said flatly. "It'll be gold."

"Will it?" Lucifer asked, sounding intrigued. "I always saw Valora preferring more vivacious colors, like pink. But what do I know?" He shrugged, the gesture somehow exceedingly elegant. "Oh, yes, I know quite a bit." His lips curled into a charming smile, one befitting his stature.

"Are you aware of the destruction that little whore just caused?" Necros asked, folding his arms across his broad chest. "She's taken down half of Caluçon."

More, I thought, calling the life strands to my mind, seeking the ones I'd yet to destroy who'd earned their fates. I'd released them when Adrik required my energy, knowing I could find them again.

Harness it, Adrik whispered. *We're going to need all of it, Valora.*

For Lucifer, I realized. *I don't understand why he's acting this way.*

He's the Devil. He acts however he wants.

"I do," Lucifer murmured out loud, his obsidian gaze twinkling with the stars of the night. Whether it was in response to our internal exchange or to Necros, I wasn't sure. And the Devil didn't clarify. "Nothing occurs in the Underworld without my knowledge. I am the Creator, after all." He glanced upward, sighing loudly. "Not that I'd had much choice in the matter. Alas, here we are. Serving our fates as required."

"We can fix this again," Necros said, his focus landing squarely on me. "You know I can control and wield her power. I'm happy to serve as the conduit once more."

Lucifer chuckled. "I'm sure you are, Necros, but you're not the one she's chosen." His smiling eyes went to Adrik. "You're everything we desired and more, King of Shadows."

"We?" Adrik repeated, his dark brow inching upward.

"Yes." The feminine response came from the shadows as a female with long, dark hair and sable eyes slid into view.

Adrik's lips parted. "Lux."

She bowed her head, just enough to show respect

without belittling her position of power. I'd never seen the Queen of Noxia in person, but she was every bit as beautiful as I anticipated. And energy seemed to pour off her in waves now that she'd revealed herself to the room.

Necros frowned. "Are you here to retrieve your wayward son? The one you claim as your own who is not who he seems?"

Lux's lips curled in delight, her head shaking back and forth, amusement gracing her gorgeous features. "Oh, no, King of the Dead. I'm not here for my son." Her dark irises flitted to mine. "I'm here for my daughter."

"*Our* daughter," Lucifer corrected, his tone indulgent.

My mouth worked without sound, my confusion reaching a precipice that left me dumbfounded before them. *What?*

"That's not possible," Adrik interjected. "I would have known."

Lux's smile held a touch of sadness. "Influencing the minds of children is easy, Adrik. You know that. All it takes is a little illusion to hide what their eyes truly see."

He stared at her for a long moment, then released a laugh of disbelief and shook his head. "There was never a prophecy. You've been fucking with my head since the beginning."

"No prophecy?" Lux tutted at him. "The King of Shadows will destroy the King of the Dead through the use of the Daughter of Light's heart." She glanced at Lucifer, the male claiming to be my father. "Lucifer Morning Star, the lightbringer, the father of our lands, the fallen one who brings light to the darkness."

"You masterminded all of it," Adrik accused. "Every detail down to this very one."

"It's true we may have crafted the prophecy to guide you all, but isn't that the point of a destiny?" Lucifer asked, sounding curious. "To create the paths for you to walk, with a little nudge along the way?"

"Why?" I finally managed to demand, my voice a rasp of sound. "What about Graystall?"

"The justice bearers are all my creations, hence their ancestry in the stars. They are the ones I use to guide the Underworld, to enforce order where required. It wasn't hard to convince the Queen and King of Graystall to raise you as their own and make you their heir apparent, darling child. We even gave you the Queen's eyes." He glanced indulgently at Lux. "Hmm, but I do believe they darken to a deep blue shade when she engages her fire, similar to your irises when you call upon your own flames. Yes?"

"Yes," she agreed, smiling at me. "A gift I bestowed upon her while she grew in my womb."

"Among many others, in addition to my light." His focus shifted back to me. "Which is why you possessed too much power, even as an infant, for you to truly prosper. So I provided you with an appropriate upbringing to ensure your understanding of humanity, justice, the principles of right and wrong. It was the only way to guarantee that you could properly lead. Otherwise"—he turned to Necros—"you would have ended up like him."

"That's one hell of a risk," Adrik cut in. "What if she grew up just like him?"

"But she didn't," Lucifer replied with a smile. "And the beauty of it is, his actions ensured that she didn't. While yours crafted you into the perfect candidate to serve at her side. With a little grooming from my beloved."

Lux bowed her head. "It was my pleasure to raise such a fine king for our darling queen."

I couldn't believe what I was hearing.

"This was all a way of *raising* me?" The forced marriage. The rape. The *agony.* A part of me wanted to laugh. The other part desired destruction of the worst kind. But as the flame rose on my fingertips, Lucifer blew it out.

"If you'd been raised as mine, you would have never seen the Underworld as you do now. You have a heart, Valora. That heart is what will help you rule. And yes, it was crafted beneath a wave of cruelty, but now it will thrive in a sea of warmth. *Your* warmth." He looked to Necros. "I believe you've served your purpose. Valora, I release you of your vows to this vile creature. What is yours is now yours again, including your loyalty, fealty, and protection."

A vise around my heart released, causing me to shudder, as Necros fell to his knees with a look of astonishment on his face. "*What?* After everything I've done for you? In your honor?"

Lucifer snorted. "We both know it was never for me, King of the Dead." He glanced at Lux, a curious note in his voice as he added, "How aptly we named him."

"Indeed," she agreed, smiling. "His reassignment with the Reaper will be well-appointed."

"You slaughtered my kingdom," Adrik growled,

the words for Lucifer and Lux, not Necros. "To what? Create a new regime? To guarantee my loyalty? To craft the perfect mate for your daughter?"

"All of the above," Lucifer answered calmly. "The Shadow Kingdom needed to fall for you to value your place just as much as Valora values hers." He canted his head, his expression thoughtful. "Corruption is the consequence of power, of which you both contain more than any other in all of the Underworld. To curb that corruption and influence humanity requires great sacrifice. As you both now know."

"But we never wanted this," I whispered, shaking my head. "I never desired…" I trailed off, hearing the lie before I finished speaking.

Because I *had* desired power. Many times. But mostly to protect myself and others who required it from vile men like Necros.

"And you feel that way because of your instilled humanity," Lucifer murmured, obviously inside my thoughts. "You're my most beautiful creation, Valora. Strong, powerful, and a living, breathing star. You could destroy the Underworld if you chose to, but I know you won't. Not after everything you've endured and learned through experience."

"What's to stop me from destroying you?" I wondered aloud, furious with the knowledge of being his puppet.

Adrik seemed to agree, his link to me thriving with support at my comment.

"Your heart," Lux replied softly. "One day, you'll understand what we've done and why. When your child is born, you'll understand the sacrifices we made on your behalf. For you're not the only one who suffered all these years, Valora. And fortunately, you'll never feel the pain of a mother giving up her child—for the greater good."

When? I thought, glancing at Adrik.

His pale skin seemed to whiten to a near-ashen color. "Child?" It came out on a whisper of sound.

Necros ruined the moment by chuckling, his presence becoming more of a nuisance than a fright. "Impossible. She's barren."

Lux's lips flattened as she regarded him. "Why do males always assume it's the female preventing pregnancy?"

"A flaw in our creation programming," Lucifer sighed. "And yes, Adrik, you are the father. Contraception is a mortal invention. Valora merely needed to choose and she chose you."

The world spun around me, Adrik's arm catching me before I could fall. But he didn't seem to be faring any better, his shock at the pronouncement leaving us both stunned.

"Once you've sent Necros to the death planes, the kingdom and all the surrounding regions will become yours to rule as you desire. But I have faith you will both prosper here." Lucifer smiled. "The fates are in my favor, after all." He held out his arm. "Shall we, My Queen?"

"One thing before we go," she said, approaching me cautiously. "Valora, I know you hate what we've done. But you will heal. You already are. Twenty-one years is a blink of an eye for someone who will live as long as you. I just want to say, I'm so proud of the woman you've become, and the queen you will be.

When you're ready to learn more, you know where to find me." She turned to Adrik, her smile growing. "I'm proud of you, too. You're everything I've always dreamed of for our daughter. Strong, noble, and kind. The perfect king."

She started toward Lucifer, her heels clicking against the soot-littered ground.

"What about Grigory?" Adrik asked. "Is he…?"

Lux turned, her grin magnificent in its beauty. "Mine?" She nodded. "Yes. And he will take his place soon, once he's finished living his destiny."

Lucifer chuckled. "I love how that's playing out."

"She is quite feisty, isn't she?"

"Reminds me of someone I know," he murmured, wrapping his arms around her.

They disappeared with a rumble of power that sent us all to our knees.

Necros was the first to recover, his rage blowing through the room on a harsh tornado of power that swept Adrik up into the ceiling and sent him crashing down to the floor.

His head lolled, his body momentarily stunned from the display of unexpected force. Necros followed up the explosive blast with one meant for me that I blocked. His third attempt was lost to my flames.

He growled in fury. "Is that any way to treat your husband, *wife*? The male who raised you and provided you with shelter. The one who gave you jewels and dresses and a life."

He must have missed the part where Lucifer denounced our vows.

I narrowed my gaze. "I've let you do horrendous

things to me thinking it was your right as my husband. Something *you* taught me, I might add. But now I see the truth. You're a weak demon with little hope left. It's a poetic end to a life that has meant nothing but cruelty."

"I'm the one who's fed and clothed you since childhood. I made you my queen when everyone else abandoned you." His laugh was cruel. "You're nothing but a pawn to Lucifer. Surely you see that?"

"Just as I was a pawn to you?" I countered. "You only *raised* me for my power."

"A power Lucifer gave me. The man who calls you his daughter. What does that say about our fates?"

That I never had a choice.

That we were always meant to end up here.

"That today is the day you die," I said out loud, stirring my power into the air to create a force field around myself and Adrik. I sent a third wave of energy to the only remaining guard—the one who chose me over Necros—and shoved him from the room, needing him to run and find shelter.

This was between me and my soon-to-be-dead husband now.

"We'll see." Necros sent shock wave after shock wave at me, but each one bounced off my fiery shield and hit the walls of the palace, destroying the foundations of Adrik's former home.

It was almost laughable how Necros's energy compared to mine. My fear for him felt ancient, infeasible. Now all I experienced was boredom from the clearly lesser demon.

Oh, he was more powerful than most.

He just no longer compared to me.

And he didn't have a conduit to my flames.

I'm Lucifer's daughter.

Queen Lux is my mother.

I will bow to no one again.

What they did to me was wrong. But I also understood it. They wanted me to have a connection to humanity, to keep me grounded and prevent me from becoming someone like the cruel, arrogant being before me.

They gave me compassion.

But not for this man.

Necros deserved to die, and painfully. For all his heinous acts against me and those who opposed him.

I held my hands up high in the air, lifting Necros on a cloud of smoke until the tips of his heavily booted feet barely brushed the ground. He struggled, his energy battling mine, but it was no match to the angelfire brewing within me.

"Too many clothes." I had no desire to see my husband naked ever again, but my plan required it. A surge of flames demolished his garments to ash, leaving his skin undamaged. "Isn't it degrading to be in such a vulnerable position?"

"Nudity has never bothered me," he countered, sounding just as cocksure as ever while his power futilely roared with a vengeance.

He knew I intended to kill him.

He knew I would win.

But he seemed to be hell-bent on maintaining his dignity as he went.

"How many males have you broken in this position?" I wondered aloud, tilting my head. "Hmm,

I can count several dozen I've witnessed alone. Would you like to see what I learned from those experiences, husband of mine? To see what you've taught me to do?"

A flicker of uncertainty flashed in the depths of his eyes, followed swiftly by mocking disbelief. "You don't have it in you."

I brought my fingers up to my lips and hushed him. "*Shh.* My time to rule now, dead king. And I'm concentrating on your demise."

A stray tendril of blue embers curved its way out of my body and around Necros. I didn't allow it to burn him, but to simply coil like a snake around its prey. It lowered over his abdomen and toward his manhood.

He tried to swipe it away with flares of his own. But failed.

"Do you know the part of you that I hate the most?" I circled his flaccid cock, arching a brow. "All the times you defiled my body and made me do things to you I despised were experiences I tolerated as your wife. But then you shared me. And that, Necros, was your biggest mistake of all, because I learned about pleasure. I was never the problem. You were, and your miserable excuse for a dick."

It was my turn to allow evil laughter to fill the room. It didn't echo off the ceilings, because they weren't there anymore. Instead, the sound flooded out into the Kingdom of Caluçon to let those who heard it know a new leader was rising.

"Say goodbye to your precious instrument. It wasn't all that useful anyway."

His eyes bulged at the words, but behind them

lurked a begrudging respect.

A respect I wanted to see die.

He did not make me.

He did not own me.

I was not *his* queen.

My vine of fire twisted around the base of his cock and burned through the flesh, cauterizing the wound as I severed the most despicable part of him.

Necros screamed, his body shaking in exquisite agony, his power dying before my eyes and then flashing again as he attempted one last time to save himself.

"I see why you enjoy this," I mused. "It's beautiful to watch someone so vile writhe in pain." I lifted the sliced-off part of his anatomy to his face, pressing it to his lips. "Open. Take it all. And swallow like a good little king."

His gaze met mine. "You'll destroy Cal—"

I shoved the offending item inside with a surge of heat, no longer interested in his voice. "The only thing I'm going to destroy is *you*, the male who murdered innocent women and children of his own realm as a test. The male who raped for pleasure, abused for fun, and murdered for power."

Darts of fire spanned from my body and pounded into Necros's flesh like a hailstorm in a thunderous downpour. I watched as his skin melted, the smell of acrid flesh filling the room. One hit his eye and burned deep into the socket, blinding him.

"Your outside matches your inside now," I said quietly. "A scarred monster."

Adrik stirred beside me but still didn't wake. I could sense his thoughts as they entwined with mine.

A fervent desire for Necros's death.

Rest, my lover. Rest.

I pictured the organs in Necros's body—his liver, lungs, kidneys, bladder, intestines, stomach, brain, and heart. They were what kept him alive. I latched onto them all, shoving my angelfire inside, needing to destroy him completely. Utterly. Resolutely. His insides burned and bloated and crumbled. His heart didn't take long, because he barely had one, and last was his brain.

"Goodbye, husband. See you in hell."

His single eye met mine, just long enough for me to see his pride.

I ripped him apart into a sea of embers dissolving to ash at my feet. That look from him would haunt me for the rest of my life. He was proud of me for torturing him. Proud that he taught me to lead in this way.

And it was vile. Disgusting. *Wrong.*

He thought he'd created a monster to live out his legacy.

And I would spend the rest of my life proving him wrong.

With a sweep of my arm, I sent his remains as high as my power allowed, into the sky above. The violet sun dissipated, replaced by a dark night littered with glistening stars.

Necros.

Where he would remain for eternity and watch my rule, unable to interfere, just observe. He didn't deserve the death planes. No. This fate served him much better.

"I'm not you," I told him now. "And I never will

be."

I'm free.

I'm finally fucking free.

A queen.

Set to rule a new kingdom.

My kingdom.

"Valora?" Adrik whispered, stirring.

"He's gone." I didn't move, my eyes fixated on the sky above.

"You killed him?"

"Yes." I nodded.

Adrik followed my gaze, his lips curling down. "You didn't send him to the death planes."

"No, I didn't." I canted my head, studying the design his ashes made in the sky. *A large star.* "I want him to suffer. For eternity."

And he would with his soul shredded into so many pieces.

Are you still proud of me? I wondered, smiling. "It's done."

The war was finally over.

And I now owned the crown.

CHAPTER TWENTY-EIGHT

ADRIK

A BABY.

Lucifer's daughter.

And a kingdom.

It resembled the foundation of a bad joke. But instead gave birth to a new life as Valora and I walked outside the palace walls. We hadn't spoken much since she killed Necros, her handiwork brightening the night sky above with millions of twinkling lights.

"What now?" she asked, surveying the demolished landscapes that once housed Caluçon.

She'd already dismissed the only remaining guard—Jeremiah—for the night, telling him to rest and report back in the morning. I suspected she would knight him, perhaps put him in charge of refining palace security. Given the bravery I witnessed from him, I approved. But he would have a hard time recruiting new employees.

Thousands had died today.

All Necros loyalists with black hearts.

And I couldn't mourn a single one.

"Do you wish to mourn for the kingdom?" I

wondered aloud, draping my jacket around her bare shoulders. She didn't seem to mind being nude, but the lack of a sun had brought on a chilly breeze that trailed goose bumps down her arms.

"No." She gazed up at the beautiful display above. "No, I do not. But I would like to rename it."

I linked my fingers through hers, pulling her alongside me. "Do you have something in mind?"

"I do," she murmured. "Nova Kingdom."

An appropriate name, given her display of power today. "I like it."

She nodded as if she already knew. And maybe she did. Valora vibrated with more power than ever, her confidence bolstered by having removed the one who'd brought her down all these years. She seemed alive, happy, and so very strong.

"What do you want to do about your parents?" It seemed so weird to me to think of Lucifer and Lux as her father and mother. I couldn't even begin to imagine how insane it was to her.

"Nothing for now." She paused at the cliffs that overlooked the fields leading to the town below. "I don't agree with what they've done. But I'm also not ready to understand it all yet."

An intelligent interpretation. "We may never understand it."

"Which, I think, is the point," she replied, leaning her head against my shoulder. "Lucifer is the Creator of this world. He's a mastermind of impossibilities. I'm not sure we were created to understand them all."

"Something tells me he only explains the ones that matter." Such as why he and Lux had crafted such an intricate scheme to match me to Valora. It raised the question of fate and if we were ever in control of our own destinies.

I suspected we were not.

But I also wasn't sure I possessed a desire to change mine.

Yes, I lost my kingdom. However, the primary reason I cared was because of Lux's insistence that I seek revenge for my family. Not because I ever loved them. I was too young, an infant, to feel the pain of their loss. And then I grew up in a life of riches and opulence. How much did I really suffer? The answer was not at all.

Valora, however, endured a far worse life. Always being told she was beneath others. Her husband treating her as a common whore. Having her powers ripped away at birth and then squandered upon revival.

"Do you hate them?" Because I wouldn't blame her if she did.

"No." She faced me, her opposite hand grasping mine to hold both my wrists before her. "I can't hate them when they brought me you."

"I'm pretty sure they made me to be yours." At least, that was what I gathered from all their cryptic words.

"Then I am quite pleased with their creation," she replied, her smile radiant with a touch of seduction. "You are the perfect king."

"For a perfect queen," I replied, lifting her hand to my lips. "I wouldn't change any of it. Apart from being unconscious during Necros's destruction." It sucked to miss that part. I really wanted to hear the bastard scream.

Mirth shone bright in her icy blue gaze. "I can recount each excruciating detail for you."

"Mmm, pillow talk." I tugged her closer, desiring to feel her warmth against mine. "Are you trying to seduce me, My Queen?"

"I am now," she replied, releasing my hands to wrap her arms around my neck. "Do you truly want this, Adrik? Do you want me?"

I pressed one palm to her lower back, the other going to her nape, holding her closely. "Do I want to live happily ever after with my queen? To rule the Nova Kingdom at her side? To raise our future son or daughter—without all the sick and twisted games?" I smiled. "There's nowhere else I'd rather be, Valora, than with you. Call it fate. Call it divine intervention on behalf of the Devil himself. Regardless, my heart is true, and it desires you."

"Happily ever after?" she repeated, her gaze twinkling. "Does that even exist in this world?"

"I think we can make it exist." I lowered my mouth to hers, brushing a soft kiss against her lips. "You're the Creator of the Underworld's daughter. If anyone can manufacture a happily ever after, it's you."

"No," she whispered, her fingers twining in my hair. "It's us. We can create it. Together."

"Sounds like the destiny of our dreams." I ran my tongue along her bottom lip. "And what of our kingdom, My Queen?"

"We rule together," she vowed. "Forever and always."

"A life I can adore, like I adore you."

She smiled. "Is that a yes, then?"

"As if I could say no," I replied, kissing her once more. *I love you, my sweet star.*

Her amusement touched my thoughts. *Who knew you could be such a romantic? Happily ever afters. Love.*

I swept her into my arms, carrying her as one should on a wedding night. "If you don't require the romance, then allow me to return us to our rooms." I paused, glancing down at her. "They are still in one piece, right?"

She laughed, her arms around my neck. "I didn't destroy everything. Just…" She paused to glance around. "Well, a lot of it."

"We're going to need a few architects," I agreed, taking in the destruction. The stone walls were fine. But a hell of a lot of dust had settled from the bodies of those she'd slain.

"We'll rebuild it all, except the forbidden areas. Those I want restored. Especially the library." Her eyes twinkled. "I want to establish an education program for those in need. We will offer classes there."

"On self-defense and power manipulation?" I teased, carrying her through the gardens that backed up to her rooms. She'd demolished all the statues to rubble, giving it a rather bleak appeal.

"Maybe," she replied. "But only if you're leading the class. Naked."

My eyebrows rose. "You intend to share me with the women of this new kingdom of ours?" I meant it as a taunt, but her nails digging into my scalp said she took it very seriously.

"Never." Her irises smoldered. "You're mine and only mine."

"Now who is being romantic?" I nudged open the door to her quarters and tossed her on the bed.

She giggled and crawled backward into the pillows, her expression darkening beneath a wave of desire. "I love you, King of Nova Kingdom," she said, her voice one of a siren calling her partner to bed. "Now fuck me like you own me."

"Ah, and they truly did live happily ever after," I murmured, stripping myself of my clothes before prowling over her in the bed. "In their own little kingdom." I kissed her soundly. "Of Nova."

"The end," she whispered, smiling.

"The end," I agreed.

EPILOGUE

ZAYA

Four Months Later…

THIS WEDDING WAS FAR DIFFERENT from the first one I witnessed in this palace. For one, the bride was willing. The groom was a significant improvement to the last one. And this room had undergone one hell of a renovation.

Hell being the operative term there.

Because *wow*.

Valora had outdone herself with the pinks and reds and blues. All the drapes were bright, the windows clean, and the walls a pristine white. The great room practically glowed and not just because of the bride and groom at the altar.

Or the Devil behind the podium.

Although, they were part of it, all lit up like the stars shining in the Nova Kingdom night.

Beautiful.

Perfect.

Happiness.

For everyone in the room, anyway, except me.

Happiness no longer existed in my world. Not after…

I swallowed, pushing the thoughts away as I met Grigory's knowing gaze across from me. He stood behind Adrik, his eyebrow arched in that arrogant way I despised.

Of all the Noxia vampires to cure me, it had to be that one.

The conceited, pompous prick of a prince who couldn't even get my name right. If he called me Zay one more time, I'd punch him directly in the nose.

Valora laughed, drawing my attention to her. She repeated the vows Lucifer had created, the words very different from her first wedding. These boasted new principles, ones that left everyone smiling.

They promised to maintain faith in each other. To respect each other. To adore one another. To lead together. To raise their kingdom with honesty and high regard for others. And to cherish their future daughter always.

A tear fell from Valora's eye at the reveal of the gender inside her growing belly.

A tear that Adrik kissed before taking her lips and completing the vow.

Such a gorgeous ceremony.

And yet, being in this place only filled me with dread.

I can't move back, I realized, my plans to stay with Valora after the wedding halting in my mind. *I can't live here.*

It was littered with too many bad memories that no amount of decorating could hide. Adrik and Grigory had worked so hard to rid the kingdom and the surrounding areas of black hearts, but it didn't change my fears. The damage was already done.

Noxia provided a fresh start, a land without pain or memories. A land I could lose myself in without anyone noticing. That was where I needed to be.

"We'll be back soon," Valora whispered, handing me her bouquet of white flowers—the same color as her beautiful dress. "Adrik is keen on consummating the marriage as quickly as possible."

A genuine smile crossed my face at my friend's enthusiasm for getting to the bedroom this time around. The pair left with a hungry growl from Adrik, his new wife giggling in his arms as he swept her from the great hall.

No one followed. New kingdom, new rules, and the newlyweds didn't want to share their private moment with anyone.

Finally. Some normality, I thought, slipping through the shadows and out into the newly planted gardens. The bramble-like structures had been replaced with greenery and flowers. I set Valora's bouquet near a particularly beautiful display and sighed as I walked through the maze of bushes, adoring the life protruding from the grounds.

"Zay?" Grigory's voice came from behind me, causing me to stiffen.

"It's Zaya," I reminded him for the hundredth time today. The millionth time since we'd met.

He ignored my correction. "Aren't you joining the festivities?"

And watch you hit on everything that moves? No, thank you. "I needed some fresh air."

"What you need is to have some fun." He waved a beer mixed with blood in my face to demonstrate his point.

I batted it away. "I was having plenty of fun before you came outside."

He looked doubtful. "More like wallowing in self-pity."

"Says the male who is refusing to speak to his mother over Valora's birthright," I countered. But to be honest, I agreed with his feelings on the subject completely. She lied to him, kept too many secrets, and put my best friend through hell. To say I disliked Lux would be an understatement.

But I knew this topic would make Grigory leave me alone because anything and everything regarding Queen Lux pissed him off right now.

"Are you trying to piss me off, Zay?" he asked, eyes narrowed. Most would fear a look like that from the esteemed Prince of Noxia, but his blood had linked us. Indefinitely. I could see inside his mind just as he could see into mine.

Another factor of his acquaintance I hated. Almost as much as his ridiculous nickname for me.

"*Zaya*," I growled through gritted teeth. "I'm going back to my room. I'll come down again when Valora and Adrik are back."

Grigory grabbed my hand and pulled me close to him. "Don't be—"

My hand cracked across his cheek, causing him to stumble backward. I jumped at my reaction, brushing my mouth with my fingertips, gazing at him with wide eyes. It'd been an instinctual reaction to someone touching me. A male. Here. On these grounds.

I'm going inside. "I-I…" I swallowed, the words trapped in my throat.

"No, I shouldn't have done that," he said, his voice softening. He set his beer on a nearby bench, his expression falling into a mask of softness that I hated. It was the look of a man handling a frightened animal, and I didn't want to be that frightened animal.

"It's…" I trailed off, unable to voice it.

"The grounds." He took a step forward, his hands before him as if to warn me of his intentions, to show his lack of a threat. "What happened to you here is a nightmare no one should have to live through. But you did. And you're stronger for it."

"Then why are you looking at me as if I might break?" I countered.

"Because I don't want to get slapped again." His lips twitched, his head angling to the side in a more playful manner. "And because you're going to dance with me."

I snorted. This arrogant side of him I could handle so much more than the one that pretended to care. "Go find another bridesmaid to fuck, Grigory."

"Oh, I will. But I want to dance with you first."

"Foreplay?" I taunted, arching a brow.

"Everything in life is merely an interlude to pleasure," he replied, his grin wicked. "Dance with me."

"No." I abhorred male touch. It made my skin crawl. And the knowledge that I had the blood of one coursing through my veins brought bile to my throat. "I don't want to dance."

He sighed. "Living a life in hiding isn't living at all, sweetheart."

"Then maybe you shouldn't have brought me back," I said quietly, stepping away from him. It was his interference that forced me to be here. I'd have likely died otherwise. What if that was my true fate and he'd altered it in error?

"Zaya." It was the first time he'd called me by my proper name. "You're better than this, and we both know it. Yes, these lands are shrouded in the darkness that tried to destroy you, but sometimes facing those demons is what we need to heal."

A shiver spread down my spine. That would never happen. This was my life now.

We fell silent, the amicable air between us oddly soothing.

I studied the sky, adoring the new stars Valora had created. It served this kingdom so much better than the violet sun ever did.

"I'm happy for her," I whispered. "For Adrik, too." Although I barely knew him, I saw how happy he made my friend. That was what mattered most.

Fireworks erupted in the night sky as if on cue, causing Grigory to chuckle.

"Seems Valora is quite thrilled as well," he said knowingly. "It must be fun being able to produce lights like that when you come. Not to mention the pride Adrik must feel."

"You realize she's your sister, right?" I prompted, laughing at his resulting expression.

He shuddered. "An image I do not need."

"You're the one talking about Adrik fucking his bride."

Another cringe. He picked up his beer and took a long swig. "You're a spoilsport, Zay."

I shook my head. "It's Zaya."

"Isn't that what I said?" he asked, winking. "Dance with me and maybe I'll get it right."

"That doesn't sound promising."

He smiled. "Trust me, sweetheart. It's *very* promising."

"You're incorrigible."

"And you love it."

Yeah, I supposed I kind of did. Not that I'd ever admit it out loud.

He held out his hand. "Please?"

This man was going to be the death of me. Or perhaps, something more. Because every time we touched, a zap of energy warmed my veins. Just like it did now as I finally agreed. "One dance."

"To last a lifetime," he replied, his dimples flashing.

He led me back inside, to a place I considered my own personal hell. Although, his presence seemed to brighten it just a little, causing my heart to beat faster for an entirely different reason.

Perhaps there was hope for me yet.

The End For Now

The Story Continues with Zaya and Grigory in Happily Ever Bitten…

Happily Ever Bitten

A Halfling.

My designation. A plague. An essential death sentence in the underworld. Until I met him.

A Noxia Prince.

He's arrogant, a playboy, and the male who saved my life. Except he never gave me a choice, his blood tying me to him for an eternity of servitude. And I'm not sure I want to pay that price.

An unspeakable past.

Monsters haunt my nightmares. Most of them dead. But a few are still alive, and so I'll hunt them. Torture them. Slay them all. Even if it brings about an early demise.

A courtship signed in blood.

One bite sealed my fate.
Except someone is playing a dangerous game, and she'll stop at nothing to see me destroyed.

Life is a journey to Death.

Sometimes the only way to truly live is to die.

About Lexi C. Foss

USA Today Bestselling Author Lexi C. Foss loves to play in dark worlds, especially the ones that bite. She lives in Atlanta, Georgia, with her husband and their furry children. When not writing, she's busy crossing items off her travel bucket list or chasing eclipses around the globe. She's quirky, consumes way too much coffee, and loves to swim.

Where to Find Lexi:

www.LexiCFoss.com

Also By Lexi C. Foss

Blood Alliance Series - Dystopian Paranormal

Chastely Bitten

Royally Bitten

Regally Bitten

Dark Provenance Series - Paranormal Romance

Heiress of Bael

Daughter of Death

Son of Chaos

Elemental Fae Academy - Reverse Harem

Book One

Book Two

Book Three

Midnight Fae Academy - Reverse Harem

Book One

Immortal Curse Series - Paranormal Romance

Blood Laws

Forbidden Bonds

Blood Heart

Elder Bonds

Blood Bonds

Angel Bonds

Mershano Empire Series - Contemporary Romance

The Prince's Game

The Charmer's Gambit

The Rebel's Redemption

Other Books

Scarlet Mark - Standalone Romantic Suspense

ABOUT ANNA EDWARDS

Anna Edwards is a British author from the depths of the rural countryside near London. When she has some spare time, she can also be found writing poetry, baking cakes (and eating them), or behind a camera snapping like a mad paparazzo. She's an avid reader who turned to writing to combat her depression and anxiety. She has a love of traveling and likes to bring this to her stories to give them the air of reality. She likes her heroes hot and hunky with a dirty mouth, her heroines demure but with spunk, and her books full of dramatic suspense.

Where to Find Anna:
www.AuthorAnnaEdwards.com

Also By Anna Edwards

The Glacial Blood Series – Paranormal Romance

The Touch of Snow
Fighting the Lies
Fallen for Shame
Shattered Fears
Hidden Pain

The Control Series – Romantic Suspense

Surrendered Control
Divided Control
Misguided Control
Controlling Darkness
Controlling Heritage
Controlling Disgrace
Controlling Expectations
Controlling the Past

Dark Sovereignty – Dark Romance

Legacy of Succession
Tainted Reasoning
A Father's Insistence

Other Books

Beauty's War - Gods Reborn - With Claire Marta
Apollo's Protection – Gods Reborn – With Claire Marta
Oliver - Part of Blaire's World
Redemption - Book Ten of the Cavalieri Della Morte
Overexposed - A Skeleton Kings Prequel
Second Chances – Romantic Suspense